EMERALD'S FIRE

Hawk turned a corner and stopped as his gaze fell on Sienna sitting on a concrete bench. He was stunned to see her, sitting with her hands clasped behind her neck, her eyes closed, her face lifted to the sun. It had been so long since he had been able to look at her this way, and his hungry gaze missed nothing.

Hawk's first impulse was to wrap her in his arms. He wanted to tell her how much he missed her, and that he never would have gone away if it had been left up to him. He stood teetering on the edge of indecision as Sienna relaxed from her stretch and opened her eyes.

The sight of Hawk took her totally by surprise. She wondered how long he had been standing there, and she noticed the longing in his eyes. It caused her heart to beat faster, and her stomach to quiver. She rose to her feet.

He had crossed the tiled area before he realized it. Urgently, he slid his arms over the cool chiffon, wrapping Sienna within them. He watched her moist lips quiver and open with unspoken words. At the moment, words were not what Hawk needed. He needed to feel his mouth upon hers, to taste the sweetness that he'd never forgotten, one that had haunted him from one end of the world to the other.

Hawk kissed her deeply. He kissed her as if to awaken her soul, let alone the memory of the love they once shared. Finally, Hawk slackened his hold, withdrew from the kiss, and stood staring into Sienna's face.

"I missed you so much, Sienna." His voice vibrated in his throat.

"You missed me? But how could that be?" She stepped back and placed her fingertips to her throbbing lips. "I've never seen you before today."

BOOK YOUR PLACE ON OUR WEBSITE AND MAKE THE ARABESQUE ROMANCE CONNECTION!

We've created a customized website just for our very special Arabesque readers, where you can get the inside scoop on everything that's going on with Arabesque romance novels.

When you come online, you'll have the exciting opportunity to:

- View covers of upcoming books

- Learn about our future publishing schedule (listed by publication month and author)

- Find out when your favorite authors will be visiting a city near you

- Search for and order backlist books

- Check out author bios and background information

- Send e-mail to your favorite authors

- Join us in weekly chats with authors, readers and other guests

- Get writing guidelines

- AND MUCH MORE!

Visit our website at
http://www.arabesquebooks.com

EMERALD'S FIRE

Eboni Snoe

BET Publications, LLC
www.bet.com
www.arabesquebooks.com

ARABESQUE BOOKS are published by

BET Publications, LLC
c/o BET BOOKS
One BET Plaza
1900 W Place NE
Washington, D.C. 20018-1211

Copyright © 1996 by Gwyn F. McGee

All rights reserved. No part of this book may be reproduced, stored in a retrieval system, or transmitted in any form or by any means without the prior written consent of the Publisher.

If you purchased this book without a cover you should be aware that this book is stolen property. It was reported as "unsold and destroyed" to the Publisher and neither the Author nor the Publisher has received any payment for this "stripped book."

All Kensington Titles, Imprints, and Distributed Lines are available at special quantity discounts for bulk purchases for sales promotions, premiums, fund-raising, and educational or institutional use. Special book exerpts or customized printings can also be created to fit specific needs. For details, write or phone the office of the Kensington special sales manager: Kensington Publishing Corp., 850 Third Avenue, New York, NY 10022, attn: Special Sales Department, Phone: 1-800-221-2647.

BET Books is a trademark of Black Entertainment Television, Inc. ARABESQUE, the ARABESQUE logo and the BET BOOKS logo are trademarks and registered trademarks.

First Printing: December 1996

10 9 8 7 6 5 4 3

Printed in the United States of America

One

Six months or a thousand years—both felt the same to Hawk. In his mind patience was no longer a virtue. It was a horrible necessity that, once he descended from the plane, had transformed into anxiousness. Pulsing energy surged in him as he eyed the overly friendly Costa Rican man with skepticism. Hawk had travelled to enough places to recognize a scam artist when he saw one, and he hoped the puzzled, greyhaired woman who had been a passenger on his flight did as well.

His hazel-eyed stare took in the scene with one sweeping, practiced glance. The area outside of Juan Santamaria International Airport was buzzing with activity and promise, and, despite the code of indifference that he had lived by for the last six months, he felt it would be a shame for the woman to be scammed so quickly after arriving on the Central American isthmus.

"I think you're mistaken," he heard her say as she shook her streaked head, "I'm sure I've never seen you before."

The man continued to insist that they were old acquaintances, in English coated with Spanish flavor, as his accomplice began to lift the woman's wallet out of her oversized bag.

Hawk's thick eyebrows rose as he witnessed the caper, and a feeling of perturbation scratched at his insides. Precise and brisk in his movements, Hawk whacked the nimble hand with his carved walking stick, halting the crime, to the woman's surprise and the shock of the pickpocket team.

"What in the world is going on?" Her gaze flickered from the bag at her side, where her wallet lay caught in a fold of canvas material, to the stunned features of the scam artist in front of her, and eventually to Hawk's steady stare.

As the words tumbled from her lips, the two would-be criminals scurried away, mimicking the style of the countless lizards that frequented the tropical streets, leaving her possessions intact and her heart racing.

"Shame on you!" she shouted, and she shook her finger at the fleeing criminals, then pressed a small hand with strong fingers against her rapidly pumping breasts.

"I'm not usually this careless." She looked up at Hawk. "I was just so excited about meeting my daughter here, and then that man came up, claiming he recognized me." Her eyes still exhibited shock, although embarrassment was quickly rising in their depths.

"It's alright. You don't have to explain to me, Ma'am." Hawk nodded his head and turned to walk away.

"Wait a minute." She reached out and caught his forearm.

Hawk faced the woman again.

"I'd like to thank you properly. What's your name?"

"They call me Hawk."

"I can't believe any self-respecting mother would name her child Hawk." Her full bottom lip was extended forward. For Hawk, the expression dredged up vague memories of his grandmother's face.

"I have to admit you're right, Ma'am. My mother named me Hennessy Jackson."

The woman nodded, showing her acceptance.

"I want to give you a little something for helping me out." She began to dig inside the large canvas bag.

"Honestly," Hawk said commandingly, "that's okay. I don't need anything." Once again, he turned his back on the woman. This time he rapidly put distance between them as he headed for the public bus stop.

"You won't believe what almost happened to me just a few minutes ago," Nanna said as she watched her daughter, Charmagne, place her luggage in the trunk of the car, then close it.

"What happened?" Charmagne asked as she walked to the driver's door and climbed inside. Nanna got in on the opposite side of the vehicle.

"A young man who reminded me of Gerald came out of nowhere and stopped two pickpockets from stealing me blind."

"Mama, don't start this stuff about Gerald again. He's been dead for two years now. You've got to come to grips with that."

"I know my baby boy is dead," Nanna retorted. "I believe I know that better than anyone else."

"I'm sorry to have said that," Charmagne apologized softly, looking into her mother's injured eyes as she started the car. "Here you have just arrived, and we're almost arguing. I guess we both miss him." She sighed. "I tend to want to bury the pain, whereas you seem to want to keep it alive. You see Gerald in everything and everybody." She steered the car into the congested street.

"No, that's not true. I don't want to keep the pain alive, Charmagne, but I do intend to keep your brother's memory alive. He was a good soul who wandered down the wrong path. That doesn't mean he's not worth remembering," Nanna proclaimed as she turned toward the window.

Charmagne released another trembling sigh.

* * *

Hawk looked at the people standing at the bus stop. He had become accustomed to travelling like the natives in all the countries he'd visited. He liked the grounded feeling it gave him. There was no way to hold illusions of grandeur about yourself under such modest conditions, no matter who you were, what you owned, or what special gifts you possessed. From the bus ride he would determine where he would stay, and once there he would wait until the appointed time.

Hawk stood apart from the silent group that had gathered near the sign, not only because he chose to, but because his physical features also singled him out from the Ticos, Costa Ricans of Spanish descent. Although his golden brown skin matched that of several of the residents, he was taller and more muscular. His neatly cultured, light brown dreads lay tied in a ponytail against his expansive back, while his carved facial features gave no clue to his thoughts, nor did his thickly lashed, hazel eyes.

"There is the man I was just talking about. Stop! Stop right here, Charmagne!" The voice rang out, and a bright red compact car forced its way up to the curb in front of him.

"Why didn't you say you needed a ride?" A familiar grey head popped outside the car window. "My daughter and I would be more than happy to give you a lift anywhere you'd like to go." She ignored the insistent tugging at her sleeve.

Before Hawk could answer, the car door swung open and the woman stepped out onto the curb, pushed the car seat forward and motioned for him to climb inside. He hesitated a moment as he thought the situation over, while the woman waited expectantly. In the end, Hawk accepted the woman's insistent kindness and climbed into the backseat. He grunted as his head hit a low overhang inside the car. When he settled himself in the back seat he felt like a jack-in-the-box that had been folded into the wrong container.

"Hawk, you can call me Nanna," she announced, "and this is my daughter, Charmagne. Charmagne, this is the young man that kept me from being just another statistic in a foreign country."

Hawk looked straight into a set of soft but vibrant eyes. He recognized the moment when skepticism was transformed into curiosity, when Charmagne evaluated him over her arm as she adjusted her mother's seat with concentrated yanks.

"Hello, Hawk."

There was a distinct pause as he answered slowly, "How are you?" Then his eyes became hooded as he focused on the silver bracelet she wore around her wrist. Just the sight of the ornament caused his chest to constrict, and memories flooded in, mental images of another slim, brown wrist encased in an intricately engraved silver bangle.

"Do you want something to drink? Or maybe some ice to help cool you down?" Sienna asked, her attractive features altered by concern.

The alerting tinkle of the doorbell caused her to glance over her shoulder, drawing her attention away from the frail woman sitting on the stool. The melodic sound was an admonition that the last customer was exiting the shop.

"Thank you and come again," Sienna called as the door closed behind them.

"I hate to be causing all this trouble." Sienna's dark brown eyes returned to the woman's face. "But some water might help," the woman responded through the trembling hand pressed against her lips.

"You just relax right here. I'll get you some water right away." Sienna checked her watch as she headed for the back of the store. She hesitated, then made a one hundred and eighty degree turn. "It's after closing time. I need to lock the door and put out the sign, before anyone else comes in."

Her stylish sandals moved soundlessly across the tile, and her thoughts remained with the tiny woman who had nearly passed out in the middle of the floor.

The woman had entered The Stonekeeper about forty-five minutes ago. Her vivid tropical dress had made her stand out amongst the more conservatively attired customers, and Sienna distinctly recalled giving her the customary welcome. No one was allowed to pass underneath The Stonekeeper's arch of grapevines draped with silk magnolia blossoms and eucalyptus without it. Sienna remembered going back to the business at hand as the woman began to browse. Several customers made their choices and went on their way, but the brightly dressed woman remained, asking prices in a dialect that Sienna couldn't quite place. She recalled the warning shout that came from another customer while she was helping a young man who had asked about a mermaid-shaped pendant with lapis lazuli in its crown. It was at that precise moment that Sienna noticed the woman weaving on unstable legs between the herbal bath section and a display case of essential oils and aromatherapy lamps. She had arrived in the aisle just as the woman began to slump, and she managed to help her to a nearby stool.

Sienna looked out at the crowded street before she flipped the Open/Closed sign over with a practiced hand. She exhaled long and deep, her shoulders rising. It had been a long, prosperous day. Dawn, her assistant, had left early, leaving the remnants of the Saturday night crowd to her. She had to admit it had been quite trying, but she appreciated that. It kept her body and her mind occupied. Although it had been nearly six months since she last saw Hawk, the silent, solitary moments still drove her to distraction, for her thoughts never failed to call up his image. His haunted eyes. His strong yet soft dreaded hair. The way his firm lips felt moist, sparking electricity against hers. How she had awakened feeling warm with hopes for their future one morning with the sun spilling in through an opening in the sheers, only to find a note of apology and him gone. It had felt as if someone had cut out her heart, the pain was so deep.

Sienna turned the lock, securing the door. She was more than a little aware of a strange emptiness that lurked inside her, and her usually compassionate eyes were glazed over with a more volatile emotion. Sienna could almost pinpoint the time when the hurt had turned to anger. She remembered how she had welcomed the hot, emotional shield with open arms. Hawk and his secrets! He had never allowed her totally into his life. He was like a beautiful, leather-bound book of which she was allowed to stroke the cover and gaze at the title page. The knowledge of what really made him who he was, though, was closed to her.

Sienna drew a deep breath and held it. In the very beginning, she had tried to keep her distance from him, to no avail. The unusual circumstances under which they met had caused their relationship to develop at an accelerated pace, and she was deeply in love before she knew it.

Short, breathy coughs from across the room forced Sienna out of her retrospection. "I'm sorry," she apologized, "I'll bring that water right away."

The woman's hands were nearly calm when she accepted the pliable paper cup. Sienna watched her drink the water with her eyes closed.

"Thank you," she replied as she returned the container to Sienna's waiting palm. "I'm sorry for causing such a problem."

"I'm sure you would have avoided it if you could." Sienna gave her an accepting smile.

"I had already made up my mind about what I buy, but I was enjoying the store so much I kept looking. You have really interesting things here."

"Well, I'm glad that you like it." Pride lit up Sienna's features as she glanced at the shop that had been open for about three years.

The woman stood up rather abruptly, which caused her to teeter on her feet. Sienna reached out to steady her.

"I guess I still a little dizzy," she acknowledged reluctantly. "But I feeling better, and I do not want to take up any more of your time." She walked over to a large amethyst geode that dominated a display of semi-precious stones. "This is what I want to purchase."

"It is beautiful, isn't it?" Sienna remarked without expecting a reply. "Actually we don't sell that many of these. They are somewhat more expensive than the other stones because of their size. I tell you what. Let's leave it right here while I write up your ticket and run the purchase. I've got a stop I have to make within the next thirty minutes, so as I'm leaving I'll take the amethyst tower out to the car for you."

Minutes later Sienna handed the woman her receipt. Afterward, she disappeared behind the counter to gather her belongings together. As she stepped around the partition, she spoke more to herself than to the woman standing a few feet away. "Now I believe I have everything I need." She looked inside her purse, which held the banking bag. "Good." Her dark brown eyes rose to the woman's face. "So, if you would just point the way to your car, we'll be on our way."

Sienna was certain the woman would not have been

able to handle taking the amethyst to her van when they finally reached the vehicle. She had parked a couple of blocks away from The Stonekeeper, in a narrow alley. Sienna knew parking was limited on Blossom Street, but she wished the woman had warned her about the distance. She would have suggested she pull the van in front of the store. It would have been much more convenient.

By the time they reached the delivery style vehicle, the woman discovered that the double doors in the back were partially open.

"I guess I left them open by mistake," she cautiously remarked, stopping several feet away from the dilapidated van.

"Are you sure?" Sienna asked as her mind turned over other possibilities. "Or do you think something may have been stolen from inside?"

"No." The woman shook her head. "There's really nothing inside to steal."

Sienna stood back as the woman opened the doors and then stepped away to allow her access. Then, just as she bent forward to place the cumbersome geode on the cheaply carpeted floor, the wind was nearly knocked out of her. Someone grabbed her from behind, pinning her arms down to her sides. Shocked, Sienna drew in a quick breath. It was as if her attacker had expected her reaction, and a cloth with a strange, pungent smell was clamped over her nose and mouth. She began to struggle. She turned her head, attempting to free her face of the cloth. When her terrified eyes widened even further, they took in the woman standing passively a few feet away. Concern could be seen in her gaze, but it was obvious to Sienna she had known all along this would happen. She was part of a set up. But why?

Sienna's knees began to buckle as the concoction on the cloth took effect. The piercing scream she wanted to give resembled a breathy, painful moan. Then all of her limbs seemed to turn into melting wax, and she tumbled into a dizzying darkness.

Two

"She comin' out of it," a distant male voice warned. "It ready?"

The words reached Sienna through a mental fog. She could hear herself taking deep breaths through her nose and her mouth, which only magnified the cloying scent inside her nostrils. Her eyelids began to flutter, and, even though she thought her eyes had partially opened, the darkness around her was almost as solid as the blackness she experienced when the nauseous fumes overtook her. Sienna's mouth was extremely dry, and her tongue felt like a foreign object.

"Here. Hold this," a familiar female voice instructed as it moved closer. "Let me take care of her."

Sienna felt an arm being slipped around her shoulders. "I am sorry they were so rough with you," the voice crooned. "Here drink this." She felt a cup being pressed to her lips.

Weak, Sienna moved her lips away from the container. She tried to shake her head, but ended with more of a loll. "But why?" Her voice was weak and raspy.

"Do not try to talk now," the woman advised. "Drink this. I know your mouth as dry as volcano ash. This quench your thirst and calm your nerves."

The ability to think coherently was slowly returning to Sienna, but it was her fear that spoke to her the loudest. She tried to focus on the face of her would-be benefactor, but it was too dark to make out her features. Was she the woman who had stood calmly by while she was being attacked? Sienna opened her mouth to respond, which enabled the woman to pour a small quantity of a fruity tasting substance inside. She swallowed involuntarily. It felt like a soothing balm on her thick tongue, but the minute quantity of liquid only emphasized her thirst.

"That was good, was it?" the female said, continuing to entice her. "Be good to yourself. I will not allow them to harm you further. Drink." She pressed the cup against Sienna's lips, allowing some of the liquid to trickle out against them. Immediately, Sienna's tongue flicked out to capture the precious drops, and almost of its own volition her mouth opened further. She swallowed the liquid in thick gulps until the woman advised her to drink the brew slowly. Sienna licked her lips again, then finished the contents of the cup at a slower pace.

"Now you should begin to feel better immediately." The woman sounded as if she were singing close to Sienna's ear. "The liquid will renew you. Give you a new beginning."

An extreme calm floated up inside her. Her lips turned up in a slight smile although she knew not why, and her eyes closed with serenity.

"I have never been fortunate enough to experience the liquid of new life," the woman continued. "Nor have I had the honor of bestowing it on another, although I knew the rites. It a very precious substance that has an exalted history. Kings and queens of Egypt had it at their disposal, and now my master, Paz, is one of a limited few who found out these secrets. But I am the one with the knowledge to make them a reality."

Sienna could feel a hand smoothing her hair, and she remained in a trance-like state as she listened to the woman's melodic voice.

"It under his instruction that we were told to find you

and, once we were certain of your identity, to administer the liquid of new life to you. You see, my master, Paz, is a worldwide collector of rare things. Him a very rich man, which enables him to obtain just about anything that his heart desires. So when him was told the last of the legendary Stonekeepers lived in the United States in a city called Atlanta, his heart was set to possess you for his own." The voice ceased for a moment. "So now, Sienna Russell, now that I have seen the mark of the crystal on your body for myself, I will carry out my master's wishes. All of what has happened to you today, and your life up to now, will be but a distant dream. You can see them fading, fading into the past. Only the things that I tell you are safe to remember. From this moment on, them will you embrace as your own memories."

Scenes of Sienna's life from the present to the past began to drift through her mind. Her days at the shop with Dawn, endless days and nights of passion with Hawk, being forced to acknowledge her position as The Last of the Stonekeepers, coming close to death on the island of Martinique because of a stone called The Passion Ruby, meeting Hawk. From there, other life sequences seemed to speed up . . . the funeral of her great-great aunt Jessi, who was The Stonekeeper before her, the shop, school, living in the orphanage, finding out her parents had died in a train wreck.

A need to resist the pleasurable wave that was sweeping her away rose up in Sienna. It urged her to hold on to the past. She could see herself in her mind's eye, both arms stretched out before her as images of her past backed away into the distance. Of all the faces, Hawk's was the most vivid, the most compelling. Maybe it was because the love she had for him burned so fervently within her. Sienna's beautiful features contracted from emotional pain.

"Do not fret," the female voice tried to reassure her.

"You can hold on to your childhood. It the images of the recent past that you must forget. Like a veil, the liquid of new life surrounds your last year in a fog, and only the things that I tell you will you remember."

Sienna fought to hold onto Hawk's image, but the tone wove its way deep into her will, soothing the hurt within her, and to Sienna this voice became her reality.

"You will enjoy your new land, Costa Rica, and your new home, my master's estate, Shangri-la. There is no place richer or more beautiful." She paused. "Your life at Shangri-la will be like paradise." She moved Sienna's head onto her lap.

"Now, you shall enter the state of the in between." She began to rub the spot in the middle of Sienna's forehead in a circular motion. "Like a sponge you will absorb the stories that I tell you. They will easily become your memories if you allow them to. But there is one thing that you must not forget." She pressed the spot of her symbolic third eye gently. "It is that you are The Last of the Stonekeepers. I want you to remember your victory with The Passion Ruby. Only the faces and the identities of the people involved will be unimportant to you. You see the thing you must understand, your value lies in your being a Stonekeeper." The woman removed her fingers. "Later, you will meet me, Tina, for the first time. It my desire that you come to think of me as a friend." She stroked Sienna's spongy curls. "Rest comfortably, child, as I tell you the stories of your life. The journey to our homeland be a short one. Paz's helicopter waits for you."

"So it's settled. And I don't want to hear another word, Hawk. You're going to stay with my daughter and me, at least until you've made better plans." Authority rang in Nanna's voice.

"I guess that's that," Charmagne commented as her eyes met Hawk's in the rearview mirror.

He looked into her friendly gaze, then closed his eyes suddenly. "Is something wrong?" Hawk heard Charmagne ask, although he did not answer.

Feelings and thoughts were reaching him from another place. It was as if he, in some way, was miles away emotionally, and he knew without a doubt it had begun. Sienna's life had once again been caught up in fulfilling her fate as a Stonekeeper, and his connection with her had been reestablished.

Sienna's feelings were of betrayal. It was overwhelming. He could feel her shock, and the fear that followed. Hawk was an involuntary, long distance sentient, and he felt helpless despite the knowledge he possessed. How cruel life could be. He would know the very moment the tide of destiny was pulling Sienna in, and the only thing he could do was wait.

It had taken time, but Hawk had come to understand he could not upset the delicate balance of the events that surrounded her. It was because there was so much at stake. He had finally come to the realization that Sienna's role as a Stonekeeper was important to humankind. It was her legacy to record human history inside the chosen gems before the millennium arrived, and with it the uncertainty of humankind's future.

Hawk understood far too well what it felt like to be forced into a situation not of your own choosing. Leaving Sienna that morning was the hardest thing he ever had to do, but he had made a solemn vow in Martinique, when her life was being threatened because of him and The Passion Ruby. Hawk had promised the powers that be that he would no longer ignore his gift of sight, and he would use it to help others if her life was spared. At the time, he had no idea this vow would mean leaving Sienna and travelling all around the world, alone.

For weeks after he left her he experienced her pain and longing, as well as his own The desolation was almost more than he could bear. Then her hurt had turned to anger. To know she held such an emotion against him was devastating. In an extremely volatile moment, he had demanded that if the powers that be held any compassion for him, this knowing of Sienna's feelings be taken away if he could not be with her. In an instant the connection was severed.

Hawk regretted he had never been able to tell her the entire truth about himself, how he had been haunted by ghastly physical transformations that forced him to become solitary, all because he had tried to deny his prophetic sight. But no matter how he had wanted to share all of himself with Sienna, he could not. He was afraid that she would no longer want him, that she would not want a man who had been cursed as a result of his own selfish quest for fame and wealth.

Still, he admitted there was another reason he had not told her. In truth, it was impossible for Hawk to reveal what he did not know. His life reeked with uncertainties. How would the transformations ultimately affect him? What would the powers that be expect from him in the future?

"Are you alright back there?" Charmagne's voice echoed alarm.

Hawk opened his eyes, but he kept his gaze away from the rearview mirror.

"Yes. I'm fine."

"He'll do just fine staying with us, at least for tonight." Nanna misunderstood her daughter's reason for asking the question. "Because if it wasn't for him, I would be just another statistic in a foreign country." She went on, repeating the circumstances under which she and Hawk met as Hawk looked out the window. "And people talk about crime in our Black communities back in the states.

It gets bad sometimes, but from what just happened, I'm a witness crime is everywhere," she announced with a final nod. "So Charmagne, I want you to know you're not escaping anything by moving here."

"I wasn't trying to escape, Mama. I was just tired of teaching, and I knew from visiting here that I could make a new, simple life in Costa Rica."

"I live in a house on the outskirts of Limon," Charmagne said for Hawk's benefit. "I believe you'll find it to be comfortable enough."

"I'm sure I will."

"I hope for your own sake that you are either an early riser or a hard sleeper," Charmagne said, continuing with her pleasant chatter. "I've turned the back of my home into a kind of bakery. I bake bread during the early morning hours and sometimes my neighbors come by rather early to purchase a loaf or two."

"You don't have to be concerned about any of that. I simply appreciate your hospitality." Hawk made eye contact with Charmagne again through the mirror, then looked away. For the first time he noticed she was rather attractive, with her short natural hair, round face and full lips. "Plus, I am an early riser, and now I'm looking forward to my first taste of freshly baked loaf bread."

"Well, you are definitely in for a treat," Nanna interjected. " 'Cause no one bakes bread like Charmagne. I don't know where she gets it from, because she sure didn't get it from me," she confided, looking over her shoulder. "And she definitely didn't learn it while she was in college studying to be a linguist."

"A linguist?" Hawk's curiosity was roused. "Is that how you came to live in Costa Rica?"

"In a way," Charmagne replied. "I love different languages, and that made me want to know about different cultures and their origins." She maneuvered the car around a truck with a flatbed piled high with bananas and a boy with gangly legs swinging off its rear. "So, I saved my money from teaching and travelled when I could. Then, during one summer trip I came here to Costa Rica. The blend of people fascinated me, but I was most intrigued by the people of African descent who basically lived near the coast, near Limon. Oh, my goodness," Charmagne erupted, "with all this excitement involving you, Mama, I completely forgot this is the beginning of the gatherings for the Virgin of Los Angeles." Charmagne steered the car behind several others that were travelling at a snail's pace. "If I had been thinking clearly I would have taken another route."

"The beginning of *what?*" Nanna leaned forward, trying to see beyond the cars.

"Oh, Mama, I've told you about this before." She looked at her mother as she continued to drive. "La Negrita. The Black Virgin, Costa Rica's patron saint," she said, attempting to spark her memory before looking in the mirror at Hawk. "Even though we can't see it right now, I'm sure the cars are being held up by the procession. Hordes of people come to the city of Cartago to visit the Basilica Of Our Lady Of the Angels, which was built in La Negrita's honor nearly four hundred years ago."

"Yes, I do remember your telling me something about this," Nanna said as the car passed through the immense crowd of believers.

"Are the miracle stories true about people drinking water from the stream behind the church?" Hawk inquired. "I read that was where the original statue of the Black Virgin was found."

"From the things that I have heard, yes. There are people who still claim they are being cured of all kinds of ills and diseases." Charmagne replied with conviction. "And as you can see, they come by the hundreds, actually the thousands, from as far away as Panama, Guanacaste, Nicoya and Nicaragua."

"Charmagne, you should have remembered this," Nanna reprimanded. "You know sometimes I suffer horribly from arthritis in both of my knees. I wouldn't be against drinking some of that water myself."

"It's not too late, Mama," Charmagne assured her. "You can still join the procession, if you want to. I can let you out right here."

Nanna studied the unbelievably long, slow-moving line of pilgrims.

"Well, maybe next time." She clasped her hands together. "I'm sure Hawk's tired after that plane ride, and he needs to get to a place where he can rest his head for a while."

"Whatever you say, Mama." Charmagne smiled to herself as they chugged slowly past the procession, down the road toward Limon.

Three

"Tina. You are back." Paz raised his eyes momentarily from the brimming gold and silver dipper. After the brief interruption he continued to fill the matching neo-Russian wine cup with his favorite wine. Tina watched as he placed the ladle back in the smoky colored intoxicant with care, making sure he did not scrape the insides of the richly ornamented imitation bucket that contained it.

It was always hard to tell what he was thinking, because he always gave the appearance of complete calm. Tina knew Paz enjoyed and therefore maintained a certain sense of order and control in all endeavors, sometimes compulsively so. It had taken years for him to master his emotions in such a way. Tina remembered a time when his anger flowed like lava. It was a time she would rather forget.

Ceremoniously, Paz downed the wine, wiping out the cup with a handsewn towel used expressly for that purpose. Afterward, he placed the cup back in its appropriate place. With his movements announcing a *fait accompli*, Paz covered the wine with a lid fashioned by his most accomplished goldsmith.

Tina watched as Paz placed a hand dramatically against his abdomen, while his dark eyes closed momentarily. Once he had told her that the wine created an internal furnace inside of him, making him feel alive, powerful. He had said it helped him understand the energy that caused volcanoes like Arenal to erupt in such disastrous splendor. It was all a part of its nature, what it was created to be. He had said the wine helped him control the volcano that raged inside of him.

"You have returned so quickly, Tinatico." His mouth spread into a charming smile. Purposefully, he used the pet name. He wanted to show his pleasure toward the only person in the world who had extended kindness to him while he was a child, barely surviving on the street.

"Yes, I have," she agreed, nodding her head, "because things went very well."

Their eyes held.

"Her is here," Tina announced.

This time Paz couldn't help but give a small display of his exhilaration, and he placed his hand upon Tina's thin cheek.

"The Stonekeeper is here at Shangri-la." Only the sound of his own voice confirming it seemed to make the deed a reality. "The person who might be the rarest human being on earth, if the legend is true. The person who could help me find The Pirate's Emerald." His words became a hushed whisper. "Tell me, Tinatico, does she possess the mark of the crystal?"

"Yes." She nodded once again.

"Where?"

"The small mark can be seen between her breasts."

"Oh-h." The single word held many implications. "But of course, I am sure fortune would not be so extravagant as to give such unique powers to a woman of beauty. It would be more than heaven could take." Paz smoothed his precisely cut mustache.

"As I've told you before, my Paz, you should never be too sure about anything or anyone until them have been tested."

"So, is that your way of saying this Stonekeeper's value goes beyond her legendary abilities?"

"I can tell you without hesitation her is good-looking, but her also has a kind heart, my Paz, and there is no value that can be placed on that."

"Rest assured, it won't be her heart that *I* am interested in, Tinatico." Flashing brown eyes made his feelings clear before Paz turned his back. "Do you think the elixir of renewal has done its job?"

Tina observed a change in his carriage, and she knew his mind was exploring brand new possibilities surrounding the woman. Paz's chest appeared to expand beneath his emerald green, silk shirt as he perched on the edge of a table, crossing his ankles below the cuffs of matching pants.

"I no reason to believe that it hasn't," Tina finally answered. ""After I gave it to her, and filled her mind with chosen memories, her fell into the expected sleep. At this time her has not awakened. It will probably be early morning when her does."

"Good." Paz stood up and clutched a key suspended from a gold chain around his neck. "Take me to where she sleeps. I think I'd like to look at this Stonekeeper while she is not aware. That way I can study her at my leisure." Slowly, he smoothed his palms one against the other.

Tina looked down at her feet before replying, "Her is in the Egyptian suite."

The well oiled, ibis-embossed doors opened with the slightest bit of pressure from Paz's hand. Tina followed closely on his heels as he entered, but she stopped just inside the threshold, keeping an observant distance. Her wise eyes travelled from the still figure on the bed to the man she had known for the last thirty-five years. She recalled the first time she set eyes on him in Tortugeuro, selling stolen turtle eggs; he was a dirty, ten year old boy. Today, he was a man of wealth, with so much power amongst the locals that it seemed to ooze from his pores.

Paz approached Sienna in the same reverent manner that he displayed with all his prized possessions. He had spent years gathering rare and beautiful objects to surround him, but this was the first time a human being was being added to that collection. Tina knew that he had studied her origins, like those of all of his priceless treasures. Paz had found out how Sienna's parents died, how she had spent most of her childhood in an orphanage, and that, Jessi Thompson, her great-great aunt, was believed to be The Stonekeeper before her. Although he gave no outward sign, Tina knew excitement boiled over inside him, because she knew Paz in a way no other person did.

He stood stark still as he looked at Sienna as she lay upon the bed, so still that as the moments passed Tina wondered what was going through his mind.

Finally, Paz leaned down and removed the silver bangle from The Stonekeeper's wrist. "The bracelet," he announced in hushed tones. Moments later, he touched her face and allowed his hand to travel downward, adjusting her scooped neck top to reveal the telltale mark. Tina heard the breath catch in his throat, and he turned eyes gleaming with amazement and something else toward her, like a child who had found his favorite toy beneath the tree on Christmas day. Collecting himself, Paz returned his attention to the steady rise and fall of Sienna's breasts. His gaze cut a trail to her trim waist encased in a wide, red belt, down to her hips that were smothered in colorful yards of material. He started to lift the end of her skirt to reveal more than the bottom half of her legs, but instead he dropped it back around Sienna's legs in a flounce of red, beige and black, emitting an anticipatory chuckle. Paz tapped his index finger against his lips as he crossed the room toward Tina, and stood in front of her.

"I want you to tell her one more thing for me." His mouth slid into a sly smile.

Tina stared at him, waiting.

"Give her the memory that we have been more than friends in the past. Tell her," he paused, "that we are lovers. That we are practically engaged." He stroked the key that lay against his hairless chest. "That should add a new twist to our . . . relationship. A pleasurable one that I had not anticipated."

Tina took in every detail of the face of the man she had watched turn from a mischievous, angry child into an attractive, yet devious man. "You know I will do what you have asked of me, Paz, but I feel I must warn you now. Of all women, this woman is special to The Earth Mother. You promised me that you would treat her well." Tina looked down again as a tinge of anger entered Paz's eyes. "Her not one of your inanimate objects that you have imported from across the sea, my Paz. Her a flesh and blood human being. You must take special care of how you treat her, lest you regret it in the end."

"I don't need your warnings, Tina," Paz snapped. "Just make sure she is at my breakfast table in the morning, with the proper memories intact." He started to walk away, then pivoted, showing Tina only half his face. "I have taken good care of you for many years, old woman, and I will do the same for her as long as it pleases *me*."

"You're bright and early this morning, Selles." Charmagne smiled, wiping her hands on her apron. "And that means you get the first loaf of the day."

"That t'is good, 'cause I haf to be on my way. My cousin David's been doing some brick work at Shangri-la. Him told me they could use a few more men. I thought I'd be one of the first to show my face this morning. That way I know I'll get some work today." Selles brushed his hand across his wooly hair.

"That's why you do so well, Selles. You know everybody, and you're not afraid to work, and work hard." Charmagne's smile brightened even further when she saw Hawk enter the room.

Selles twisted his mouth to the side and began to chew on his bottom lip, enjoying the praise. "I always try to get in on the projects them have going from time to time. Shangri-la's a good place to work, 'cause them feed you well and the pay is pretty good. Plus, it's a real pretty place, although I only worked on the grounds and have never been inside." Selles wrapped the brown paper bag around the warm loaf of bread Charmagne had given him.

"Selles," she said, interrupting his monologue. "I'd like to introduce Hawk. He arrived in Costa Rica yesterday, the same time as my mother," she explained. "I'm not too sure about how long he'll be around. He seems to be rather secretive about that."

"Wa'apin, Hawk," Selles chimed.

Hawk accepted the rough hand that was stretched out in welcome, as well as the warm slice of buttered bread Charmagne offered from behind the counter.

"I tell you, that the way some people are," Selles continued. "Take that Mr. Paz, for instance, him who own Shangri-la. There have been some strange stories about him and some of the goings on at that place. I know you've heard them, Charmagne."

"Yes, I have. Usually from you, Selles." She gave Hawk a clandestine wink as the older man looked down, nodding his head.

"But we all know how much power that man has around here. There not too many folks that would dare to cross him." Both of his thick eyebrows lifted, nearly meeting a generous fold in his forehead. "Yes, him powerful, and I know that him owns a lot of valuable things. The word is, for years him been paying some of the workers in the Columbian emerald mines to smuggle for him. I hear all this stuff from my cousin, David. But I think of all the things that him told me, what him said last night is the most bizarre story yet." Selles shook his head, and his eyes made sure he had captivated his audience with his pronouncement.

"Is that right?" Charmagne commented accordingly, well aware of how much Selles liked to gossip.

"That's right," he eagerly encouraged. "David claims them was told about some woman that's nearly Mr. Paz's fiancéee. But him says there had never been even the slightest whisper about such a woman before. But yet and still, the announcement was made that her would be staying at Shangri-la, and that them should treat her with the utmost respect." His dull eyes widened. "But I tell you," he said, leaning forward in a conspiratorial manner, "David's been dealing with Maud, who works in the kitchen up there, and her said her overheard a conversation between Mr. Paz and Tina. That the woman who practically runs the place. Maud said some really strange things were said about this woman. Her said her didn't quite understand it, but this woman suppose to have some kind of mark on her body that makes her special. But *raas*, it suppose to have something to do with stones or gems."

Hawk's teeth locked on the slice of bread because of Selles' words.

"Stones." Charmagne tried to stifle her laughter under Selles' offended gaze.

"You laughing, Miss Charmagne," Selles said, and threw back his shoulders, "but if you get to be as old as I am you'll find out there are plenty of things that sound crazy that hold a lot of truth." He turned to make his exit.

Hawk concentrated on keeping his voice low and calm as he spoke. "You say they are looking for a couple of extra men to do masonry work?"

"That's right." Selles sized up the man who leaned against the counter.

"I think I'll come along with you, if you don't mind. I could use a few extra dollars."

"You know anything about brick and tile laying?"

Hawk nodded his head slowly as he popped the last piece of bread in his mouth. He stood up straight before he looked Selles directly in the eye. "I've been a lot of places, and I've done all kinds of work."

Selles scratched the side of his nose, as he always did when he was in the midst of making a decision. "Alright then, I'm recommend you for the job. Come on with me while I drop this bread off at home, then we'll head on over to Shangri-la."

"I guess this means you plan to stay in Limon for a while," Charmagne commented, a hopeful gleam in her eye.

"It looks that way at the moment. It all depends on what happens over at Shangri-la." Hawk gave the woman a wry smile. "Thanks for the breakfast, Charmagne, and the hospitality." He paused before he spoke again. "If things go well and I get the job, I'd like to rent that room from you while I'm here."

"I believe we can work that out," Charmagne replied.

Hawk nodded, then followed Selles outside. The older man's pace was brisk as they headed down the road, but it was easy for Hawk, with his long strides, to stay abreast of him.

Waves of anticipation rose and faded in him as he thought about what Selles had said. There was a woman at Shangri-la with a special mark on her body, and it was related to stones. He knew there was a ninety-nine percent chance that the woman the rumor referred to was Sienna Russell.

But under what circumstances had she come to Costa Rica? In the months that they had been apart had she fallen in love with another man? Was it the owner of this place called Shangri-la? He had told Charmagne everything depended on what happened at Shangri-la. Those words held more meaning than she could ever know.

A vision had brought Hawk to Costa Rica, the only one he had experienced in months that involved Sienna, and he knew her second encounter as a Stonekeeper was about to begin. It was during the first cycle that he initially met her. They had come together under unfavorable circumstances, and embarked on a search for The Passion Ruby, but their search for the ruby had yielded more than the gem. Their physical attraction for one another was undeniable, and the love that grew from it was the most powerful he had ever known.

Now it was time for him to come face to face with her again. Although he feared she hated him because he had left her, his life's path was still tied to her role as The Stonekeeper, and his heart still belonged to Sienna, the woman.

Hawk drew a deep breath. How strange life could be. Out of love for Sienna he had promised to use the gift of sight he had ignored for so long, but he had not known that embracing it would force him to leave her. He knew leaving had been the right thing to do. Hawk was convinced that if he had stayed he would have destroyed the love they shared, for when the sight was upon him the power it possessed was nearly uncontrollable. It consumed him body and soul. At that time he was a pure vessel for the powers that be. He would not have been able to give of himself to her, because there was so little of the man she knew to give.

Hawk had no idea what circumstances awaited him at Shangri-la, but there was one thing he did know—time and distance had not dulled his love for the woman he had come to know as The Last Stonekeeper.

Four

"Good morning, Sienna. It is good to see you finally awake," a voice said from across the room.

Sienna turned her head in the direction of the sound. The image of a woman walking toward her was slightly blurred.

"You given us quite a scare." The woman rested her hands on the bed. "You been sleep for a whole day. But the doctor assured us it was just a matter of time before you awakened. How you feel? Does your head hurt?"

Sienna put her hand up against her temple, moving her head back and forth.

"No, I don't feel any pain, but things are a little fuzzy."

"I'm surprised, but glad. You had quite a fall."

Concern filled Sienna's eyes. "I did? Maybe that explains why I recognize your face, but I don't remember your name."

"I'm Tina." The woman gave her a slight smile. "I met you at the airport. I don't want you to be alarmed if you don't remember everything right away, because the doctor told us to expect a little of that. Meaning some memory lost, even jumbled memories. But don't you worry, Paz is going to make sure that you are well taken care of. Him feels so bad that the accident happened here at Shangri-la. Now him even more determined than ever to make sure you have a good time during your first stay here."

EMERALD'S FIRE

"Paz?" Sienna sat up in the bed, smoothing a cloud of dark hair away from her face. "The name sounds familiar."

"You don't remember Paz?" Tina acted truly surprised. "Him be so hurt to know that, although I'm sure him understand," she threw in, with her eyes downcast. "You met in the United States, and him has been to see you many time since. This is Paz's home." She extended her arm, showcasing the room. "Do you remember anything about your trip to Costa Rica?"

Sienna shook her head, puzzled by her own lack of recollection.

"Well, I am sure that it will all come back to you with time." Tina folded her hands in front of her. "And a good breakfast might set you well on your way. You know how generous Paz is," Tina looked down at her hands. "He felt so bad about your injury that him special ordered you all kinds of clothes. They are in the closet and this set of drawers." She went over and stood by a chest of drawers made of ebony. "The bathroom over there," she said, pointing, "and breakfast will be served in thirty minutes. One of the servants, called Maud, will be available to show you the way." Tina reached the door and turned back toward Sienna once again. "There is a vial of medication beside your bed." Her eyes gleamed. "The doctor says you should drink all of it this morning, and another will be brought to you before the day is over."

Sienna watched Tina exit the room as her thoughts tumbled over one another. The names and circumstances she had mentioned were familiar. Yes, a man named Paz had been a part of her life, he had even been her lover, but no matter how she tried she could not recall his face. How strange! The memories were there, but somehow she did not *feel* they were her own. Sienna's logical side argued, *How could that be?* It agreed with her memories and Tina's statements, but somewhere in her gut she was not sure.

Sienna's gaze travelled around the room, which was exquisitely decorated in Egyptian style decor with priceless artifacts. One thing was very apparent to her as she inspected it . . . no cost had been spared in creating her amazing surroundings.

She climbed out of the bed expecting her skull to ring with pain, but there was none, and her head had totally cleared. For a moment she felt relieved. Then panic over her mental state began to surface. Quickly, Sienna closed her eyes, telling herself over and over again this state of confusion was only temporary. Determined to bring some normalcy into her situation, she drew a deep breath, opened her eyes, and headed straight for the closet. She slid the glass-covered door aside and found a variety of dresses, pants and shirts hanging in neat, color coordinated rows. Below them sat a slew of shoes in colors and styles that would match any wardrobe.

Consumed by her thoughts, Sienna selected a red and yellow floral pantsuit made of chiffon, and a pair of vermillion sandals. She laid the delicate outfit over her arm, causing the material to flow as she crossed the room to the chest of drawers, where she selected a matching set of underwear.

As she entered the bathroom Sienna observed that it was decorated in the same exquisite style as the bedroom. A mural of the Nile laden with ancient Egyptian ships graced one of the immense walls, while elaborate masks of Egyptian gods such as Isis and Ra hung majestically on others.

Sienna was surprised to see that the sunken bathtub, surrounded by columns, was full of turquoise blue, scented water. She had never had a servant draw her bath before, and the thought of it felt foreign, but pleasing.

She went over the things Tina had told her in her mind

as she took off the unfamiliar white nightgown and slipped into the warm, slick wetness, unsure of herself and what was to come. Feeling extremely vulnerable, she prayed her memory would completely return, as Tina said the physician had promised it would.

The bath was a quick one. Afterwards Sienna dried off with a mauve towel that was soft and plush. She looked up to see the only thing that was familiar, her own image in a large, beetle shaped mirror. Her dark brown, almond shaped eyes appeared extremely bright in her dark pecan, oval face, and she knew it was fear she saw in them.

Sienna's hand rose and traced her heart-shaped lips, then her small but slightly protruding nose, as if reacquainting herself with her own features, a way of reassuring herself that she was the woman she believed herself to be. A nervous hand ran over her shoulder-length, dark hair, which bushed around her face. Instinctively, she reached for her own comb and brush, but a carved set of ivory greeted her touch. That was when she realized there had been no sign of her own belongings, her purse, nor the luggage she would have brought with her on the trip. She determined to inquire about the articles at breakfast as she combed through her tightly waved locks, parting them on the side, allowing the thick cloud to fall as it may.

Finally, she slipped on the expensive pantsuit and shoes. The material felt like cool silk against her skin. As a finishing touch, she dabbed on color from one of several tubes of lipstick that were arranged decoratively, along with an array of make-ups and perfumes. A knock sounded as she blotted her lips and reentered the adjoining bedroom.

"Come in."

"Are you ready for breakfast, Ma'am?" The slim woman stepped into the room with lowered eyes.

"Yes, I guess I am," Sienna replied as she crossed the floor.

Maud moved aside, allowing Sienna to exit before her. Sienna could feel the woman's curious eyes boring into her back before she turned and said, "It probably would be better if you led the way."

"Of course, Ma'am," she replied as she hurried past her.

They entered a large hall that extended in both directions, and from that alone Sienna could tell the house was immense. She followed Maud down a majestic curved stairwell. Once they arrived at the bottom, the maid gestured toward a set of double doors.

"Breakfast is being held there in the breakfast salon, Ma'am." She turned on her heels and headed in the opposite direction.

Sienna crossed the circular area and reached out to open one of the high gloss doors, but before she could, it opened. She found herself standing within arm's reach of a man. For a moment she was startled, and her gaze rose from his chest to his face, which was surrounded by light brown dreadlocks. Their eyes locked, and somewhere inside Sienna felt instant recognition. A barrage of emotions assaulted her as she watched his eyes change from hazel to a smoky green. They both seemed to hold their breath as Sienna's mind fought for clarity, and her lips trembled to form a name.

"Sienna, my darling," a rich voice purred from somewhere behind her.

She heard her name, but it was hard to extricate herself from the magnetism of the stranger in front of her. Finally, as she looked down and saw the masonry tools in his hands, another set of hands settled on her shoulders.

"Sienna, it is so good to see you up and about." Paz pulled her into his arms. "When I heard that you had fallen and hit your head, it gave me quite a scare. Tina tells me you are still suffering from the effects of it. You are having problems remembering some things."

Sienna's arms remained at her sides as she looked into Paz's attractive face. She searched the dark eyes of the man she believed to be her lover, but there was nothing there that sparked even an ounce of emotion.

She took a step backward, turning to look at the hazel-eyed stranger.

"Are you still working in there?" Paz asked with authority, his irritation showing.

"Yes, but the job is almost complete."

"Good, because I don't want you stirring up dirt and dust while my beloved and I are eating breakfast." Paz looked at the worker, who stood a few inches taller than he did. Curiosity surfaced in his eyes. "I haven't seen you around here before."

"I was hired this morning, along with Selles."

"I see." Paz mulled over the information. "What is your name?"

"Hawk." He said it low, with a breathiness that sounded like the wind, his gaze riveted on Sienna's face.

Paz's eyes narrowed. "Since you are new around here, Hawk, I'll forgive you your insolence," he snapped, "but there is a kind of caste system in my home. Let me explain it to you." He leaned forward in Hawk's direction. "A worker knows his place, and that involves, among other things, keeping your eyes lowered, except when you are being spoken to." Paz put his arm around Sienna's shoulders as he pushed open the other door. "Now hurry and finish your work. I want all of it done before the dinner tonight," he ordered.

Sienna allowed herself to be led into the breakfast area, where a table was set entirely in silver. She did not like the way Paz had spoken to the man named Hawk. There was no need for any human being to treat another in such a condescending fashion. But there was also something about the man that had struck a chord inside her. It was apparent that he was only a worker, but somehow he seemed more familiar than Tina, and even Paz.

Sienna noticed how Paz's arm felt like a possessive clasp as he escorted her to a chair. She was glad when he let her go, and pulled out the miniature St. Anne for her convenience.

No sooner had they settled themselves, Paz sitting in front of her, than a servant entered the room. In silence he began to open one covered dish after another, displaying the fare as well as offering to serve it. Steam rose like genie smoke above the table, releasing aromas that Sienna did not associate with breakfast. She examined each of the dishes with subtle curiosity, and Sienna could tell Paz took pleasure in introducing each of the portions the servant offered.

"Now this is *gallo pinto*, which is always served during breakfast. It is a combination of rice and beans fried together. You can have it with eggs or ham." He paused as the servant hoisted another dish. "That is *sopa negra*. It is made with black beans, and can be served with poached eggs. As you can see, there is a variety of fruits," Paz announced with a sweeping hand, "and this is a bread that my people call *pan bon*. You usually find it on the coast. That is where most people of Jamaican descent live. I suggest you have *sopa negra*." He motioned for the servant to administer the dish along with the egg.

"No," Sienna responded, "I don't believe I want that. I'd like the bread, please," she informed the male servant.

Distress rose on the servant's dark face at her contradiction of Paz's order, and he looked to his boss for further instruction. Sienna saw Paz nod his head ever so slightly before the bun was put on her plate. She did not like the feeling that gave her. Was Paz so controlling that the servants didn't dare to heed anyone else's request without his permission? And had she allowed him to control her to the extent of choosing the foods she ate? Her brow wrinkled as she looked down at the designs swirled inside the batter on top of the bun. Just the thought of such control seemed to go against her very nature. She watched in silence as the servant poured steaming hot coffee into silver cups buffed to perfection. Paz did not appear to be aware of her mental dilemma. He was consumed with his own explanation of the origin of the dishes.

Moments later, Paz looked up from his meal, his gaze following the movement of someone who had entered behind her. Finally, the man Hawk came into view. His muscular body moved in graceful lines as he knelt several feet behind Paz. He began to scoop up grout, smoothing it between new pieces of Italian tile that trimmed the face of a small rock garden. Sienna watched him for a moment before she returned to eating her meal.

She was extremely aware of the worker's presence as Paz talked about her stay at Shangri-la and the things he planned for them to do. The main thing on his mind was a party he had scheduled for that night.

"I want the entertainment and the food to be just perfect, because all kinds of people will be attending, residents of Costa Rica and some of the surrounding countries. Most of them, like me, are collectors. Of course my closest acquaintances know all about you," he commented with his eyes feasting on Sienna, "and they are dying to meet you."

"Oh. And why is that?" Sienna asked, her feelings about Paz still unclear, her dark eyes darting to Hawk as he worked slowly behind him.

"Because they've never known me to talk so much about any other woman." He gave her a beautiful smile. "And that is because there has never been another woman who has been as important to me as you have, Sienna."

"So I take it from that we have been seeing each other for a long time."

"Yes. It is close to a year now," Paz lied.

Immediately, Sienna looked back down at her plate. "I feel so strange because I don't remember anything about us." She shook her head. "It is as if I know certain things have taken place . . ." she said, pausing as she attempted to say the right thing, "but my feelings don't seem to go along with my memories." She looked up again, only to see Hawk staring straight at her from behind Paz's back. Their gaze held for a moment, until she forced herself to focus on Paz's face.

"Well, I don't think you should fret about that. I'm sure it's all related to the trauma you have suffered." He reached across the table to touch her hand. "And now that you are better, we will be able to spend more time together, to rekindle the feelings you have lost."

The meaning behind his words was perfectly clear. Slowly, Sienna removed her hand from under his.

"I was wondering about the things I must have brought with me on this trip," she told him. "Where are they?"

A sinister darkness appeared to rise in Paz's eyes as he watched her. It chilled Sienna as well as confused her, but she continued to press the issue. "I'm talking about my purse and my luggage."

"Oh, yes." Briefly, Paz's heavy lids hid his eyes and his thoughts. "I'm sure Tina is taking good care of them."

"I would like to have them put in my room," Sienna announced rather shakily. "Maybe seeing some of my own things will help jog my memory. I'm sure I have an address book with phone numbers and names inside. Perhaps some information about my own private physician. I probably should give him a call to let him know what has happened to me, in case things have not gotten better by the time I return home."

Paz brought his hands up and folded them against his chest.

"Darling, don't you remember? Before coming here we both had decided you would not be returning to the states. Things had gotten pretty serious between us, Sienna, and you were going to make your home here with me at Shangri-la." An injured look passed over his handsome features. "I can't tell you how much it hurts me that you have forgotten what has passed between us." A smug expression followed on the heels of the hurt one. "And here at Shangri-la you won't find a single telephone. I abhor the bothersome things. They are a necessary evil when it comes to work, but I consider my home to be my personal paradise. Only the things and the people that I want to have around me are allowed here. Telephones are an intrusion. Without them I can keep the world at bay."

Sienna was shocked by his pronouncement, and she stared at the man who sat across the table from her. Although she could not think of a reason why he would lie, her intuition warned her not to trust him.

Suddenly, she felt like an unwilling prisoner in a strange place, a strange land. Out of a nervous habit she reached for the silver bangle that she was accustomed to wearing around her wrist. It was not there. "My bracelet. I always wear a silver bracelet." Alarm showed in her eyes and her voice.

"Now, *that* I can help my darling with. I have it right here." With slow deliberation Paz retrieved the ornament from his pants pocket. He held it in front of him, his gaze travelling over the detailed carvings lovingly. "You kept twisting it on your arm as you slept. I thought perhaps it was bothering you. So I removed it." He passed it to her. Sienna replaced the bracelet on her slim wrist, and she thought she saw Hawk's broad shoulders stiffen as he listened to the exchange.

"It is quite unusual," Paz commented as he placed a slice of papaya in his mouth.

"Yes, it is." Sienna stared directly into his eyes as her fingers traced the markings on the ornament.

"You probably don't remember, but one day you said you would eventually tell me the entire story behind it. You said it was quite unbelievable, and that I, being a connoisseur of rare things, would be able to appreciate its origins more than the average person."

Sienna remained silent, for it seemed that just touching the bangle unearthed memories. She allowed herself to open up to the bits and pieces of her life like a flower thirsting for water. All of a sudden she was certain that in the recent past she had been through a great deal because of it. The images of those whose lives had been caught up along with her own were blurred, but one thing was clear. From birth she had inherited a unique responsibility that was connected with the bangle. Like several women before her, who had worn it, she was a Stonekeeper, destined to return gems with unusual powers back to the earth. There was a time when she did not believe that to be true, but now she knew within the depths of her life that this was her legacy. She had experienced its power not long ago.

Sienna embraced this understanding with all her heart, because these were the only memories that truly felt as if they belonged to her. Strength and clarity welled up within her, and as the realization became clearer Sienna's hand automatically rose and pressed itself against the mark that lay between her breasts. Her heavily lashed eyes shone with the weight of her understanding.

"Is something wrong, Sienna? You have the most amazing look on your face." Paz leaned closer. "Have you remembered something important?" Sienna watched his dark eyes take on a piercing look, like those of a snake waiting to strike.

"No." The conscious lie was barely a whisper, and she placed another piece of the *pan bon* in her mouth as she questioned her own response. She could not bring herself to tell Paz what she was thinking and feeling. Yet, she had taken this man to her bed! At least that's what her thoughts told her, although her heart denied it. Sienna chewed slowly. The bread seemed to turn into heavy dough inside her mouth as all of her instincts cried out not to trust him.

"I thought perhaps the bracelet had sparked your memory. That, perhaps, you had remembered more of the legend you once shared with me." He sat back, wiping the handkerchief over his mouth, his eyes filled with disbelief. "Now if I remember correctly," he pressed, "it involved something called . . . a Stonekeeper."

The sound of metal clanging against tile caused both of them to jump. Paz whirled around to confront Hawk with a venomous look upon his face.

"Are you still here?" he ground out between his teeth, his impatience with Hawk and himself for forgetting his presence very apparent.

"Yes, I was just finishing up," Hawk replied, with his back facing them.

"Well, do it, you slow, animal-eyed bastard, and get out of here." Paz spaced out the last four words as he held a cup of cooling coffee in his hand.

Sienna watched Paz vent his anger and his authority against the worker. She could see the man, Hawk, taking a deep breath as if he were trying to contain himself. Then she saw him begin to turn toward them, a blaze of emotions in his eyes.

All she could think of was halting the confrontation that was imminent. This poor worker would receive no mercy from Paz. No doubt he would lose his job, and she felt Paz would find ways even more extensive than that to punish him. She was sure that, with the money he apparently had, his influence in the area was substantial, and workers like this one depended on the jobs he provided for their welfare. She couldn't imagine what possessed him, but she could see that Hawk was on the verge of having his say. Sienna stood up abruptly to stop him.

"I'm going back to my room." Both sets of eyes were riveted on her. "I don't feel well," she announced, her voice even, a glimmer of defiance in her eyes. "I also feel I need to tell you, Paz, I'm confused by all of this, and I really don't—" Sienna's lips began to form the word "believe," but she saw an unnatural gleam rising in Paz's eyes, so she said, "think I'm adjusting to this very well. I believe I need more time to rest."

Paz placed the cup back in the saucer just as the servant reentered the room with a fresh pot of coffee.

"I will walk back with you," he offered.

"No. Please. Don't cut your breakfast short on account of me. I can easily find my way back." She pushed the chair up to the table, donning a reserved smile. She was distinctly aware that Hawk was gathering his equipment, preparing to leave.

The servant offered to pour more of the aromatic coffee, and Paz's hesitation to continue his meal was short-lived. He gave the servant the go-ahead, nodding his approval toward Sienna.

"I hope we get to spend some time together before the party tonight, but I'm sure most of my day will be occupied with preparing for the gathering. So just make yourself at home."

Sienna nodded, crossing her arms in front of her protectively as she backed up, turned, and walked out. Her heels clicked loudly against the glossy marble floor as she crossed to the staircase. She ascended it rapidly, fear mounting with every step, for she knew without a doubt that she did not love Paz, and she never could have. The gut feeling warning her against him was too strong. So why was she at Shangri-la? Had she become involved with him, afterward realizing he was not the man for her, and hadn't had the nerve to tell him? According to him, she had come to Costa Rica with the intention of remaining there. How unnatural that felt. Not only did she know she was not in love with Paz, but her feelings toward him bordered on repulsion.

Sienna stood with her hand on the bedroom doorknob, ready to open it, when a strong urge to turn around made itself known. She looked down across the catwalk and saw Hawk staring up at her as he stood at the entrance to the mansion. His yellow-tinted gaze cut into her, but there was some emotion behind it that she did not understand. Once again she felt a strong affinity with the worker, and an inclination to cross the hallway to the rail rose within her, but the sound of feet approaching on the marble floor made her hesitate. Quickly, she opened the bedroom door and stepped inside. Sienna peered out through the opening as she closed the door behind her. Hawk was gone, but she watched Tina walk to the center of the foyer just as Paz opened the door to the breakfast salon. His napkin was still in his hand as he glanced up toward her bedroom door, then began to speak to Tina in a hushed tone. Sienna thought he appeared highly frustrated. His hand movements were emphatic, while Tina's hands remained folded in front of her as she listened. Moments later they went into the breakfast salon, Paz leading the way with ardent strides.

Suddenly, the bottom of a lace tablecloth sitting near the main door began to flutter, as if someone had pulled the heavy door closed. For a second she wondered if Hawk had been standing outside, listening. What would be his reason for doing so?

With a final click Sienna closed her own bedroom

door. She walked over to the bed stand, where a new vial of the medication Tina said the doctor had prescribed for her lay. Sienna studied the tiny container, and made up her mind. Until she was clear about her own feelings and her stay at Shangri-la, she would not trust anything or anybody. She threw the medicine out of the window.

The words from a distant memory rose up, egging her on. *If it does not feel right, question it. Your intuition is your connection to the source.*

Five

There were so many doors that Sienna didn't know which one to choose, so she selected a swinging door that opened into another hallway. Unlike the others, this one was void of the plethora of paintings and artifacts that were usually displayed on the walls.

She had grown anxious sitting in the unfamiliar bedroom. The silence that surrounded her, along with a replica of a sarcophagus and figures and painting of beings from the Egyptian underworld, helped her feel as if she were in a tomb. The lapse in memory also helped Sienna to feel that parts of her were dead, and she had grown tired of trying to recall more of her past.

Sienna had no idea what Paz would feel about her unauthorized rambling through the mansion, which was proving to be quite vast. Frankly, she did not care. She was determined to find out more about Shangri-la, and in doing so perhaps find out more about herself.

There was not even the slightest squeak as she pushed against another swinging door. Like the rest of the hinges in the mansion in general, everything appeared to be in immaculately maintained condition. When Sienna entered the room on the opposite side of the door, she found herself in an immense kitchen. An island, the length of a dining table that would seat fourteen, cut through the center. Above it hung pots and pans of all sizes and types, and below them stood three women cutting up mounds of vegetables. Two double ovens occupied by a variety of meats were built into the wall, and were being carefully attended by a stout woman with her sleeves rolled up, and a heavy hair net slopping onto the side of her face. Sienna scanned the rest of the area with unbridled interest, stopping only when her eyes met the gaze of an adolescent hauling several cakes of butter from a steel door refrigerator. Shock and amazement dawned in the girl's round eyes as she continued to stare openly.

"Dorothy, what the matter with you?" a stern voice called from inside a walk-in pantry.

The girl turned toward the pantry, then faced Sienna again.

"It's her," she replied in a breathy voice.

"What are you talking about, girl?" The voice sounded as if it were emerging from a tunnel. Finally, an attractive, deep brown-skinned woman appeared.

"Oh," the woman remarked when she spotted Sienna, "I see." She advanced, wiping her hands on a tiny, white apron. "May I help you?"

By now the teenager had crossed the room to stand with the other workers, who had gathered into a gawking clump.

"I was just giving myself a tour of the house," Sienna replied. "I'm Sienna Russell." She reached out her hand in greeting.

The woman looked down at her hand before her gaze returned slowly to Sienna's face. She did not return the courtesy.

"Meaning no disrespect," she said, smoothing the hair near the side of her face, "I don't think Paz would like you travelling 'round in the house without an escort." Her face held a forced subservient look, while her eyes glowed with defiance.

"I don't think it's part of your job, Mary, to decide

what *Master* Paz thinks," Tina remarked as she entered the room.

Mary turned around, antagonistic words flowing as she went.

"But you know full well Pa-Master Paz would not like—"

"That's not for you to decide, Mary." Tina cut her off, sternly. "Despite what you may think, I believe you should remember what your position is in this household."

They locked eyes for a moment before Mary looked down at her shoes.

Tina focused her attention on Sienna. "I must say I am surprised to find you here, in the kitchen, Sienna. Master Paz told me you planned to rest in your room for a while." A slight smile touched her lips. "Obviously, I forgot to show you how to use the intercom system. Through it you can make your needs known to any of the areas of the house."

"As a matter of fact, I did stay in the room for quite some time," Sienna replied, "but then I decided to explore the grounds." Sienna wondered if this was Tina's way of telling her she was not free to wander on her own. "I hope that isn't a problem."

"No. No problem at all," Tina assured her, maintaining the same smile.

"That reminds me, Paz told me you have put my purse and my luggage away. I'd like to get them, if you don't mind."

Tina's expression did not change, except for a slight quivering about her mouth. "I'll get someone to bring them to your room. But it may take a few moments." Tina paused. "If you like, I can show you around some of the gardens. Each suite has a view of a garden complimentary to the style and country in which it is decorated."

"My goodness, Paz is such a creative, extravagant man," Sienna said placatingly as she scanned the kitchen once again, noticing how one of the kitchen helpers appeared to be visually searching the area around her neck, "but you don't have to show me around. I'd like to venture out on my own."

"Alright." Tina bowed her head. "But I must warn you, the grounds are vast, and you could get confused in the maze of hedges. You are still recovering from your fall, you know."

"I'll keep that in mind, but at the moment I feel fine," Sienna assured her. "Now, if you can show me to a well marked starting point, I'm sure I won't have any problem finding my way back."

Tina began to lead her out of the kitchen. As they progressed, Sienna saw a splotch of color out of the corner of her eye. She turned toward a nearby window, where a circle of blooming orchids were planted. A statue of a man wearing knee-length pants and a jacket that stopped at his waist rose several feet into the air from the center. One of his hands was hidden inside the front of the jacket, while the other wiped his brow.

"Can I enter one of the gardens from there?" Sienna pointed.

"Yes, you can, but it not lead to any of the gardens that I mentioned to you. It leads to the first garden that Master Paz had cultivated. It was created long before the mansion was completed, and it runs close to a nearby neighborhood. It is not as elaborate as the others. I am sure you would like them much better." Tina pushed against the swinging door.

"From what I've been told I will be here for quite a while." She studied the woman's face. "So I'm sure I'll get around to all of the gardens in time. But since I'm here, I might as well start with that one."

"If you insist," Tina replied. "That door will put you on the pathway." She pointed. "I suggest that you return in plenty of time to prepare for the dinner and entertainment tonight. Master Paz likes to start early, and him doesn't like for anyone to be late. But, of course, I'm sure you of all people know that." She smiled, turned and walked away.

"I hear Timothy and some of the others got away wit' a big bit t'is time," David said under his breath as he unwrapped the plantain leaves to reveal a tamale made of ground corn and pork.

"Say what?" a young man beside him retorted, leaning in closer to hear his companion's remark.

"Can't you hear, Archie? I said, I hear Timothy's group hit big t'is time." David bit off half of the snack.

"Oh." The youngest man shook his head. "Mon, I bet them goin' to be lookin' pretty at the place tomorrow night," he said, and kicked at a broad-leafed plant near his foot, "while here we sit, work as hard as them do, and don't live nearly as good. If I had my way I'd be gettin' some of t'em emeralds meself and—"

"And do what, boy?" an old man with a straw hat said, cutting him off. "Be sidin' up wit' Satan, too? Takin' what's not yours and puttin' it in your pocket, then bring it to The Paz, and him make more money than you can imagine. Him gettin' rich while you the one riskin' your life in the mines."

"I hear that how The Paz made his money in the beginnin' and, *raas* . . ." Archie's muscular arm waved dramatically, "we workin' for him now for a bit of money. So Satan may not be too bad of a partner. I don' want to be an ol' mon like you, Rumsey, broke body and pocket."

Hawk watched Selles walk over to a tree near the center of the group.

"There's no need to talk to one another t'is way." Selles looked into each one of their faces. "We all one people, and we need to act like it." He looked over at Hawk, as if to remind the group a newcomer was in their midst.

David changed the subject. "Some of the big money men are beginnin' to arrive already. I saw two of t'em bein' dropped off in front of Shangri-la. T'em had some womenfolk wit' t'em."

"I bet none of t'em be their wives," Rumsey remarked.

"Course not. My Maud says all kinds of carryin' on ends up happenin' in the house during and after these parties. Some of the t'ings her sees and hears her told me I better not repeat." David's shoulders lifted with pride because he knew the most about The Paz's private affairs. "And her says that's what The Paz likes. Him wants to keep his business partners happy. That's why him bring in t'e women, and why him hire someone outside Shangri-la to find special musicians and other entertainment. Her say everyt'ing have to be just right, or t'em catch *raas* after all the guests have gone."

"I remember when The Paz was much younger." Selles picked the remains of the meat from the *pati* out of his teeth with a tiny twig. "Him never could have thrown a party like this back t'en. Him had the money, but him no social standin' or education. So him sent himself off to some university outside of the islands, and t'at daughter of the snake doctor, Tina, looked after his business while him was away." He flicked the twig off into a bed of flowers. "When him came back he was speakin' and actin' high and mighty. And been doin' so ever since."

"High and mighty sounds fine to me," Archie interjected. "To me, the Paz is the only Black man around here who don' fit the sayin' *'Chineman run business, but Black man keep shop'*. Him got more business than you can lick a stick at."

"But look what de mon do wit' his money. Buy t'ings t'at are no use to nobody." Rumsey's negative view had not changed. "Shangri-la be more of a museum t'an a home, and now him bring in t'is woman, too. What him gone do, sit her up on a shelf? Showin' off t'at mark t'ey say she got?"

Hawk's eyes narrowed.

"The word is him got more than t'at in mind." David grinned and nudged the man beside him.

"Well." Rumsey's leathery brown, puffy fingers massaged a knobby elbow. "Him known for goin' through his women helpers, so you better keep a close eye on your Maud," he said, throwing another verbal dagger before continuing. "But we all have heard him believes t'at woman got some kind of special ability t'at will lead him to The Pirate's Emerald. T'e Paz been believin' in t'at buried treasure for years. T'ey say t'at why him put t'at pirate statue on the grounds." He thumbed in the direction behind his back. "It be his way of honorin' t'e dead, as well as lookin' for his blessin', in hopes him will help him find t'at stone. You would t'ink him had enough, wit' his take from the mines."

"The Paz is not by hisself in believin' t'ere is treasure in t'ese parts," Selles added. "T'ere are many stories about pirates bein' all around here in t'e old days. I heard t'ey would rob the folks in Bocas, and rob the Indians. T'e pirates would make t'e Indians tell where t'eir gold was before t'ey killed t'em. For some reason t'e pirates seemed to favor buryin' the treasure t'ey stole near the coast."

"*Raas.*" Archie stood up. "I don't want to hear anyt'ing else about emeralds, treasure or money, 'cause none of it is makin' my pockets any fuller." He started toward one of the paths. "T'ere's still time, so I'm goin' home for a little *guarapo*. We took it out of the calabash last night. My uncle boiled t'e milling corn about ten days ago, so it should be ready for drinkin'."

"I could use a little boost myself." David stood up and joined him. All the other men followed suit, except Hawk.

"You goin' to stay?" Selles asked.

"Yes," Hawk replied as the entire group looked on.

"We will be back in about twenty minutes," Selles informed him. "I will meet you in the Japanese garden, which is off the east wing of t'e house. It won't take us but a little while to finish t'e work t'ere, and we will be done for t'e day."

Hawk nodded, then watched as the men disappeared down the path. All morning, ever since he saw Sienna, his thoughts had been a jumbled mass. He had not known what to expect when he had gone out for the job at Shangri-la. He had hoped that it would lead him to Sienna, but the circumstances under which they met were stranger than any he could have imagined.

Hawk began to wander through the meticulously cut hedges. He recalled how they had stood no more than two feet apart, and yet it appeared she did not recognize him. Instead of recognition and the surfacing of emotions that he could understand, such as shock, happiness or anger, the look in the eyes that he knew so well was one of confusion. It was as if she had been fighting with her own inability to recognize him.

Hawk's hollow jaws grew rock hard as a grinding feeling began to churn at the base of his stomach. Paz had said Sienna had recently hit her head, and was suffering from some kind of trauma. He had also said he and Sienna had been involved in a relationship for nearly a year. Hawk stopped and looked up at the sky as he thought about it. That would mean Paz and Sienna had met just before *he* met her. It would also mean that during their brief three month relationship she had been in communication with Paz, although there had been no indication of anyone else in her life. Crinkles formed in Hawk's forehead. The bottom line was, Sienna had not been completely truthful with him, and she had not loved him as he had loved her.

Consumed by the realization, Hawk began to walk, with little thought of his destination. To believe Paz would mean that Sienna had come to Shangri-la willingly, a woman coming to her lover with the intention of staying. Hawk couldn't help but wonder if her hurt and anger over his desertion had contributed to this. He wrestled with his guilt.

Selles and the others had their doubts about Paz's story when it came to Sienna. Rumsey had said Paz believed Sienna could lead him to some kind of buried treasure . . . The Pirate's Emerald, he had called it. Despite all other appearances, Hawk knew from his vision that Sienna was in Costa Rica because she was The Stonekeeper.

He visualized the symbols inscribed on the silver bracelet that Aunt Jessi had given to Sienna, and their message. They stated an emerald would be the second stone recovered by The Stonekeeper. Yet Rumsey's revelation abo The Pirate's Emerald provided an-the code. It was all consuming. In ignorance, he had held the crystal against his heart, and he said the words that were written on the rock, ignoring the warning. *Take not these crystals into your hands lightly, for they hold the power of sight. Cast them away from you if you can not bear this worldly burden. Hold them near to your heart if you claim it as your own. But remember, in the end justice can only be found with The Stonekeeper.* Hawk would never forget those words for as long as he lived.

The outbreak of the hideous rash had been instantaneous, followed by the voices that seemed to come from everywhere and nowhere at the same time. That was the first time, but many more times followed after that. Hawk ignored the voices that called to him, and eventually they lessened in intensity, but the painful rash grew larger with each occurrence.

Hawk could not reveal his bizarre circumstances to his intellectual co-workers at the museum, so he had quit his job and resorted to consulting as a way to take care of himself. The event had totally changed his life, but there was one thing he was determined his view of life. Overall, he had learned that people were people, be they from the jungles of the Amazon or the fashionable streets of Paris.

Hawk had been able to deal with his nomadic lifestyle because it was born out of love. It was out of love for Sienna that he had promised to honor the gift, and it was because of his love for her that he had stayed away.

Hawk had known that he would be forced to leave Sienna from the moment he touched The Passion Ruby. As he held on to the fiery, red gem, he could see his life so clearly. He had felt pride deep within him, realizing that he possessed many virtues, but he could see that his life also held many challenges, and he would be forced to face his demons head-on. It would mean making his gift and himself available to people in need, just the opposite of the almost solitary life he had been living. But worst of all, it would mean living without Sienna.

Hawk recalled how the powers that be had made it clear: *When the time comes, you must walk the path alone. If you are true to this instruction, the gift will flow like nectar upon all that you touch, but if ignored it will be a fiery acid of destruction. Still, you must remember, in the end justice can only be found with The Stonekeeper.*

Hawk turned a corner and stopped as his gaze fell on Sienna, sitting on a concrete bench. He was stunned to see her sitting with her hands clasped behind her ne‍‍‍‍, her eyes closed, her face lifted to the sun. Hawk watc‍‍‍‍ as a powerful breeze gave life to the wide sleeves of he‍ red and yellow top, transforming her into an illusion‍ butterfly. The feelings that stirred inside him as‍ watched her were earth-shattering. It had been so‍ since he had been able to look at her this way, a‍ hungry gaze missed nothing.

Sienna's eyelashes lay above her velvety brow‍ in a fan of uniform curls. They were as lon‍ as Hawk remembered, and as dark as the profusion of ‍pongy curls that billowed out around her face and shoulders. To Hawk, her body was pure symmetry. The elongated lines of her neck curved down into high breasts that rose and fell into a smooth, trim waist. The sight of Sienna, so unaware, unearthed memories and desires.

Hawk's first impulse was to wrap her in his arms. He wanted to tell her how much he missed her, and that he would never have gone away if it had been left up to him. As he stood teetering on the edge of indecision, Sienna relaxed from her stretch and opened her eyes.

The sight of Hawk took her totally by surprise, and her hands automatically clutched at her sides, grabbing handfuls of chiffon. She wondered how long he had been standing there, and her brow furrowed when she noticed a deep longing in his eyes. It caused her heart to beat faster and her stomach to quiver.

Sienna rose to her feet, turning her head slowly from side to side, an outward demonstration of her inner confusion. What was it about this man that made her react in such a way? She searched her mind for a logical answer, but there was none. Her mind told her he was simply a worker at Shangri-la, although her gut feeling begged to differ.

Hawk knew she was trying to make sense of her feelings, and the more he watched, the more compelled he felt to go to her. Logic warned him to keep his distance. It was obvious she did not recognize him. Hawk knew he would have to approach her as if she were a skittish animal. He would have to use soothing words to communicate his feelings, while telling her about their past. But it had been six months since Hawk had seen her, held her, and the need to touch her was more than he could bear.

He had crossed the tiled area before he realized it. Urgently, he slid his arms over the cool chiffon, wrapping Sienna within them. He looked down into her eyes, dark brown eyes that searched his desperately as they glistened with a hint of tears. He watched her moist lips quiver and open with unspoken words. At the moment, though, words were not what Hawk needed. He needed to feel his mouth upon hers, to taste the sweetness that he had never forgotten, that had haunted him from one end of the world to the other.

Out of a need that he had never known before, Hawk placed his mouth against Sienna's as his breathing started to come in long, staggered bursts. It was hard for him to believe that he was actually holding her, kissing her, so to reassure himself he rubbed his firm lips slowly against her softer ones. When Hawk felt their yielding moistness he wrapped Sienna tighter within his embrace and kissed her deeply. He kissed her as if to awaken her soul, let alone the memory of the love that they once shared.

Sienna felt her entire being succumb to Hawk's display of affection. She closed her eyes, feeling as if she were tumbling inside a spiral. Her senses whirled as she was drawn deeper and deeper into the kiss until her awareness of being a separate being disappeared. Sienna felt as if she and Hawk were one, and that she had been united with the one person in the entire world who was her other half, her twin flame.

Finally, Hawk slackened his hold, withdrew from the kiss, and stood staring down into Sienna's face.

"I missed you so much, Sienna." His voice vibrated in his throat. "Six months is such a long time."

Hawk's words caused the pleasurable cloud around her to dissipate, and she struggled to understand her feelings, which contradicted her logic.

"You missed me? But how could that be?" She stepped back and placed her fingertips against her throbbing lips. "I don't understand why I allowed you to kiss me. I've never seen you before today, yet I wanted you to kiss me." Her last words trailed off.

"You allowed me to because you *do* know me, Sienna. For three months we shared our lives. You were the most—"

"You're telling me that you and I were lovers?" Fear, coupled with confusion, blanketed her features.

"We were more than that," Hawk replied.

"You said it had been six months since you've seen me, yet you claim that we meant so much to one another. Why would we have stayed apart for so long?" She backed away even further.

"It's a complicated story. But I tell you we were—"

"Someone is lying." She looked down at her hands as she clasped them together. "Paz claims we have been involved in a relationship for the past year." She wrapped her arms protectively about her. "He says I came to Shangri-la because of the relationship we have shared."

"I know that." The color of Hawk's eyes changed slightly. "But I believe he is not a man to be trusted, and all I know is what *I* am telling you *is* the truth."

She stared deep into his eyes, which remained steady. Sienna saw an urgency there that tugged at her heart, yet she struggled against her illogical feelings for the worker. She had already decided she did not trust Paz, and it would make no sense at all to trust this man who was a total stranger.

"How do you expect me to believe you, when I don't remember any of the things you have said? I can not imagine how I could forget you, considering the kind of relationship you claim that we have shared."

Hawk stiffened at the distrust he saw in her eyes. "I was listening to the conversation that you had with Paz in the breakfast room. He said you had an accident, and from what you said there are many things that you do not remember." He held her face with one hand. His touch had become rough with disappointment and impatience. "But there must be some part of you, Sienna, that has not forgotten me."

Her skin burned where he held it, and her natural reaction was to push Hawk's hand away. When she looked into his eyes this time, that inner knowing prodded her to tell him of its presence, tell him that there was a basic part of her that seemed to remember. Out of fear, Sienna chose to ignore it, because of the harshness she saw in his eyes and felt in his touch.

"I told you, I don't remember seeing you before today."

She swallowed when she observed Hawk's jaws tremble with restrained emotion and his hazel eyes ignite with a fiery glint. "Right now," she continued, taking two steps away from him, "I have to rely on the few things I do remember, and I refuse to trust anything else." She lifted her chin and looked him dead in the eye. "Therefore, from where I stand, you are simply a worker on my fiancé's estate who has overstepped his bounds." She crossed her arms in front of her again. "This time I won't report you, but there'd better not be a next time, or I will turn you in quicker than you can say your own name."

Hawk didn't know what he had expected, but these distrustful, unkind words struck him hard. His eyes narrowed, and he spoke between lips that barely moved. "I remember a time when you would have trusted your heart." The low words admonished her, and the throaty laugh that followed held no humor. "I see it didn't take much for you to change from one of the most compassionate people I have ever met to a snobbish cynic. Or maybe I never knew you in the first place, and gave you more credit than was your due," he said out of his pain. "Yeah, perhaps outside of being The Last of the Stonekeepers, one of your other specialties is making a man believe he is the most important person in your life while you secretly juggle other men, like Paz, on the side."

Sienna's dark eyes registered surprise at his reference to her being a Stonekeeper, and Hawk raked her with a seething gaze from head to toe.

"Once, I told you you were different from all the women I had ever met. I believed it then, that you were special among women. But perhaps I had spoken too quickly, and you were far more common than I dared to imagine."

Male laughter swelled in the distance, and they both turned in the direction of the approaching sound. It was a scattered moment. So many things had been said, but from the look in their eyes there was no doubt, regardless of Sienna's denial, that even more things had not been said. Their gazes held for a prolonged moment before Hawk turned and vanished among the hedges.

It was only after he had disappeared that Sienna realized she had been holding her breath. His words had touched an emotional chord inside her, and above all his acknowledgment that she was The Last of the Stonekeepers rang in her mind. Paz had merely mentioned that the bracelet was connected with the legend of The Stonekeeper, but it was Hawk who had actually acknowledged that she was The Last of the Stonekeepers.

She stood staring at the empty space where he had stood, her mind recreating the look in his eyes as he turned and walked away from her. How could he have known that, unless he had known her in the past?

"H-h . . ." Sienna almost screamed his name, so urgent was her need to speak to him again. But she stopped herself. She knew it would be dangerous for anyone to know that they had spoken privately.

Sienna rehashed the scene in the breakfast room earlier that morning. It was obvious Paz did not know there was a past connection between them, and that Hawk wanted to keep it that way. She would do the same.

She began to retrace her path back to the house. With each step Sienna determined that she would find a moment alone with Hawk. He had become a key to her past and her present.

Six

"Mary," Dorothy called with her shoulders stooped, peering around and through a line of musicians walking across the kitchen. "I don't know what to do with this big dish of *sopa de pollo y okra*, chicken and okra."

"Say what?" Mary retorted as she opened the door again for a guitarist who had forgotten his pick. Another man completely covered in a ninja-like costume entered as well.

"Wait a minute, wait a minute," Mary said, stopping the masked man, "Who are you?"

"I'm here to tell fortunes for the party," Hawk lied.

"Do you have t'e paper t'ey give you to—"

"I can't hold it much longer," the younger girl cried. "It is too heavy."

Mary looked from the strangely dressed man to the wobbly teenager behind her. *How was her suppose to run the kitchen, make sure the dishes were properly placed in the dining hall and screen the entertainers as them came! Part of this was Tina's responsibility, but her was off somewhere smiling and enjoying the music and the guests. Well, her wouldn't break her neck trying to make sure everything was perfect to make Tina look good.*

She waved the man inside, quickly closed the door, then crossed the large kitchen to assist the nearly overwrought Dorothy.

Hawk proceeded through the kitchen, exiting just as

he had seen the guitarist do. He had no idea where he was going, but at the moment that didn't matter. His biggest obstacle had been getting inside the house as part of the entertainment. Now, with that behind him, he would simply play the rest of the evening by ear.

Strains of a lively calypso mounted as he walked down the empty corridor, leaving one swinging door behind only to be met by another. He emerged on the other side, into a room where several men were imbibing a variety of drinks served by accommodating waiters. Curious eyes turned in his direction, but Hawk simply nodded calmly and continued on his way, as if his presence in the room was as natural as their own. Inside, his senses were on high alert.

Hawk peered into another room with a circular table besot with spectacular fruit and vegetable arrangements, along with a plethora of breads, cheeses, spreads, and dips. The only people inside were a lone musician and an amorous couple whose actions, in his opinion, seemed better suited for a bedroom than a social area. A wry smile touched his lips underneath the smooth, cloth mask when he noted how intensely the *quijongo* player blew on his wind instrument, trying to appear oblivious to the couple's carrying ons. Hawk realized he was the originator of the calypso that had drawn his attention minutes before.

Hawk continued through the room, out into a wide corridor. Animated crowd sounds filtered into the hall as three women, all pleasing to the eye, opened a set of buffed doors.

"There is no need for disagreement," Hawk heard Paz say just inside the portals. "Let me take your minds off the business at hand, and raise your curiosity as well as your envy." A meaningful pause ensued. "I want to show you some original pieces of the Dead Sea Scrolls that I was ingenious enough to acquire several years ago. I must admit they are not emeralds, but to some people they are much more valuable. They are right down the hall, if you care to follow me."

The sound of Paz's voice grated on his nerves for more reasons than one, but it was too early in the game to meet him head-on. The evening had just begun. It was at moments like this that he loathed the uneven deal the powers that be had dealt him. His power of sight could not be used to help him, only to help others. So his fate tonight, as always, was totally left up to his ability to think and act quickly.

"Would you like to know what the future holds for you?" Hawk smoothly linked arms with two of the women as they stepped into the hall.

At first they were startled, but as they summed up his muscular frame in the spandex-like suit all of their expressions lit up with curiosity.

"Only if you promise to let me see if the real thing is as enticing as it appears beneath all that clothing, when we get through," one of the women cooed, causing the other two to laugh.

"Be careful. You just may get what you ask for," Hawk replied as he pulled the women to his sides, bowing his head close to one of theirs as they slipped back into the room, giving Paz and his companions enough space to leave.

In a glance Hawk surveyed the humongous room, where a band was playing on one end while a female contortionist tied herself in elaborate knots on a small stage on the other. A generous crowd drank and munched in between. He chose a vacant alcove with walls nearly covered with mirrors. The only furnishings were a table and two chairs. From the alcove he could see the door leading to the hallway, as well as most of the ballroom floor.

Hawk pulled up two more chairs for his clients, and

doused the flames of nearby sconces that provided illumination for the tiny spot. He replaced their glow with a solitary candle from a small table of *hors d'oeuvres*. The single flame would keep the corner dim.

"O-o-oh. Isn't this a kind of eerie, cozy atmosphere?" the black haired one asked. "Just right for telling fortunes or making love. I prefer the latter."

Once again the women laughed in unison.

Hawk extended his hand toward the woman. "May I have your palm, please?"

"From the light in Cheryl's eyes, you can have more than that," the woman with the French roll and corkscrew curls chimed in. "All you have to do is ask."

"She's right, you know. I've always had this fantasy about making love to a masked man."

Hawk looked at the small hand that lay in his, and despite the woman's invitation all he could think of was that this was a time for firsts. He had never asked for anyone's palm to bring up the sight. He did not need to. Nor had he ever donned the black suit without a feeling of self-disgust and a need to hide, not only from the world but from himself.

It had been months since he had actually worn it, and the initial feel of the mask against his face brought up memories. Painful ones. For it did not matter that the material was smooth and cool. Whenever it pressed against where the hideous rash had distorted his features during the initial months of his use of the sight, it was a blistering reminder of his lot in life.

Since the rash had subsided, he had continued to carry the suit with him as a kind of macabre reminder of who he had become, and that he could never live a normal life until his debt to the powers that be had been paid. As Hawk gazed at the lines in the woman's hand, he thought of how ironic it was that he, a true visionary, was pretending to read someone's palm.

* * *

Sienna watched the wax slide down the sides of the shortening candle like coagulating water. She noticed how there had been a steady flow of people watching and seeking the services of the fortune-teller, and she longed for a moment's peace from Paz so she, too, could test his ability.

From the moment she had come downstairs, it was obvious to Sienna that Paz had been notified, for he was at her side in a matter of minutes, and had not left it since. They had mingled steadily with his guests while he introduced her as the woman in his life. Some of the poignant stares made her uncomfortable, particularly the looks she received from a curious group of men who wanted to ask her personal questions that seemed inappropriate. Paz thwarted their inquiries by informing them that Sienna had not been feeling well, that perhaps, later on, she would feel up to conversing with them at greater length. Sienna had felt somewhat perturbed by his conjecture, but other than that the evening had proven to be quite relaxing.

There had been a steady stream of conversations, usually revolving around personal collections, for it appeared that all the men present were collectors of some sort or another. Sienna gleaned from the objects they collected that cost was of little consequence, and she wondered how they had managed to accumulate such vast discretionary incomes.

Sienna noticed that the women, like the men, held something in common. It was a rare moment when one of the them, usually hanging on her companion's arm, joined in the discussion. Their silent stances made them appear mere ornaments. She surmised, from the number of men who wore wedding bands compared to their ringless dates, that the women were temporary decorations, to be disposed of at will. No sooner had the thought crossed her mind than she realized the steady egress and ingress of affectionate couples and groups. Could it be possible this gathering of Paz's associates was also a set up for their decadent pleasures?

"That soothsayer seems to be a very popular diversion tonight," Paz commented as he redirected Sienna's attention away from Hawk's table over to him. "He even seems to have captured your attention, my sweet. I must commend the person who hired him when I get a chance."

"I just thinking about that," Tina inserted. "I don't remember a fortune-teller being on the list of those who would be entertaining tonight," she informed him, looking at the small crowd of men and women who awaited their turn.

"You can not be on top of everything, my Tinatico." Paz's words reflected his pleasure at how well the evening was progressing. He turned another beguiling smile in Sienna's direction.

She had to admit that Paz looked extremely attractive in the white suit he wore, and she found herself wondering why she did not feel what she obviously should feel for him, if their lives were so intertwined as he had told her.

Minutes later, Sienna watched in silence as a man approached them with his gaze fastened on her. Before he leaned over and whispered in Paz's ear, his eyes studied her breasts, which were partially exposed through a super sheer, white lace panel. Their darkness contrasted vividly, as did the mark between them. After listening intently, Paz nodded and the man walked away.

"Here, have some champagne," he directed as he removed a crystal goblet from a waiter's tray.

Before Sienna could react, he added, "I hope you took the evening medication that Tina left for you." He touched her cheek. "You know that I am looking forward to your speedy, complete recovery, my darling."

Sienna replied with several static nods of her head as she took the champagne. She hated to lie, and the motion seemed to jar a heaviness that was growing inside her head, causing her to wonder if she should have taken the medication, instead of being suspicious.

"A group of my acquaintances would like to speak with us privately," he informed her.

"Us?"

"Yes." Paz pressed his hand against the small of her bare back as he directed her toward a door several feet away.

"Perhaps you should go alone," Sienna replied, turning to face him. "I can't imagine my playing an important role in the conversation. You probably want to talk about business, anyway, so I'll stay here and have my fortune told."

"No," Paz insisted almost harshly, "It is important that you be by my side." He attempted to soften his stance with a smile. "After all, they have known me for a long time, and they are curious about the woman who has almost managed to pin my bachelor's wings."

Once again Sienna felt pressure on her bare skin, which was accessible because of a deep V-cut in back of the white fitted gown Paz had requested she wear. She had no choice but to comply with Paz's wishes, even though a warning was sounding deep inside her. To do otherwise would mean causing a scene.

Several men were seated when they entered the room, but they got to their feet when they saw Sienna. It was a plush, minute conference room with just enough chairs for Sienna, Paz and the men at hand. She counted eight. Most appeared to be sober despite the multitude of drinks on the table, except for one emaciated looking man in an expensive tailored suit.

"Good evening, gentlemen. I would like for you all to meet my fiancéee, Sienna Russell," Paz announced.

For a moment they all looked startled, glancing around the table at one another, then up at Paz and back at her. Finally, they acknowledged him with nods and accented words. Paz walked over to the table and pulled out a chair. "You sit here, my darling." Sienna sat down, and the entire room followed her lead.

The conversation started with generalities, and she surmised that most of the men were from nearby countries like Panama, Nicaragua, Colombia. Eventually the talk progressed to importing and exporting, and just when she decided what she had said to Paz was true, that her presence would be of little importance, one of the men threw a question her way.

"What do you think about the natural resources found here in Costa Rica and the surrounding lands?"

The room became pregnant with expectancy as all eyes turned in her direction. For some reason, the question felt like a set up to Sienna.

"To be honest, I don't know that much about the natural resources in this area," she responded cautiously. "I would assume the land is rich for agricultural purposes—"

"Farming may be the biggest contributor to the economy in Costa Rica now, but, from what I understand it has other hidden treasures," another man with extremely bright eyes interjected. "There was a time when this area was sought out by world travelers looking for precious metals like gold."

"Are there still gold mines here?" Sienna asked, trying to turn the attention away from her.

"In small quantities. It's not like it was when the Indians who first inhabited the land knew where the gold mines were. They honored the metal because they believed it had spiritual value. They felt that way about many things. But the foreigners they shared their knowledge with honored nothing more than their own pockets. They were pirates. Many a story of buried treasure has survived as a result of their exploits." His gaze followed the faces around the table. The thin, inebriated fellow leaned forward as if to speak, but Paz cut him off.

"It seems that time has had little affect on human nature," Paz said, smiling. "Of course, everything doesn't have to have monetary value in order to be precious." He touched Sienna's hair. "We all have our personal treasures."

Sienna closed her eyes as his hand made contact. She wanted to withdraw from his touch. Maybe it was because of the lascivious looks his action elicited around the table.

Suddenly, without provocation, disconnected scenes from her recent past flashed behind her eyelids. Tina in a crumpled heap on a floor . . . seeing herself carrying a large amethyst geode . . . feeling and smelling a cloth being placed over her nose and mouth as she stared into the dim insides of a van. Sienna opened her eyes with a start.

"Sienna is a rare jewel," Paz continued, "she is beautiful as well as intelligent, and her talent and worth go far beyond what meets the eye. She even comes with her own personal story." His pampered hand stroked the bracelet around her wrist, remaining there.

As Paz spoke, Sienna got the distinct impression that she was on display, like a Ming vase in a case, or a rare painting. *Comes with her own personal story. What was she, a Christmas present?* It was all that much more disconcerting because of the strange pressure in her head. Sienna blinked several times, attempting to clear the mental fog, only to focus on Paz, who continued as if he were gloating over a prized possession, not a living human being, especially not a woman that he loved and cared for.

"Take Sienna's bracelet, for instance. It is no ordinary silver bangle." He lifted an eyebrow as if he had played a hold card. "There is a legend that goes with it. The legend of The Stonekeeper. Every four generations a woman is born with the mark of the crystal between her breasts," he began. "Tell them the rest of it, Sienna," he commanded. Paz smiled at the look of surprise on his companion's faces, which caused him to miss the vexed, confused look that surfaced on Sienna's. She had no intention of completing what he had started. He had said during breakfast that she had never told him the legend of The Stonekeeper. Now, in boasting before his peers he had proven himself to be a liar.

Sienna examined the self-satisfied expression Paz wore. It was then she realized this was simply a game to him, one that he and his friends had played before. Maybe the last time it *was* a Ming vase, or a rare statue acquired from the grave of an Egyptian Pharaoh. But Sienna knew the entire scene was really about their inflated egos. The more material possessions they acquired, the larger their egos became. In the game of life these were men with money to burn, and most of them felt superior because of their financial status. She surmised that the act of acquiring money in and of itself was no longer a challenge, and they missed the rush it used to create. To replace it they had invented a unique way of generating that excitement. Now they derived a kind of pleasure from competing with one another in an elaborate collector's arena, and this time, she, Sienna, happened to be the item on display.

She studied the men around the table. The intense anticipation she saw on their faces confirmed her assessment. There was no doubt Paz was not alone in his craving to hear about the bangle. Perhaps his motivation was slightly different, for she was sure that in his mind he was now the king of the roost, the man who had found and acquired The Stonekeeper. However, that did not curb the curiosity of his associates.

Some of them leaned forward, waiting for her response, their gazes traveling between her face and the mark between her breasts. For the first time Sienna really knew what a man looked like when he coveted the possession of another. Eight examples stared her directly in the face.

"Go ahead, tell them, darling. Tell them the entire story surrounding The Stonekeeper," Paz prodded, realizing she had not responded.

This time her continued silence was noted by everyone.

"Ah-hah hah." The drunken man's laugh erupted into the room. "Paz's prize canary doesn't want to sing, does she?" He smacked the table impatiently. "Dammit, woman. Tell us what we came here to hear. He has waved you under our noses long enough," the inebriated man proclaimed. "Are you The Last of the Stonekeepers or not?"

"I *said* tell them, Sienna," Paz ordered, forgetting his ploy as he faced being embarrassed in front of his peers.

Sienna was astounded by what she heard. It had all been a set up from the very beginning, orchestrated by Paz. *Well, they're in for a big surprise,* she thought as she looked at their carnivorous faces. She was not going to be used in this demeaning manner. As a matter of fact, she had no intention of staying in this room a second longer.

Sienna rose to her feet, her mind a calculating mass. But where would she go? In her condition, she couldn't remember her own address, and she realized that Tina had never come up with her purse and luggage. She claimed they had been confused with those of another guest, promising it would be cleared up before the night was over. Now, for sure, Sienna did not trust Tina or her promises. "I have no intention of telling you or your friends a damn thing." She looked at Paz, anger and mistrust dancing in her eyes. "I will not be put on display like an animal in a cage. I don't know what you've been accustomed to, but you've got the wrong sister here." She stormed out of the room.

Seven

Hawk ended the palmreading he had just begun when he saw Sienna's reflection pass through the mirror, with Paz in hot pursuit. He could see Paz's lips form Sienna's name, an angry expression on his face, but he couldn't hear his voice above the loud music. They cut a path through the crowd, and several people moved back, turning curious looks in their direction as they made their way toward the door.

"Eez that all?" the man asked as he looked down at his outstretched palm, then back up into Hawk's masked features.

Hawk did not answer him. His total concentration had become focused on Sienna and Paz as they disappeared through the door. In one fluid motion Hawk pushed his chair back, rose to his feet and stepped up onto the teetering table, evoking a cry of disbelief from the man who had sat across from him.

"What the hell happened?" The man's words blended with the background noise as Hawk forced his way through the crowd. He, too, was heading for the door.

When Hawk entered the hall the corridor was empty. For a moment he experienced indecision as to what direction to take, but the sound of Paz's voice calling Sienna's name vehemently pointed the way. The voice was rich with anger, and Hawk thought the fervor beneath it vibrated with each syllable, like a Japanese gong. He could tell the volatile emotion was coming from a place deep within, and he wondered what Sienna had done to rouse it.

Hawk pursued the sound until he came to the end of another hallway. Hurried footsteps then became his guide, and when he emerged into the huge foyer Paz's voice resounded once again.

"How dare you embarrass me in front of my colleagues!" The words were breathy and full of strain as he pushed against Sienna's bedroom door, which she was attempting to close. "Who do you think you are, anyway? No woman of mine will ever talk to me the way you just did," he threatened. "And I don't care if you *are* The Last of the Stonekeepers, I still will wring your pretty little neck if you go against me ever again." Paz's true nature continued to flow like molten lava. "This is my house, and no door shall be closed against me!" he bellowed, and, with an apparent surge of strength, he forced his way in.

Hawk's gaze remained glued to the opening, where Sienna's door remained ajar. His heart lurched when he heard an object crash to the floor, and he took the steps two at a time.

"It has taken a long time for me to make it to where I am," he heard Paz say. "It was only a few years ago that men like that would not have shared the same room with me, God forbid a table. And for once, *I* was the one they envied. Me, the boy who stole and ate only turtle entrails to survive. I could see it in their eyes. They wanted to possess what *I* owned. And you had to go and spoil it all."

"What *you owned?*" Hawk heard Sienna's incredulous reply as he reached the door. "You may own this house, and some of the other people in it, but I guarantee you don't own me."

"Why you, smart-mouthed American w-,"

Hawk interrupted Paz's foul retort and the backhand that was advancing toward Sienna's defiant face. His action tipped Paz off balance, and he stumbled to one side. Paz turned toward his assailant with anger and resistance distorting his features, but the two emotions gave way to shock when he stood face-to-face with Hawk in his black mask.

"What is this?" Paz's cheeks inflated with astonishment and fury.

"Come stand beside me," Hawk instructed, ignoring Paz's question.

"Say what? Who in the hell are you?" Paz demanded, his eyes narrowing at the quandry before him.

Hawk could see Sienna with his peripheral vision. The loose, dark hair that surrounded her face made the ashen look beneath her brown skin more apparent. She looked back and forth from Paz's face to his masked features. Confusion and fear jostled for position in her eyes.

"Remember the garden," Hawk said.

Sienna's head jerked back in his direction, and recognition surfaced on her distraught features. She knew it was the man Hawk behind the disconcerting mask. Sienna hesitated for no more than a second before she took a step in Hawk's direction. Her body language was clear. She hadn't decided to come to his side out of love. It was a matter of survival.

"Where do you think you're going?" Paz stepped in front of her, blocking her way. "I spent a lot of money, and went through plenty of trouble bringing you here to Shangri-la." He looked down at her, ownership emanating from his eyes. "So the soothsayer turned bodyguard thinks you're in trouble." He jerked his head in Hawk's direction. "Well, that's one fortune he got right tonight." Paz grabbed Sienna's face, roughly forcing her to look at him. "And I know exactly why you were able to make such a big impression on him." His gleaming eyes followed the curves of Sienna's body, outlined to perfection beneath the formfitting dress. "You made the same impression on me when I first saw you. But I can tell you right now you're not going anywhere with him or anybody else, unless I say so."

"Take your hands off of her." Hawk's demand was low, menacing.

Paz looked at Hawk as if he were dirt beneath his feet. "Have you lost your mind? You better get out of here before I really lose my temper," Paz threatened. "And when I get through with you, I'm going to make sure you don't work anyplace else for a long, long time." He turned back to Sienna. "I'm going to get some kind of satisfaction out of this situation tonight," he said, grabbing one of her breasts possessively, "and then I'm going to make sure that you apologize to all of my friends, in whatever manner they will accept."

"Don't touch me." Sienna gritted her teeth and forced his hand away, but before the last word was out of her mouth Hawk had spun Paz around, striking him with a *hsing-i* blow which sent him sprawling on the floor.

"We've got to get out of here," Hawk commanded as he grabbed her by the hand and started across the room. When they reached the door, they nearly collided with Tina. It was obvious that they had taken her by surprise, but Hawk noticed how she was able to maintain an uncanny calm.

Tina's dark eyes took in the mask and Sienna's anxious features before travelling to their locked hands, which were clasped between them. The only time she reacted at all was when her eyes widened as she observed Paz on the carpet behind them. Without a word she stepped aside and let them pass.

Hawk descended the stairs as quickly as he could with Sienna in tow. In a matter of moments they were outside, being embraced by the moist but warm night air. Sienna found it difficult to run in heels and the fishtail dress. As she considered her predicament, she didn't know what was more disturbing, her physical or mental condition.

Hawk had her hand in an iron grip as he headed into the underbrush. When they exited the house they dashed through one of the maze-like paths of Shangri-la's gardens, and into the forest-like terrain for better cover. Now, as the plants and vines pulled at her legs and the tree branches swiped at her face, she questioned her reasons for going with him. At the time Hawk had appeared to be the lesser of two evils, but as they became engulfed in the dual darkness of night and thick foliage, Sienna was no longer sure.

She stumbled and nearly fell when she tripped over an extremely thick vine. It took her grabbing Hawk's wrist and a lifting of his forearm to keep her from joining the vine on the forest floor.

"Wait! You've got to stop," Sienna called. "I can't go on like this." She pulled back, refusing to run. "Exactly where are we going?"

"I only know one place to go." Hawk removed the mask, causing his neatly cultured dreadlocks to frame his face and shoulders like a lion's mane. "I'm pretty sure they won't accept your being there without asking a lot of questions. But we'll deal with that when we get there."

"Well, I've got several questions of my own to ask." Sienna stared up at him with only a sliver of moonlight for illumination. She was amazed by the electrical current that buzzed inside her just from the sight of him. Even under these stressful conditions Hawk seemed to resemble some great Egyptian god. Sienna couldn't help but be aware of the black jumpsuit that molded to his frame. The material flowed in and out of the ridges of his tendons and muscles like carved onyx. As she looked at him now, she did not doubt she was physically attracted to him, but it was hard for her to believe that they had been in love. Could she have forgotten that? Or was he a liar, like Paz had proven to be?

"I'm quite sure you do, but this is not the time or the place to ask them. By now Paz has gathered his senses, and I'm sure he's madder than hell. Don't doubt for a second that he won't be sending someone out to find us."

All of a sudden, as the forest grew lighter, Sienna could see Hawk's features more clearly. Through instinct they both turned in the direction of the artificial light. For a moment she was confused. Was it coming from the house? Then the source became evident. A vast lighting system throughout the hedge-enclosed gardens of Shangri-la had been turned on. Hawk was right. Paz had already begun his search.

Before Sienna knew what he was doing, Hawk had stooped down before her, his hands embracing her lower thighs. Taken aback, Sienna formed the words to question his motives, but at that moment a ripping sound filled the air. He had torn away the bottom portion of the dress that encumbered her movements. For a second he remained there, his gaze lifted toward her face, his hands centimeters away from her flesh as they rested on her stocking-encased limbs. Their gazes held, and the heat that scorched her during that time was a consuming flame. Sienna felt as if her breath had been stolen away as she watched his gaze travel down over her shoulders, her breasts, her waist, then finally rested on her hips, at eye level. Finally, Hawk stood up, remaining mere inches in front of her.

"Better?"

Sienna didn't trust her voice to answer. She simply nodded her head and looked away.

They began to run again. This time she didn't question if he had lied to her, for she knew without a doubt that there was some unique connection between them. He had taken her breath away with just a look, and had stolen her individuality with a single kiss. Sienna was afraid to imagine what part of her would be lost if they ever made love. According to Hawk, that, too, was a part of their past.

She followed him in silence as they headed out of the forest, crossed a narrow dirt road, and entered a tree-sprinkled field. The farther they went, the more Sienna was aware of how foreign the landscape was, and with everything that had happened fear rode her as easily as dandelion seeds ride the wind.

It was a horrible feeling to lose her memory, but she was grateful for the snatches of her life that were beginning to return. Sienna trusted that eventually she would totally recover.

A wave of emotion rippled through her as her thoughts transferred to Hawk. She stole a glance at the man who trotted along beside her. His profile was powerful. Strength was apparent in the high nose, his broad but firm lips, and his hair that now cut a path away from his face because of the wind. Strangely enough, at that moment she knew what frightened her most. It was not the loss of her memory, or being a stranger in a foreign land. Sienna feared how much of her had been lost as a result of loving him, if what Hawk told her was true. If their love had been as strong as he professed, why had they not managed to stay together? Had she left him? Or had he left her?

Despite her limited memory, abandonment was something Sienna knew well. It was like an imprint upon her soul, an unwanted lifelong companion. Although her parents' death had been an accident, on many days she had felt abandoned inside the walls of the orphanage. Just the thought of having been abandoned, by a man who claimed he loved her and that she loved him above all else, created a nearly immobilizing pain. Sienna prayed that life had not jilted her twice in such a fashion.

They approached several houses situated off a branch of dirt roads. She searched the darkness as they came up on one of the buildings from the rear, her heart hammering as she considered the full weight of her predicament. It was obvious that Paz had brought her to Costa Rica for his own purposes, and that he had intended to use her to accomplish his own selfish goals. When she recalled the way those men had looked at her, dismissing her humanness, and seeing her, The Stonekeeper, as some kind of collectible oddity, she was aghast, and her pride had not allowed her to endure their voyeurism for a single second more. She had voiced what was in her heart with little thought of the consequences. Truly, she had not known that Paz would react as he did. There was a volatility that burned inside of him. She could feel it as he approached her in the bedroom. At one point, because of the outrage she saw in his eyes, Sienna had feared for her life. She dreaded to think what might have happened if Hawk had not appeared. But what had she gotten herself into by going with him?

She knew from a place deep within that she had always been self-reliant, but now she was totally dependent on him. She knew no one in Costa Rica, and she feared that by daybreak all of those villagers who were loyal to The Paz would be on the look-out for her. Her only hope was the man who tugged her along beside him.

Sienna felt Hawk grab her by the waist and pull her down into a shadow beside the concrete block home. A nearby calabash tree provided even greater cover.

"Now, you stay here. This," he pointed upward, "is the window to my room. I'm going to go inside, and very shortly I will open it for you to climb in."

Sienna did not want to be left alone outside the strange building, and she began to feel the weight of everything that had happened within the last twenty-four hours. Many questions clouded her mind. She wanted to ask Hawk what he thought would happen if someone caught her, and what he thought Paz would do if she were returned to him. She held her tongue and nodded her agreement, and he stood up and disappeared around the corner of the house.

Sienna waited, crouched in the darkness. Suddenly, someone darted from behind a bush a quarter of a mile away. She pressed her shoulder up against the cool concrete as she watched, wondering if it was one of the searchers instructed by Paz. Moments later, another person ran out into the road. They were joined by another, and laughter filtered through the air. Sienna realized they were just some of the local children playing hide-and-go-seek, and the air gushed from her lungs in relief.

The rattling sound of a loose windowpane caused her to look overhead. Hawk was easing the old window upward. Afterward, he extended his arms to help her climb inside. He pulled her through the window as easily as a mother lifts a baby from its bath, before delicately allowing her feet to touch the wooden floor. Hawk still had one arm around her as he placed his finger up against his lips, warning her not to make a sound.

Eight

"Did you find out who that soothsayer was?" Paz's eyes flashed as he nursed his swollen jaw.

"Not yet," Tina answered. "We still trying. A call was placed to the recruiter, but there was no answer. And you know it takes at least thirty minutes coming and going to reach the public phone." Tina held her hands folded in front of her, and her head was slightly bowed as she looked up at The Paz. "And I checked the list of entertainers again. He was never on it."

A light tapping sounded from the door.

"Who is it?" Paz growled.

"Mary. I heard you wanted—"

"Come in," he ordered.

Mary stepped into the library. First she looked at Tina, then her gaze rested on Paz, who sat with one leg propped up on the edge of an ornate desk.

"Tina says at one point during the evening you were in charge of letting in the entertainers and checking their paperwork. Is that true?"

Mary looked at Tina, then back at Paz, "Yes."

"Did you let in the man wearing the black ninja-like outfit?"

"Yes." Mary's eyes widened slightly with her monosyllabic response.

"Did you check his paperwork?"

Mary's back and neck stiffened visibly as indignation

rose in her molasses-colored features. "Well, I believe I glanced at it, but I can't say for sure." She looked at Tina once again, her bottom lip protruding slightly. "I have to say it rather hard trying to run the kitchen, making sure everything laid out pretty on the serving tables, and check all the entertainers paperwork," Mary bolstered herself with each word. "I thought it my job to head up the kitchen, not run the house," she added boldly.

Paz walked over and stood in front of her. With his teeth gritted, he pressed his middle finger into the center of her forehead. "Your job is whatever I want it to be, and don't you forget it." He tapped the last words out on her skin.

Immediately, Mary's eyes glistened with unshed tears. Another knock sounded at the door.

"Come in," Paz whirled around and commanded. This time a man in uniform stepped into the room.

"I understand you have had some trouble here tonight, Mr. Paz."

"You understand correctly, Mr. Rankin." Paz deliberately decided not to use the word *lieutenant*. In his eyes this man's authority did not supercede his. He was a pawn to be used, just like all the rest of the villagers. "And I want something done about it right away."

"What the problem?" The policeman began to finger his belt buckle in a nervous fashion.

"My fiancéee was kidnapped from my house tonight by a man who entered my home under false pretenses. He was acting as a soothsayer, a palmreader, but I do not believe that was his true profession." Paz exchanged the soggy towel holding the melting ice cubes for the fresh one Tina offered. She gave no reaction to Paz's lie. "They left about thirty minutes ago, and I want the police to find them."

"You say him kidnapped her?"

"That's right. I tried to stop him but I wasn't able to." He placed the new ice pack on his bulging jaw.

"I see." The policeman reached in his pocket and pulled out a pad and pen. "I need a detailed report on what happened, and a description of the kidnapper."

"A detailed report!" Paz brayed. "I just told you what happened." His flaming eyes scorched the officer as he took several menacing steps toward him. "While you're standing here attempting to take down some stupid little notes, they are getting farther and farther away. I need you, and some of your men, to go after them *now.*"

"Alright, Mr. Paz." The officer took a tentative step back. "But I still need a description of the kidnapper."

"He is about six feet, six feet one. Strongly built," he spat.

"What his face look like?" The officer asked him.

"If I knew what his face looked like, I would have told you." Paz raised his arms, exasperated. "He was wearing a black mask." He flopped down into a rusty, velvet-covered armchair. "I did not see his face. The only thing I could see was his eyes, and they were a strange color. Maybe a smoky green, or a hazel."

"Was this man a *mestizo*? Of Afro-Caribbean descent?"

"I don't know what he was. His hands were brown, and here in Costa Rica that could mean anything." Paz's own brown hand sliced the air. "I don't even know if he had an accent. He was speaking so low I could barely hear him."

The lieutenant shifted his weight onto his other leg. "What your fiancéee look like?"

"She is a pretty woman. Dark, crinkled shoulder length hair. Large, dark, almond-shaped eyes. Her skin is the color of fine redwood. She is about five four, five five, with a body that would make you cheat on your loving wife."

Mary crossed her arms beneath her breasts in a hasty fashion, while Tina continued to look down at her hands.

"And she has a mark shaped like a crystal between her breasts."

The most intoxicated of Paz's colleagues suddenly walked through the door, which had been left partially open by the officer. A quick, nasty remark was on the tip of Paz's tongue when he saw the uninvited man, but he fought to keep himself in check.

"May I help you, José?" Paz asked, his breath quickening.

"No. I simply thought that I might be able to help *you*. Has something happened to your . . . fiancéee?"

"Yes, it has. But I will discuss it with you and the rest of my guests later."

Paz turned away from José, silently dismissing him.

"I have a couple of my own men that I want to send along with you." Paz addressed the policeman again. "They will meet you at your car, Mr. Rankin."

The officer nodded and left the room, with José in slow pursuit. Mary started to cross the room behind them.

"I want to see you later on tonight, Mary, when all the guests are gone. Don't make me have to wait too long." The implication of Paz's words was clear.

She turned and looked at him, her arms still crossed. At that moment a couple of the tears that she had managed to keep at bay trickled over the rims of her eyes. She left the room with her mouth tightly sealed.

He plopped down in the plush armchair. "I want to be alone for a few moments, Tina."

She nodded slowly and began to cross the floor. She stopped just inside the library door.

"I watched you since you were a young boy, manipulating and maneuvering people to your advantage. I helped you in the very beginning because I needed you as much as you needed me, to survive. Many nights I have regretted some of the things that we have done. Through the years I have always been by your side because I have come to love you like my own son. But now, My Paz, your actions involve the one The Earth Mother has chosen as one of her special ones. I assisted in bringing her here because I longed to see The Last of the Stonekeepers. It was my human weakness joining with your own. But you promised me you would not harm her, and I pray that you were telling the truth. It would not be wise to harm her, My Paz, not wise at all." Tina closed the door behind her.

Paz remained sitting and staring at the door, then his face began to tingle from the extreme cold created by the ice pack. He pitched the lumpy bundle into a crystal bowl, nearly knocking it over on impact. He had wanted to throw it at the old woman as she closed the door behind her, but once again he had restrained himself. He noted that as the years went by he was getting better and better at doing that.

Paz mulled over the things that Tina said. It wasn't often that she spoke out. As a matter of fact, he could actually count the times she had on one of his hands. Since the first time he met Tina, they had been an effective team. When he was a young boy they had stolen together, posing as a needy mother and son, and when things didn't go quite right they had gone hungry together. Tina had shared all that she had with him, and he with her. She was the only person, he believed, that really cared about him, money or not.

Paz touched his tender jaw. He could feel a horrible gash above the corner of his mouth, he wondered if it would heal without leaving a scar. Yes, he had promised he would not harm Sienna, and truly that was not his intent. But she had wronged him by running away, and she had to pay for that, and be taught a lesson.

Deep in thought, he surveyed the library shelves. A

colorfully decorated box that sat on the end of one of them seemed to beckon. Paz approached it slowly, reaching down inside his shirt to extract the small gold key that hung from the end of a gold chain. With it he unlocked the box.

He had not known the papers were inside when he acquired the object. Neither, evidently, had the previous owner or perhaps he simply had given no credence to what was written there. But Paz most definitely believed the story, for he had spent several years in search of proof that The Pirate's Emerald might still exist. The letter had provided such a clue, describing the carved emerald in detail. It said it was shaped like a head of a cuckoo bird, with priceless pearls for eyes.

Some believed it had been a part of the treasures of Montezuma, but that in and of itself did not matter to Paz. He craved the emerald for what it symbolized. It was the perfect mascot for the empire that he had acquired.

He thought of how the cuckoo never builds its own nest, but instead steals the nests of others and claims them for its own. Just about everything Paz owned had been acquired through theft of some kind. Most of the objects had been stolen, or through some unethical means the owners had sold them to him at a price that resembled a crime. He made a point of robbing the people he surrounded himself with of their dignity. He liked it that way. It made him feel superior. At Shangri-la he was king, and it felt good to know his power even filtered out into the surrounding area.

But Paz had an even more compelling reason for wanting the emerald. It would confirm his worthiness with those who had always considered themselves to be his betters. Men like the members of *Anansi*, the men Sienna had disrespected no more than an hour earlier. Although some of them also dealt in illegal products, they came from what Paz called real money, old money. He needed them to truly accept him. In his mind, only then would the stench of his deplorable beginnings be washed away. That's where Sienna came in. Sienna, The Last of the Stonekeepers.

Paz's handsome features hardened when he thought about the time and money he had spent following the clues in the letter. In the end, the place where he believed the stone should have been hidden had been empty. He had finally admitted he had misinterpreted the clues, and had come to a dead end until Tina told him what she knew about The Last of the Stonekeepers. She was important. A Stonekeeper had been referred to in the papers hidden in the box. It was the one thing in the passage about The Pirate's Emerald that puzzled him. It said: *Justice, or the emerald, can only be found with The Stonekeeper.*

Tina had always been full of tales that were hard to believe. As a child, he was frightened by them. As an adolescent, he was quite the skeptic. Through the years, though, she was able to gain his respect. Because of her, he had seen things the average human being might not ever see.

He remembered how she told him she had grown up in a family that believed in spirits, spirits that talked to them through their dreams and through nature. Tina said it was because of her connection with the spirits of nature that she came to know of The Stonekeeper. Then, no more than a week later, one of his associates who dealt in illegal gems came to visit from Martinique, bearing a tale of a stone called The Passion Ruby. This man also spoke of a woman called The Stonekeeper. For Paz, that was like a sign from God.

After that he knew he had to find this woman, for who could find The Pirate's Emerald, other than a person with such unique powers? So he tracked her down and had her brought to Shangri-la, using his own methods. He could not imagine how else she could have come to find The Pirate's Emerald for him. And how else would he, Paz, add the only collectible that was human to his unsurpassed repertoire?

He had tried to make it easy on her, allowing Tina to administer the elixir. Had she been cooperative, he would have taken care of her beautifully, even wooed her, coaxing her in the way that only a man can, into finding the emerald for him. At the same time he would have made her want to stay, for surely she was a woman that he would have been proud to call his own. He would have pulled out all the stops in claiming her body, therefore making her a slave to her sexual desire for him, and him alone.

Paz's lips lifted into a wry smile. That, too, had been one of his talents when he was younger. Through the years, he had found many a rich female tourist, suffering from boredom as her husband conducted business, who was willing to spend cash on a handsome, seductive native. That had added to the wealth that he had so skillfully acquired.

But Sienna had not been cooperative. She had been defiant from the very beginning, and now she had taken it upon herself to run away from him. To run away with a man who had struck him, a man who would pay for such an act.

A strange sensation of recollection surfaced, and Paz squinted his eyes as he locked into it. There was something about the masked man that seemed vaguely familiar. Something about the way he stood, the way he carried himself. Paz tried to reconcile the feelings with logic, but after a few strained moments he gave up. As he left the room to rejoin his guests, he kept the thought in the back of his mind. Could it be that the masked man was no stranger after all? Paz was determined to find out.

Nine

Sienna pressed her hands against Hawk's chest, putting distance between them. Her extraordinary predicament, the darkness of the room, and Hawk's closeness were wreaking havoc with her mind and her body. Even now she could still feel the hardness of his pecs against the top of her breasts, and how perfectly her body molded along the length of him. She stepped away, her high heels creating a disturbing clatter against the bare, wooden floor. Sienna's eyes widened with surprise and apprehension as she looked into Hawk's face. She wondered if her unconscious movements had roused suspicion in the occupants of the house.

Hawk looked down into her anxious features, then gently picked her up and placed her on the twin bed. Once again, he knelt down before her, this time to remove the shoes from her feet. Sienna felt the strongest urge to reach out and stroke his hair, to trace the tiny curls that framed his face. Instead she murmured a soft, "Thank you," before deliberately inspecting the room.

The furniture consisted of a chest of drawers, a wooden chair, and the bed upon which she sat. A duffle bag and a carved walking stick occupied one corner. She watched as Hawk turned on the only lamp they had. It was small, and rather old. The single lightbulb painted the room in a dim, yellowish light.

Hawk crossed the room again and sat down beside Sienna. His long legs stretched out in front of him. He leaned back, placing his head against the wall.

To say the least, Sienna felt awkward sitting on the bed in the tiny room beside Hawk, who claimed to be her former lover. It would be so much easier if she really knew what to believe. A part of her wanted to believe him, and a part of her actually did, but she was still afraid to trust what her mind could not verify. As it stood, all she could rely on was her intuition, and what it told her caused her to tremble. Sienna's gut feeling acknowledged that he spoke the truth, but it also warned that there were many things about this man that she had never known.

Hawk's hoarse whisper disrupted her thoughts.

"I believe Charmagne, the woman who owns this house, is out. But I don't know about her mother. That's why I had you wait outside while I came in alone," he informed her. "I think it's best for them not to know that you are here. We will stay for the night, but I think we need to head out tomorrow before dawn."

"But where will we go?" Sienna asked, feeling the pressure building inside her head once again.

Shadowy images pressed their way to the front of her thoughts, blocked pieces of her life that yearned to come forward and reclaim their part of her history. She strained for a clearer view, to recognize the places, the people, the time, only to have them to recede again.

"The nearest airport is outside of San José. We have to head back inland to get to it. I'm assuming that's what you want to do. Leave Costa Rica."

"I can't think of anything better," she replied, although she felt as if that was not the answer he sought.

"I guess you can't." Hawk paused for a moment. "Maybe when you have recovered, all of this won't seem so trying. I don't know if you realize it or not, but there is a reason outside of Paz's machinations that you are here. It is the same reason why I came to Costa Rica."

Sienna turned and looked at Hawk's profile. Although he was speaking to her and they sat so close, it was all that he offered. At that moment she realized that somehow she had come to believe, at least hope, that Hawk was in Costa Rica solely because of his feelings for her, that forces beyond his control had kept him away, and now, finally, he had come to reclaim her. Sienna rested her head in her hands and began to rub her forehead. How fanciful could she be? A weary smile touched her lips, and she decided not be so hard on herself. Of course, under the circumstances, it was easy for her to adopt such false illusions. The truth was, though, that Hawk had his own reasons for being in Costa Rica, and whatever they were they had nothing to do with love.

"Would your being here also have something to do with my being a Stonekeeper?" she asked facetiously. "It seems to be the main thing everyone else around here is interested in. And one of the only things that I remember about myself that seems to be perfectly clear."

Hawk turned and looked at her directly in the face. "Yes, it does."

His response shocked her. He had spoken to her of love, yet his sole reason for seeking her out was because of a legacy she had never wanted.

Suddenly, images of a sandy beach and her fighting for her life fluttered through Sienna's mind. A large red stone, a ruby, had actually been instrumental in saving her life. Sienna knew that at that very moment she came to accept that she was a Stonekeeper. She knew she had actually denied it up until that time. But what Sienna recalled most vividly were the thoughts and feelings that she had experienced as she held the ruby against the mark between her breasts. She had seemed to be the receptor of all human emotions and thoughts for miles and miles, until the ruby drew them out of her and into its crimson depths.

"But I want you to know, Sienna," Hawk said, drawing her back into the present, "that I am also—"

"Hawk, are you back?" a female voice called from beyond the door.

"Yes, I am." He placed his hand on Sienna's knee in a silencing gesture.

"I saw the light under your door," the woman continued, "and if you're not asleep there's something very important I need to tell you."

"Alright," Hawk stood up and hastily began to remove the black jumpsuit. "Just a minute."

In a matter of seconds he was standing before Sienna in nothing but a pair of bikini briefs. She tried not to stare, but her eyes seemed to follow his every move of their own volition. It was hard for her to believe how beautiful he was. Every part of him was taut, defined, and when he moved his muscles rippled and stretched underneath skin that was smooth as molasses.

Hurriedly, he placed the mask inside the jumpsuit, folding them together, then placed them inside the duffle bag. As he advanced toward the door he pulled on a pair of jeans, fastening them as he went.

Sienna was on her feet, contemplating what should be her next move, when Hawk motioned for her to go into the closet. Once she was there he opened the bedroom door. She stood quietly in the dark, grateful that a sizable splinter of missing wood provided a view of Hawk and the woman he had called Charmagne.

"Oh, it looks like you were already in bed," she remarked as she took in his bare torso.

"That's okay. What is it?" His tone was deceptively nonchalant.

"On my way back from town I heard that Paz's fiancéee

was kidnapped tonight, and the man who did it might still be in the vicinity. They say he is dangerous."

"What?"

Sienna held her breath as she listened.

"You know, Paz, the man who owns Shangri-la." Charmagne tried to make herself clearer. "The place where you worked this morning."

"Yes, I know."

"Well, his fiancéee, the woman that Selles told us about in the bakery, was kidnapped. A man posing as a palmreader at Paz's party is said to be responsible."

"Is that right?" Hawk's voice held a peculiar edge.

"Yeah."

"What does he look like?'

"Nobody knows." Charmagne shrugged her shoulders. "Because he was wearing some kind of cloth mask."

"What's going on in here?" another woman called.

"Oh, Mama, I'm sorry, I didn't mean to wake you up."

"You didn't wake me. I was going to get some water." Sienna saw an older woman appear outside the door.

"I was telling Hawk a woman was kidnapped tonight from the estate called Shangri-la. It's not too far away from here. I believe I've told you about it." She pulled her mother's collar out of her robe. "The woman who was kidnapped is the owner's fiancéee."

"Oh-h." Nanna wrapped her terry cloth robe closer around her body. "I believe I heard some of the women talking about him today. Humph-h." She pursed her lips. "From the things they were saying about him, it's a wonder she didn't run away. The man's a lunatic." She waved her hand and turned her back as she continued on her way.

"Now look, Mama, you can't be going around saying things like that. I'm surprised those women were talking so openly about him. Although I must admit whatever you heard was probably true. The bottom line is, he can make trouble for a lot of the folks who live around here. So it's best not to say anything if you can't say something good."

"If he walks like a duck, he is a duck," Nanna replied, her voice fading as she progressed.

Charmagne rolled her eyes toward the ceiling. "Lord, there is no controlling that woman." She shook her head. "But it's a fact. Mr. Paz doesn't have that good of a reputation amongst the regular folks around here, yet quite a few of them depend on him for their livelihoods." She heaved a healthy sigh. "I just thought I'd let you know what was going on because, to be honest with you, it makes me feel real good having a man in the house tonight." She gave his body an appreciative visual inspection. "They say the fella could be violent. It's no telling what will happen to the poor woman he has with him. So, I thought I'd warn you, just in case he decides to come this way. You know what I mean?"

A slight smiled curved Hawk's lips, and he acknowledged her with a pronounced nod.

"So if you hear me hollering over there, please don't hesitate to come running." An inviting spark entered Charmagne's eye. "I've got to tell you if Mama wasn't here, I'd simply insist that you allow me to stay in here with you. That way I'd know nothing would happen. At least, nothing that I didn't *want* to happen." She raised one eyebrow.

Instantly, a knot formed in Sienna's stomach. There was no doubt Charmagne's request for help was also an invitation, and Sienna wondered what Hawk's reply would be. Her emotions ran even higher when she realized that Charmagne was like countless women, like herself, who found Hawk to be extremely attractive. As she watched them, she recalled what he had told her. It had been six months since they had seen one another. Sienna's face grew hot as she imagined the number of women who might have been a part of his life during her absence.

"I don't believe that you will have any problem, but I'll be listening just in case you do." Hawk leaned against the door frame.

"Alright, then. I guess I'll see you in the morning," Charmagne replied, obviously disappointed.

"That reminds me," he said, straightening up to his full height, "I will be leaving out rather early tomorrow morning. I don't know what time. It depends on what I am able to work out during the day, if I will end up coming back tomorrow night."

"Oh. So you might be leaving for good?"

"It's a big possibility," Hawk admitted.

"Damn," Charmagne said softly under her breath. Then, on the spur of the moment, she stepped forward, wrapped both arms around Hawk's neck and kissed him lingeringly on the mouth. "That's in case I don't see you again, but also to let you know that I hope that I do." Charmagne turned and walked away. Hawk hesitated just a second before he closed the bedroom door and hooked the latch.

Sienna ventured out of the closet at the same time. She tried to muster the same feeling she had before Charmagne came to the door, a feeling of aloofness, distance, but the truth was she was feeling rather angry. Angry because of the mess her life appeared to be in. In a matter of days she had suffered a loss of memory, complicated by everything else that had happened in Costa Rica, and now she was experiencing jealous feelings over Hawk, a man her mind did not recognize but her heart seemed to know quite well. Until a few minutes ago she had been unsure if she had any feelings for him besides a physical attraction, but just seeing him in the arms of another woman had made things crystal clear.

All of a sudden Sienna knew how tired she was of being

an unwilling puppet in this madness called her life. She felt the urge to lash out, to pull the blankets off the bed, kick the contents out of the duffle bag. Instead, she went and stood in front of the window and looked up at the waxing moon. She was comforted by the sight of it, because she was aware it was a time when the orb, a symbol of femininity, was gaining strength and power. Sienna stared intensely at the gibbous moon dusted with a layering of clouds. At the same time, she called out mentally to the powers that be. *If I am truly The Last of the Stonekeepers, so precious to Mother Earth, then I demand an end to this confusion. To this madness.* She ran her fingers over the engraved symbols on the silver bracelet. *I am willing to step up to whatever task is mine, but it must be under my own volition, with a healthy mind and body.*

No sooner had the words left her mouth than the clouds began to part ever so slowly, allowing a full blast of the moonlight to shine upon her. She squinted with amazement as she watched. Was that nature's response to her cry? Or was it simply a coincidental timing of the motion of the clouds? Sienna was not sure, but to her it seemed a sign, and she felt stronger and more self-assured than she had before.

"Do you have a large shirt that I can put on?" She had turned away from the window, addressing Hawk. The jealousy that she had felt was still there, but it had been tamed by a self-confidence that was invigorating.

"I believe so." He cocked his head to the side as he answered her, but still he did not move.

"May I borrow it?" Sienna smoothed her hair away from her face as she spoke.

"Sure."

Hawk dug down in the duffle bag, producing a cotton, striped shirt of navy blue and white.

Sienna walked boldly toward him and took it from his hands, "Thank you." She entered the opposite corner of the room, offering him her back. She would not be so bold as to undress directly in front of him, but she would not hide in the closet, either. He was the one who claimed he knew everything about her, had caressed her body, so there was no need to hide.

She unzipped the white gown, pulled it down off her shoulders, then wiggled to maneuver it past her hips. With a calm she barely felt, knowing Hawk's gaze was on her, she donned his button-down shirt, which hit her just below the knees. Afterward she removed her stockings. Then she turned to face him.

Sienna was not prepared for the look of carnal longing and desire that was etched into every line of Hawk's face. Her immediate reaction was to look away from the blaze that burned in his bright, amber eyes, but she changed her mind, and as naturally as her curly lashes had swept downward she raised them again, with a slight lifting of her chin.

"Is there something wrong?" she said, baiting him.

The tip of Hawk's tongue slid over his bottom lip before he huskily replied, "No."

Hawk could tell there was something different about her, a shift in attitude, and he wondered what had brought it on. Although she was covered now, he could still imagine the curve of her brown waist and rise of her hips beneath the material. His breathing had accelerated as a result of watching her dress, and he made a concentrated effort to slow it down.

"Good. Because, definitely, since you're so open with me and we know each other so well, I didn't think that there would be a problem with my actions." The swirl of confidence and anger egged her on. "It was obvious you had no qualms about undressing before *me.*"

"It's according to what you call a problem, Sienna. But I caution you, things have not been easy since we have been apart, and it's been a long time since we've been . . .

together. It's been a long time period, if you know what I mean."

"Are you trying to imply that you have been celibate since we were together?" She walked over and tucked her dress into the duffle bag. She did not want him to see the hope that she would not be able to hide.

"Although I think that's important," he returned, "I think the real question is, have you decided to accept that I was part of your life in the past, and that we were lovers and much much more?" His gaze bore into her as if he dared her to deny it.

"Do I have a choice?"

"Yes, you do. You can deny it if you want. But I don't believe there is anything that could happen to me so that I would not feel something special for you. Unless that feeling was never there to begin with."

Sienna could feel the emotion behind Hawk's words. So what was he implying? That she was the kind of woman who had gotten involved with him but had deceived him about her feelings?

"Well, let's say I have accepted it. Where does that put me? Am I reclaiming a man who left me in the first place? Or are you reclaiming a woman who deceived you in and out of your bed?" Anger exploded inside of her as she spoke. How dare he imply that she might not be trustworthy. She needed no mental verification to know the kind of person she was.

Hawk watched Sienna as she climbed onto the bed, crossing her legs beneath her. He didn't like the way she talked, and the images her last question evoked. He recalled how Paz had warned her. *No woman of mine will ever talk to me the way you just did.* Hawk wondered if Sienna had truly been Paz's woman in every sense of the word, even while they had been together. He could barely stomach the idea that she had been with another man, even in his self-initiated absence. Just the thought of her cheating on him was more than he could take.

"I'm in no mood for any of this. I simply wanted you to know where I stand." He retrieved a leather tie from the top of the chest of drawers and began to tie his dreadlocks into a ponytail at the base of his neck.

Sienna had expected more than this sullen response, and she looked out the window once again, gathering her thoughts. Why hadn't he assured her that she could be trusted? That he believed in her and what he claimed they had?

"I'm tired," Hawk announced, turning off the light. "And as you can see, our living accommodations are somewhat limited. I guess I could play the gentleman and offer to sleep on the floor while you take the bed, but I'm not up to that. So we'll have to share." He walked over and stood in front of her. "Unless you would like to sleep on the floor?"

"I don't think so," Sienna retorted.

"It's settled, then."

Hawk unfastened his jeans and sat down on the bed before he slid them over his bare feet. Afterward, he lay down, placing his head on part of the only pillow. He had to bend his legs to avoid touching Sienna's backside with his feet.

Sienna sat quietly in the darkness. She wanted to lie down, but she couldn't bring herself to do it. She placed her elbows on her knees and took her face in her hands.

"You know," he said, his voice touching her in the moonlit darkness, "I never envisioned that our reunion would be like this."

"How did you think it would be, Hawk?" Sienna's voice reflected her weariness of spirit.

Silence filled the room before he spoke again.

"I had hoped that no matter what had happened in our lives, that once we saw one another the love would be the same between us. That nothing would keep us from loving one another."

The tone of his voice revealed such bleakness that it caused Sienna's heart to yearn for the love of which he spoke. An uncomfortable ball formed in her throat, and tears welled up in her eyes and began to trickle down her cheeks. She tried to halt their flow, but their source was a deep well of sadness, one that she did not even understand. The loss she felt was so profound that her shoulders began to heave with the depth of her sorrow.

It would have been so easy to turn and crawl up into his arms, but her uncertainty about him would not allow it. Although he was only a few feet away, the space between them felt immeasurable. Sienna closed her eyes as the tears continued to flow. Then, slowly, she felt Hawk's arms come up around her.

"Ah-h Sienna. My Sienna. What has happened to us?" He drew her back against his chest and leaned his face against her hair. "Sometimes it's not easy being a human being. To be able to feel the things we do, then feel the loss when we believe they are no longer there."

Hawk's soothing words caused Sienna to softly sob even more, so he sat back against the wall and drew her into his arms, like a mother cradling a child. He turned her face toward his chest to stifle the sound. "It's okay, baby. Let it go. Let it all go."

He pressed a lingering kiss against her forehead, then at her temple. His lips felt so good against her skin. His arms felt so strong around her, and so familiar. Sienna molded herself closer against Hawk, wrapping her arms about his neck as if the closer they became the easier it would be to believe in him.

"You can't imagine how much I've missed you. How I've longed to hold you in my arms just like this," he whispered in her ear before kissing away a tear that had just begun its descent.

Sienna soaked up the words and the love she could feel from him like a flower thirsting in the desert. She gently nuzzled her face against his lips that were kissing her cheek, her ear. At that moment there was nothing inside her that doubted that he loved her and she loved him.

Finally, Sienna offered her lips to Hawk and he accepted them, placing small kisses at the corners, the peaks. He tasted every portion of her lips before he parted them with his tongue and kissed her deeply. There was no haste in his exploration of the wet cavern she offered, and when Sienna's tongue joined him in his quest, the feelings that emanated through her were like strains of the sweetest music.

"Oh, sweetness, how I have waited for this day." Hawk wooed her, his lips touching hers ever so slightly. "I don't want to do anything that you aren't ready for, but Baby I must tell you that I want you. No, the truth is, I need you." This time, when he kissed her, his mouth trembled with urgency.

Sienna responded by pulling him down toward her. Her tears had dried up now, and she was thankful for the comfort and the love he was giving.

"Our being here together feels so right," she whispered shakily. "To hear you say that you need me sends waves of pleasure through every part of my body." Sienna paused. "And Hawk, I can not deny that I want you, too." The consensual words flowed so easily. "Here in your arms is where I want to be."

They hugged for a prolonged time. Then they stretched out upon the bed, staring into each others' eyes. Time seemed to stand still, and when they finally found what only lovers can find in each others' gazes, Hawk pressed Sienna down on the bed beneath him.

This time when he kissed her his tongue was a seething brand. He wanted everything she had to offer, and more.

His body moved against hers in an initiatory dance, ebbing and flowing against her yielding one, causing the shirt she wore to rise high up on her hips.

"Oh, Sienna." His words were husky as he marked her body with kisses, starting with her mouth, the tender places behind her ears, and the spot at the base of her neck. As he travelled lower, the intensity of his need was apparent as he fumbled with the buttons on the masculine shirt. Eventually his ardor gave way to impatience, and he pulled it up over her head.

A long, deep sigh emerged from Hawk when he looked down at Sienna's bare torso, her breasts standing taut, like bronze mountains with chocolate peaks. He stroked the mounds lovingly before stretching Sienna's arms over her head and holding them there.

"Baby, I want you to know I've waited so long that I have no intention of rushing now, no matter how bad my need is. I'm going to savor every moment, every part of you." He pinned her to the bed with a smoldering gaze. "And when we are finally one, I plan to stay there, pleasing you, until you cry out your pleasure, and then I will know that I've done my job."

Sienna's breaths came in tiny bursts as she listened to his words, and she could feel the heated energy from his muscular frame even before he lowered his body onto hers. At that moment Hawk's mouth and tongue seem to come alive in a lascivious way, cutting a wet path down her neck and across her shoulders. Sienna moaned as he nibbled and licked his way to the top of one of her breasts, creating enticing suckling sounds. Then his head began to waver from one breast to the other as if it pained him to draw away from one, ignoring the other. Sienna arched her back in wanton welcome, which caused Hawk to escalate his actions. Animal-like sounds rumbled in his throat as he moistened the area leading to her navel and the soft, feminine pucker below. When his mouth reached the curly triangle between her legs, Sienna could barely tolerate the pleasurable, anticipatory sensations that were surging through her. Finally, Hawk's tongue found its mark, and an involuntary gasp eased its way from between Sienna's lips. Hawk offered her his hand as a shield for the sound, and she kissed his palm, eagerly masking the sensual noises she continued to make.

Hawk explored her thoroughly, and the moment he perceived an increase in her pleasure he lingered over the area until her body rose and fell as rhythmically as the sun.

Hawk's actions had brought her to the peak of pleasure, and she was no longer in control of her mind or her body as her senses exploded into a kaleidoscopic array of ecstatic pieces.

Hawk knew that she was spent, and he took her in his arms for a final time, whispering in her ear, "How could you ever forget me, Sienna? How could you ever forget us . . . this?"

As the last sound of the word left his mouth and his lips rested against her ear, Hawk filled her softness to the hilt with a hard, pulsating force. Although his desire was more than ready to overflow, he determined he was not ready to release its power, so he subdued it by lying still within her. Finally, when Hawk knew that control was his again, he began to pleasure her, and this time, when he settled in, he knew he would not be left wanting.

The rhythm of his body was the rhythm of the universe, steady and unending. So virile was he that he drew Sienna's desire up from the valley into which it had plunged after ecstasy, and started her on the road to bliss again.

Sienna's senses and mind were still whirling from before, and all that she could do was clasp her arms around his body as his rigidness coaxed her into sexual abandon. In that place, there was no space and time, only a driving force to an explosive, mind-boggling end. When it came, they held each other so tightly that the breath of life left their bodies for a split second, causing them to be one with each other, and with everything there was.

In the end Sienna and Hawk collapsed, rag-like and still, on the tiny bed, and when they finally opened their eyes to gaze upon one another there was a wholeness present that had not been there before.

Sienna's mouth opened as if she wanted to speak, but no sound emerged. After several excruciating moments, though, she finally said as her dazed eyes looked deeply into the satiated depths of his hazel ones, "I remember. I remember everything."

Ten

"We heard about what happened to your . . . fiancée," the overweight man told Paz as he lit a fat cigar. "Although we were sorry to hear it, we found the timing of her kidnapping to be a strange coincidence, considering it happened so shortly after her outburst."

Paz lowered his gaze before he spoke. "Your heartfelt concerns are truly appreciated, gentlemen," he said graciously to the same men who had gathered in the room once before, "but I must say I don't quite understand what it is you are trying to imply."

"I would think it is rather obvious," said José, the only one present who still had a drink in his hand. "Knowing you as we do, meaning your background and all, we hope the little lady you call your fiancéee wasn't brought here under false pretenses just so you can keep your hands in our pockets and worm your way into our organization."

"False pretenses? What kind of false pretenses?" A light sheen of perspiration broke out on Paz's brow, and he wondered if the members of *Anansi* had caught wind of how Sienna had come to Shangri-la. Although he knew they also had a hand in illegal dealings, on paper they were all legitimate, thanks to money laundering and the like. They were pillars of their communities, and Paz knew they would not take kindly to, nor could they afford, being connected with anyone who was a known criminal.

They would distance themselves from him in a heartbeat. He would be blackballed.

Paz had worked so hard to gain the status and money that he had in recent years. They had become outward symbols of who he was, at least what he had always wanted to be. But something deep inside had never changed, a nagging feeling of unworthiness in the eyes of the world, solely because of the cards life dealt him from the very beginning. If these men severed their ties with him, in his mind it would mean the end of his respectability. At this point in his life he could not weather that.

"Perhaps she was not the legendary Stonekeeper of which we have heard so much," José continued. "Perhaps she was just a woman that you hired to pose as such."

Paz had to control the smile that threatened to crack his intentionally offended countenance. "I can assure all of you that, my fiancéee, Sienna Russell, is as authentic as they come. It pains me to know that you would consider it to be otherwise. I would not have the audacity to make up such a lie. And, as I have promised you, once she has been returned to me she will lead us to The Pirate's Emerald, which because of your generosity will become the *Anansi's* talisman. I'm sure it will be given a place of honor in our hall."

"I hope you're telling the truth," a squat man with sunken eyes pitched in. "You know the *Anansi* is an elite group. We have been more than open to your becoming an official member ever since you told us that you would be bringing her here. She is of great interest to us, and remember, her leading you to The Pirate's Emerald is the key to your membership." His eyes appeared to sink even farther into his skull. "But I must say we were more than surprised to hear that she had become your fiancée. Such a union between the two of you makes me wary. You said you needed the money to bring her here, and to convince her to participate in the search."

"Do not worry, gentlemen, I can be trusted, and there is no law that says a man can not fall in love, even if the woman he loves is the fulfillment of a legend. I guarantee you Sienna will lead us to the emerald, and we will be some of the most renowned collectors in the world."

"We're going to hold you to that promise, Paz," José warned. "Call me as soon as you find her. That way, the membership will be kept abreast of the situation."

Paz's eyes gleamed like polished, smoky topaz as he looked around the room. "Of course, gentlemen. Of course."

Paz waited in his posh bedroom impatiently. He looked at the clock again. "She should have been here by now," he hissed into the darkness.

The hands on the miniature clock ticked loudly, escalating his impatience and his anger. Finally, he swung his feet over the side of the bed and reached for his satiny robe. The door to his bedroom opened slowly. Mary stepped quietly into the room.

"I told you to come as soon as all of the guests were gone. That was nearly an hour ago," Paz reprimanded.

Mary didn't say a word. She began to remove her apron, but remained in the vicinity of the door.

"Did you hear what I said?"

"Yes."

"Well, where were you?"

"I had to make sure the kitchen was in order before I came," she replied.

Paz threw the robe onto a chair. "Wrong. You should have come and taken care of me first, and then tended to that."

Mary folded her clothes in a neat pile, placing her shoes beside them.

"Why in the hell are you doing that?" His impatience overflowed. "Get over here."

Mary's jaws became rock hard. She wanted to cuss at

him. She was grateful for the dim lighting in the room. By the time she approached Paz on the bed there was no sign of her displeasure. She knew that Paz could be cruel when he wanted to, and she had learned how to calm the sadistic side of him when it surfaced. Mary also surmised he wasn't really angry because she was late. He was angry because the woman, Sienna, was gone, and it riled her to think of it. Before two days ago she had never heard of the woman, and when she was told that there would be a permanent houseguest the woman was introduced as Paz's fiancéee! His fiancéee of all things.

Paz grabbed Mary by the waist and pulled her down in front of him. "You know what I want," he commanded, his voice raspy. His hands continued upward, grabbing her hair and forcing her head down.

Yes, she knew. The first time he had forced her to perform the act she had actually thrown up on him and herself. Maybe it would not have been so bad if it were the *only* thing that she did that the women in her tiny village near Tortuguero had always denounced as profane. But there were other things. Many others.

Hastily, Mary set to her task, conjuring up the images that always drew her away from the act. She gladly recalled the earlier times when Paz was the ultimate enticer, making her want to please him because he appeared to be so eager to please her. It made it easier for her to fulfill the sexual desires that she considered unnatural. Those times had been quite infrequent as of late, but she had still believed, hoped, that maybe he had some real feelings for her.

Mary knew that Paz was near his time and she hastened her movements. When the climatic cry issued from his lips she waited to receive his offering, as he had always insisted that she do. This time, she heard the name "Sienna," gush from his slackened lips.

"What? What did you say?" She sat back on her heels,

looking up into his pleasure-contorted face. She waited for him to answer, and when he didn't she could not hold her temper. "Did you say another woman's name as I held you like that?" Incredulity marred her attractive features.

Finally, the glaze disappeared from Paz's eyes, and he looked directly at her. "Who are you talking to like that?" He lingered in the pleasurable feelings. He looked down his nose at her. "And so what if I did?"

Considering all the things that Paz had done in the past, Mary still could not believe the cold harshness of his answer. Most of all, she could not believe that she had actually thought there might be a loving future with this man. A man who had taken her virginity at the age of sixteen, and had kept her as a worker in his household for the last seven years, only elevating her to the head of his kitchen within the last six months.

During those years Mary had learned much. She had not seen any of the world outside of her village Tortuguero, and Puerto Limon, but she had heard plenty, thanks to the visitors that frequented Shangri-la. She longed for the fancy clothes and airs that many of the female guests possessed, although she realized, like everyone else, that most of them were no more than high paid *putas*. Watching them had taught her that granting sexual favors for a man with status and money could yield a young woman a good living.

Still, underneath all that, her moral roots were deep. Suddenly, the innocent features of her younger sister, Junie, loomed in her mind, and she prayed that *she* would never have to even taste the humiliations she had lived through. Yes, in recent years she had willingly done everything Paz had asked of her, but her eye had been on the future. She had actually believed that with time he would see her worth outside of his sexual needs. Now, as she looked into his disdainful eyes, she was beginning to fear she had been deluding herself.

"I can not believe you would say that to me." Mary's words were barely a whisper.

"I can say or do whatever I want to you." He manipulated himself to rekindle his desire. "That's what you're here for. All of you. Now turn around and finish up what you started."

She stared at the face that she had always considered the most handsome she had ever seen. Now it no longer appeared to be so. The new pinkish-white cut near the corner of his mouth altered it, but she knew that was not the reason. Perhaps Mary was seeing the real Paz for the first time. Scorn rose up inside her, uncoiling like a snake preparing for the strike.

"You get one of those scruffy workers who beg at your doorstep every morning to be head of the kitchen." She rose to her feet. " 'Cause tomorrow I won't be here. And I finished doing these filthy things for you." Mary's hands were animated as she spoke. "You act as if my body has no feeling, as if I have no soul."

"You're not going anywhere," Paz retorted menacingly, and he placed his hands outside of his bare thighs as if he were about to stand.

Frightened about what he was about to do, Mary picked up a geometrically painted bowl from the night stand and threw it. Paz tried to protect himself, but Mary's aim was true. He doubled over as the pottery struck him, his painful outcry filling the room.

Seeing what she had done, Mary ran across the bedroom and grabbed her belongings. Hurriedly, she pulled the dress over her head while Paz remained stiff, immobile. She was glad that she had hurt him, but even then she was sure his pain was nothing compared to the humiliation she had suffered.

"You will regret what you have done to me," she warned before closing the door and running down the hall.

Paz's face remained scrunched up with pain as he sat

waiting for the excruciating throb to subside. Eventually he would get the woman, he assured himself, but in actuality she had done him a favor. In her anger she had provided the crucial piece of the puzzle that had haunted him. She had mentioned the workers who were sometimes hired during the morning. *He* had said he had been hired that morning, and had arrived with the old man Selles.

A clear image surfaced of the disrespectful, animal-like eyes that stared at him that morning outside the breakfast salon. Paz knew for certain that they were the same eyes that peered at him so violently from inside the black cloth mask, the eyes of the man who might have marred his smooth facial features for life.

He tried to stand but the pain would not allow it, and another image filled his mind. He recalled the way Sienna had stared at the worker. Was she more attracted to the lowly worker than she was to him? Could it be that in the short span of twenty-four hours she had allowed him to get next to her? And to think he had desired this woman more than any other.

An angry taste rose into Paz's throat and entered his mouth. He would pay them back for making a fool of him in his own home. He vowed to make it his business to personally track them down.

Once again Paz attempted to stand. This time he was successful, although the sensations were still agonizing. Slowly, he donned his robe. With tentative steps he crossed the room, heading for the servants' wing. There he would find someone who knew where Selles lived, and after that he would gather some men together and be hot on their trail.

Sienna sat up slowly, oblivious to Hawk, who still lay beside her. She stared into empty space as she recited portions of her life that had been lost to her. Sienna spoke as if she were telling a story as she rediscovered events that had taken place in her life during the last twelve months.

"And that's when I met you." She looked over into Hawk's pleased but somewhat veiled features. "You were with me when I discovered The Passion Ruby in Martinique, all the way to the end." She threw her arms about his neck and kissed him jubilantly. "And after that we had such great times together. We were hardly ever apart, and then I woke up . . . one morning . . . and you were gone." She looked at him as if he had struck her. "Gone. All that was left of you was a note." She began to draw back from him. "A slip of paper that possessed none of the warmth and loving nights that you provided, and did nothing to satisfy the loss I felt. You apologized for leaving me, but you did not explain why you left." She stared at Hawk's face, which appeared to be as hard as sandstone.

"A part of me wanted to die, and did, when I never heard from you again." Sienna wrapped her arms around her. "I remember it was a slow, painful death because I could not let go. I waited and waited, refusing to believe that you would hurt me so much. But in the end I had to face the truth, and that's when my belief in love died."

The rush of recollected emotions made Sienna feel as if she were plummeting down an emotional waterfall, and she doubled over under their influence. "The only thing that saved me was a budding, red, hot anger that eventually grew into a fireball inside me. It allowed me to hate you for introducing me to such a powerful love, only to snatch it away."

She turned to Hawk with all the fury and hurt that had been stored up for the last six months, "Why did you leave?"

"I *had* to." He looked her dead in the eye.

"You had to?" Her face contorted from lack of understanding. "But why? Did you have another woman? A family that you never told me about?"

"There was only my wife, Rashida. And as I told you, she died before we even met."

"So why did you le-eave, without saying a word?" Her dark eyes beseeched him.

"There are some things about me that I never told you, Sienna." Hawk placed his hand upon her shoulder, but felt it stiffen. He removed it. "And I'm still unable to tell you, even now."

She made a noise in her throat that resembled a cough as she looked him up and down. "I remember having a similar conversation with you months ago. Then, just like now, you made it clear that you could tell me if you chose to, but you refused to do it. This is exactly the same situation."

"Baby, it's not as simple as that."

"Simple. I'm not looking for simple, Hawk. As complicated as all of this is, do you think all I can handle is simple?" She did not wait for an answer. "Once I turned twenty-five I had to face that I was something called a Stonekeeper. A thing, that was for me, straight out of fairy tales, mythology. But I've come to accept it, and my life has never been the same since. What could possibly be any more complicated or unbelievable than that?"

"We all have our roles, Sienna." He stared out of the window. "In my eyes your being a Stonekeeper is an exalted thing. Even though they may not know it, you are precious to humankind all over this earth." He looked back at her, his features hardened. "Some of us have a darker cross to bear."

His insistence on not telling her infuriated Sienna. She had loved this man like she had never loved any other human being. Without telling her why, he had left her. Now here he sat, six months later, in front of her face, after they had made love, and he was still able to keep a part of himself away from her, a part so important it had torn their relationship asunder. Sienna held her two fists close to her breasts and shook them.

"Isn't it just like a man to think there is no hurt like his own? But of course, being hurt, or having a problem never happens to a man, because he's too perfect for that," she went on in a singsong voice. "Whatever happens, don't let anything disrupt this perfect image that he has of himself. He can't bear it. He doesn't want anyone to know." She got off the bed, stood up and flung her arms out dramatically. "And o-oh, don't let something *really* happen in his life, he'll never tell anyone. He'll just hold it, and take it to his grave to save his manly pride." She paused for emphasis. "So you don't have to tell me, Hennessy "Hawk" Jackson, what it is that made you just vanish, disappear." She began to speak out of pure frustration. "You can rest assured you don't know everything about me either," she said, patting her chest, "and I'm going to keep it that way. I'll harbor my own little secrets, be they about Paz, or whomever or whatever else. It's not your concern."

His eyes narrowed. "It's not quite the same, Sienna."

"It's the same to me. And you can believe from now on that whatever I do I won't be as open and naive as I was before. If you can keep a secret like that, so can I."

"Don't go that way, Sienna. Don't threaten me like that." The pulse became visible in his temple. "I consider you to be mine."

"Yours? After six months of not seeing me?" She shook her head from side to side slowly. "Like I told Paz, nobody owns m—"

Before Sienna could finish her statement, Hawk had pulled her down on the bed, pinning her beneath him. Desperate because of the curse that bound him to silence and a germinating jealousy, Hawk sought to manipulate her the only way he felt he could. He knew he could not control her mind, her spirit or her mouth, but memories of the hot love that burned between them insured him he could be the master of her body.

"I may not own you, but dammit, I'm going to make sure that every time you have the slightest thought about another man, the way I make you feel will wipe that thought right out of your mind."

Hawk's mouth descended on hers with a scorching passion. Sienna squirmed in protest beneath him as his tongue excavated the moist cave, uncovering a seed of desire that she was not even aware of. He pressed his body against hers, drawing her mind away from the reason she taunted him. She tried to cling to the anger and frustration of moments before, but the tumultuous sensations that began to course through her blocked them out. It was as if his mouth and his body were stoking a fire that appeared to be cold but was sparked by the slightest carnal movement, and once again flames began to rise.

Hawk knew the moment Sienna's body had decided to give itself to him, and a deep moan slid from between his generous lips. His hands began to touch her everywhere as if to assure himself that she was there, once again, beneath him.

"Don't turn away from me, Sienna." He wrapped his arms beneath her upper back, causing her breasts to push forward. He rubbed his hard chest against their softness. "I won't let you," he declared as he stared down into her overwhelmed features. "I'm going to do everything in my power to ensure that you never give yourself to anyone but me."

He moved his hardness against her, making her aware of its full capability. Over and over he teased her with its closeness, as he kissed and licked her mouth, her neck, her breasts. As the minutes passed, Sienna's passion became like a liquid fire. Hawk could feel her wetness move against him, cajoling him to take her, but he refused.

"I've got to hear you say that you want me. I need to know that you accept me with all my dark secrets, my faults," his words were hoarse, guttural.

"Please Hawk. Please."

"No, Baby, it's me that's asking, pleading. Tell me that you want me, that you'll never want anyone else," he said as yellowish-green eyes locked with her dark brown ones, his lips mere inches away from hers.

All of a sudden Sienna experienced a deep, open need for him that felt as if it would drive her mad if it were not filled. Her words were breathy, staggered when she finally spoke, "I only want you, Hawk. I only want you."

Hawk's mouth claimed hers as his rigidness claimed flesh smooth as silk, totally filling her excruciating need. Like the bird for which he was named, his body swooped, rose and dove in pursuit of the prey he had in sight, the complete surrender of the woman beneath him.

He rode Sienna's passion like a hawk on undulating winds, more than familiar with the wavy motions, a master navigator of the familiar water. Over and over again they rose and fell, but this time when Sienna ascended to her peak Hawk climbed with her, determining the way as he increased his momentum. When she finally gave in to the burst of unsurpassed pleasure, his movements became frenzied as he reached for his own fulfillment, and the certain knowledge that he had done all he could to cast her over the brink.

The passionate cry rose from so deep within Sienna that she could not hold it, and she plummeted with Hawk, smothering the telltale sound with a kiss.

Once he released her, Sienna turned onto her side, and Hawk pulled her limp body back toward his. Every so often, a reminiscent tremble coursed through her, a reminder of how much her body could have a mind of its own. Sienna was aware of Hawk's arm as it held her tightly, and she was also aware that she still knew so very little about him. Her pride wanted to rally against him, to let him know how unfair it was, but her body was spent from the love they had made, and her mind cried out for a moment's peace. Sienna's eyelids grew heavy as she gave into sleep, but she found even in slumber there was no rest for the weary.

Eleven

Sienna ignored the rocking, but it came again. She opened her eyes to an unfamiliar room, and for a moment she wasn't sure where she was. Then she realized it was Hawk shaking her, and it was his voice speaking softly that began to clear the haze.

"Sienna, it's time to go."

"What?"

"We need to leave before it turns light."

"Oh. Yes." She closed her eyes momentarily. "I was dreaming. It was almost the same dream that I had so many times after my twenty-fifth birthday, but this time all the people in it were children."

Hawk searched her sleepy features intensely. "I don't know if you remember my telling you this, but some people believe a recurring dream is definitely a message from the powers that be to the dreamer."

"Yes, I remember your saying something like that." She laid her forearm across her eyes.

"So tell me the dream. What was different about it?"

Sienna was silent as she reached back, trying to recapture the action filled moments that dominated her sleep.

"Once again I was in a desert, and this time I was there of my own choosing. The sun was so bright it was blinding, but then it appeared to shift and I saw them."

"Who?"

"The children. Before . . . in my other dream, there

were two immense lines of my ancestors." She turned sleepy eyes upon him. "But in this dream they were all children. I found myself at the apex of the two lines that they formed. It joined together like a V." She touched her fingertips together as she explained. "And as I stepped forward they all stepped forward, and as I began to walk they followed. I knew they wanted my guidance but I was afraid, because I didn't know where I was going. All that I could see in front of me was this endless desert plain. Then, the plain ended. It was like an optical illusion, and I realized we were on a vast plateau. I stepped to the edge of it, and I could see how it plummeted into a lush green forest that glowed like an enticing, brilliant emerald in the midst of miles and miles of light brown sand. It was at that moment that I knew where I was to lead them. I was to lead them into the center of the forest, to reclaim it. It was their home." Sienna became quiet.

"The forest gleamed like a bright emerald." Hawk rephrased her observation in a hushed voice as he touched the bracelet that clung to her wrist. "I recall that the hieroglyphics on the bracelet tell of an emerald. It is the stone that appears after the ruby."

Sienna paused, then nodded her head. "It was also written after the words *passion* equals *ruby* on that piece of paper I found in Aunt Jessi's journal. It said *emerald* equals *greed.*"

"Yes, and now we know, without doubt, the bracelet is a kind of map. Or maybe guide would be a better word." Hawk's voice held a touch of awe. "It associated The Passion Ruby with Martinique, and that is where that stone was found. I am sure it also indicates where the emerald will be found." His tone dropped to a secretive low. "May I decipher the hieroglyphics on the bracelet that tell where to look for the emerald?" Hawk asked softly.

Sienna got up from the bed and began to pace the

floor, slowly. The remnants of sleep were no longer with her, and she pondered what lay ahead. She could feel her heart fluttering as she recalled how near to death she had come by dealing with the ruby. Although she was triumphant in the end, it was a helluva scary ride getting there.

She stopped in the middle of the floor and was suddenly filled with derision. It had all begun again. Being caught up in a whirlwind of events, finding herself in a foreign country and . . . Hawk. It was the cycle of The Stonekeeper.

Sienna did not want to think about how the night before had turned topsy-turvy. Regaining a clear memory of her life was dramatic enough, but to realize on top of that that Hawk had left her, never telling why, was a double blow. She had felt righteous indignation, and she purged it by venting her anger against him. But it was a definite slap in the face to discover that even under those circumstances she would allow him to make love to her. It was as if nothing else mattered when he touched her. All she could think of was how much she wanted him, no matter what he had done.

Sienna looked at Hawk as he waited for an answer, in all his naked glory. The mighty decipherer of hieroglyphics. The master of *hsing-i*. Lover *extraordinaire*. The man that had nearly destroyed her. She tried to imagine what was going through his mind as he watched her. She finally concluded he was not waiting for Sienna, his lover. No, he was waiting for Sienna The Stonekeeper, for it appeared that in his life *she* held far greater importance. Maybe it was The Stonekeeper that he loved. It was certainly the aspect of *her* being that seemed to draw him like a bear to honey.

"No, you may not decipher it." She rubbed her palms up and down her velvety, brown, thighs. Even in the dimness she could see how her movements caused desire to surface in his eyes. "Let me take a wild guess." She paused, "Could it be Costa Rica?"

"I would say your guess is quite accurate." He looked down at the bed.

"How do you know?" Sienna countered. "What part do you play in this modern-day myth?" She stopped as she thought about her own question. "It has to be an integral part, or you probably would not have come back to me even now." It was a sinking realization. "You haven't come back to Sienna Russell, just a sistah whose trying to make it with a nature shop on Blossom Street in Atlanta. You've come back to Sienna Russell, The Stonekeeper."

"In my mind there is no separation of the two," Hawk replied.

"Well, there sure is a separation in mine." Sienna spoke loudly, bracing herself against the thought that Hawk might be using her. "Are you here because—"

"Hush," Hawk sat up, his body on alert.

Sienna stopped to listen to a distant thudding, but Hawk was already at the bedroom door, his ear close to the wood.

"It's sounds like several voices out there. Put something on," he ordered as he grabbed his jeans and crossed to the window to look out.

A light tapping sounded at the bedroom door, startling Sienna. Hawk grabbed her arm pulling her behind him.

"Yes?" he called.

"Hawk. It's Nanna." They could barely hear her whisper through the wood. "There are some men here looking for you. They are in the outer room with Charmagne." She paused as if listening. "I know you have someone in there, and I want to help. Open the door."

Hawk turned and looked at Sienna. She nodded her agreement.

He opened the door slightly, allowing the old woman in. Nanna looked at Hawk and then Sienna, her face settled in serious lines. "They banged on the door a few minutes ago and it woke me up. I was in the hallway when they told Charmagne why they were here. She had them wait outside until she could put some decent clothes on. So you got to get out of here. Look, come to my room, and we'll think of something from there."

Paz's men were there looking for her and Hawk! The realization flowed like cold ice water in Sienna's veins. Somehow, Paz had found out that Hawk was the man behind the mask. Full of anxiety, she looked at Nanna, who had offered to help them. She prayed that her offer had not come too late.

Hawk grabbed the duffle bag and the walking stick as he gently shoved Sienna ahead of him. Stealthily, they followed Nanna to a room on the opposite end of the hall. Once they were inside, she latched the door behind them.

"I heard her tell them that she thought that you were gone, but I'm pretty sure they're going to want to see for themselves." Nanna put her hands on her hips. "I heard them tell Charmagne that you kidnapped this girl, and all they want to do is turn you over to the proper authorities."

"It's not true," Sienna protested. "Hawk didn't kidnap me. I came with him willingly."

Nanna gave her a visual going over from head to toe, then a light dawned in her eyes and she pursed her lips.

"I didn't think it was." She shook her grey head vigorously. "I couldn't imagine a boy like Hawk doing something like that. But they're out to get him, anyway." She pointed her finger in Hawk's direction. "And one of the men out there is that fellow Paz. Now from what I've heard about him, I wouldn't trust him no further than I could see him. Maybe not even then."

The sound of footsteps and a door being closed temporarily interrupted their conversation.

An important message from the ARABESQUE Editor

Dear Arabesque Reader,

Because you've chosen to read one of our Arabesque romance novels, we'd like to say "thank you"! And, as a special way to thank you, we've selected four more of the books you love so well to send you for FREE!

Please enjoy them with our compliments, and thank you for continuing to enjoy Arabesque...the soul of romance.

Karen Thomas
Senior Editor,
Arabesque Romance Novels

Check out our website at
www.arabesquebooks.com

3 QUICK STEPS
TO RECEIVE YOUR "THANK YOU" GIFT
FROM THE EDITOR

Send this card back and you'll receive 4 FREE Arabesque novels! The introductory shipment of 4 Arabesque novels – a $23.96 value – is yours absolutely FREE!

There's no catch. You're under no obligation to buy anything. You'll receive your introductory shipment of 4 Arabesque novels absolutely FREE (plus $1.50 to offset the costs of shipping & handling). And you don't have to make any minimum number of purchases—not even one!

We hope that after receiving your books you'll want to remain an Arabesque subscriber. But the choice is yours to continue or cancel, anytime at all! So why not take us up on our invitation to receive 4 Arabesque Romance Novels, with no risk of any kind. You'll be glad you did!

Call us
TOLL-FREE
at 1-888-345-BOOK

"What other rooms do you have in here?" An abrasive male voice demanded.

"My bedroom, and another room where my mother sleeps."

"We need to see those as well."

"Now wait a minute," Charmagne protested, "I've already allowed you to come in my house this time of morning and look inside the room where he had slept. I told you in the beginning that I thought he had already left. Now you see with your own eyes that he's not here. That should be enough."

"Do you have something to hide?" Sienna recognized Paz's clipped tones.

"No, I don't."

"How is it that you know this man?" he pressed.

"He was a roomer in the house, that's all. He needed a place to stay, and we had one."

"I see."

Hurried footsteps advanced down the hall.

"Wh-what are you doing?" Charmagne cried. "You have no right to search my room."

"Just stay calm," Paz advised her. "We just need to make sure."

The knob on the inside of Nanna's door rattled before the loud knocking began. Hawk and Sienna got behind a curtain that was used as a divider.

"What is it, Charmagne?" Nanna called as she pulled off her robe and hung it on a nail.

"Mama it's alright—" Charmagne began before the heavy voice interrupted.

"Sorry, but we need to look in your room."

Nanna opened the door wide enough for the man to see inside.

"Who in the world are you?" She leaned back and looked up at him, with her hands on her hips. "And what are you doing at my daughter's house at this time in the morning?" She began to cough until she started to gag. "I guess you've done it now." She coughed again, leaning closer to Paz's henchman. "Charmagne, why didn't you tell this boy that I got the T B?"

The man's eyes quickly searched the room. He stepped back, leaning away from the door, before he said, "She's alone."

"Alright," Paz acquiesced. "Let's go. Wait. Do you know where he was heading?"

"I don't know anything," Charmagne snapped. "Evidently, the man's a drifter. He could have gone anywhere, and frankly I didn't think where he was going was any of my business."

Sienna heard their footsteps fading as they progressed farther down the hall. Finally, she heard what she thought was a door closing.

"Are they gone?" Nanna asked, yelling out of her room.

"Yes," Charmagne called.

Hawk and Sienna started to come out from behind the curtain, but Nanna motioned for them to stay put.

"Can you believe that?" Charmagne asked as she approached.

"Yes, I can. I believe anything that goes on nowadays. No matter where you go, you've got people like that. That's why I started coughing like I had something he could surely catch and die from, just to give them a taste of their own medicine."

Charmagne chuckled. "Mama, you've always been such a character. I remember how you wore that red pantsuit to church the Sunday after the deacon scolded me about wearing it, and told me to never wear it again." She burst into a gale of laughter. "And what about the time you ran Cynthia Patterson out of our house because you thought she was making eyes at Papa."

"It keeps life exciting, baby." Nanna patted Charmagne on the back. "Now, after this I could use a glass of water. Then I believe I'll lie down for a little while longer."

"You go right ahead. I'm wide awake now. I think I'm going to take my shower and get started," Charmagne informed her. "I don't believe I can go back to sleep."

"I understand. I probably won't go back to sleep, either, but with these old bones I feel like I could use just a little bit more rest."

"Alright."

Sienna heard the door close, and she and Hawk stepped from behind the curtain. Moments later Nanna reentered, carrying some *patacones* and *patis* in open foil. "We had these for dinner last night." She pointed to the French fry-shaped *patacones*. "They are mashed and fried plantains. These are filled with a spicy meat," she said, indicating the *patis* before closing the foil around them. "You'll need them later because you'll be getting hungry."

Sienna watched as the older woman bent over and started digging in a basket of clothes.

"You're going to need something else to wear besides that," she said, as she looked at Sienna's bare legs underneath Hawk's shirt. "Here." She gave Sienna a pair of jeans and a cotton blouse closer to her size.

"Thank you," Sienna replied, and Nanna fanned her away as if no thank you was necessary.

"Why didn't you tell your daughter that we were still here?" Sienna asked as she held the clothes next to her breasts.

"What, tell Charmagne and pull her into the trouble I may have gotten myself into?" She shook her head again. "No-o, I wouldn't do that. I want to keep my baby out of this. She's got to live here with these people when I'm gone."

Sienna could tell Nanna's thoughtfulness had not gone unnoticed by Hawk, for a slight smile touched his lips. The rare expression reminded her of when they first met. Hawk didn't even seem to know how to smile. It had taken a while before he began to laugh and smile freely, but once he did his laughter was infectious. It filled Sienna with joy to feel his joy. When Hawk left, it was one of the things she missed most about him. Sienna stepped behind the curtain to put on the clothes.

"Now, let me see here," Nanna mumbled as she sat down in a spread-covered armchair, opening her purse. "I don't have much Costa Rican money to give you," Nanna explained, "because I haven't exchanged a lot of U.S. money over to *colones.*"

"Nanna, don't worry about it," Hawk reassured her. "I have money."

"You sure?"

He nodded as Sienna continued to watch through an opening in the curtain.

"Why are you being so kind to us?" Hawk inquired, his voice low. "I know I helped you out at the airport when we first arrived, but you did more than pay me back with the ride, and by Charmagne renting a room to me. Why do you continue to stick your neck out like this?"

Nanna was silent for a moment. "You remind me of my youngest son, Gerald, that I lost in a drive-by shooting two years ago." She studied his face for a moment longer. "And I guess I just hope if any of my kids ever need help, somebody will help them, just as I am helping you."

Sienna came forward, tucking her blouse into her jeans, looking from Hawk's contemplative features to Nanna's expressionless face.

"O-oh, I bet Charmagne's going to tear the house up looking for those jeans and that blouse." Nanna made a comical expression. "Oh well, they're going toward a good cause. Even though I'll never tell her what that is."

Sienna smiled, stepped up, and gave her a hug. She felt so soft and pliable in her arms, just like she had always imagined a grandmother was supposed to feel. Sienna clung to Nanna longer than she had expected, and when she pulled back the older woman looked her directly in the eye.

"Look, sugar, I don't know what you're doing over here or how you got yourself into this mess, but I just want to tell you, if your heart is good, and I think it is, you just have to have faith that things are going to work out. Don't doubt." She raised one palm in front of her face, then lowered it. "Not for even a second. Just know that you're going to be taken care of, and you will be."

Sienna shook her head vigorously, an unwanted knot forming in her throat.

"Look here," Nanna said, turning to Hawk, "you be careful, and take care of this girl, because ain't no love like a good woman's love."

Sienna glanced at Hawk from behind lowered lashes.

Nanna continued. "You do what you need to do to keep her. Love is too precious of a gift to let it slip through your hands. You hear?"

Hawk nodded, touching the older woman on the cheek.

"Now, although I'd love to ask where you're heading I'm not going to," Nanna announced, "because if push comes to shove I don't want to know." She began to struggle with lifting the window sash, but Hawk came to her aid.

He was the first to step over the windowsill and onto the ground outside. Next, he assisted Sienna as she swung both legs over and descended to the packed earth. She noticed how Hawk had already become like one of nature's animals, his eyes scanning the landscape, his body ready for action. As they began to move away from the house Sienna turned just in time to hear Nanna say, "Goodbye, now, and God bless."

Twelve

Darkness had covered the land the entire time Hawk and Sienna made ready for their escape, but now, as they skirted an open, grassy space, an iridescent pink light announced the coming of dawn. The outline of palm-thatched houses they had left behind rose up like specters out of a fog. It was only after they were safely within the cover of a rich forest that they slackened the pace.

Sienna and Hawk crouched in uncomfortable silence as they caught their breaths. It was the first time they had faced one another with no one or nothing to shield them from the events of the night before. Sienna glanced at Hawk's cloaked features and wondered what thoughts lay behind them. He spoke before she could ask.

"So what will it be?" He turned and looked at her. "Do we head back for San José? Or do we launch a search for the emerald?"

"My, I couldn't have a larger selection of choices, could I?" Sienna retorted with irony.

She looked down at the bracelet around her wrist, and she wondered which of the hieroglyphics represented the word emerald, and the country Costa Rica. She was quite aware that the powers that be expected something from her, but she resented Hawk for pointing it out. Because of how their night had ended, she expected that they would first address their personal dilemma, and try to bring it to some closure. It was hard for her to think of anything else, to be beside him knowing the incomplete past that they shared. But evidently it was not the same for Hawk. She resented how it was so easy for him to ignore the mental schism that lay between them. Once again, she was the one left in misery. "I still want to leave the country"

"Even after the dream?" He attempted to mask his disappointment, but Sienna could feel it was there.

"Yes, even after the dream." She rose, distancing herself from him. "What am I supposed to do with that?" She threw him a frustrated gaze. "Just go running willy nilly in the jungles of Costa Rica asking the natives, 'By the way, I'm a Stonekeeper, have you seen an unusual emerald?' Yeah. Right."

"How quickly you have forgotten," Hawk said under his breath as he tightened the leather thong on his dreads.

"Forgotten what? My mind is working fine now, and I remember *plenty*." Her inference was obvious.

Hawk ignored the barb. "With the ruby you were always given signs, and I believe the dream is just that."

"Okay. Maybe it is, but they're going to have to do better than that. It's not plain enough for me. You know how Malcolm X would say, 'Make it plain'? That's what I need. Maybe it's good enough for the clandestine purposes that spur you on, but not for me."

Hawk rose to his feet, frustration evident in every part of him.

"Look, Sienna, you are just bucking for an argument. If I—"

"Sh-h." This time it was Sienna who silenced him. "Do you hear that?"

Hawk squinted his eyes, listening.

"It sounds like someone crying." Sienna lowered her voice.

A more audible sob rose from behind them, and Sienna began to creep in the direction of the sound.

Hawk reached out his hand to hold her back, but she shrugged him off, intent on discovering the source of the distressful noise. Sienna moved forward carefully, pushing aside green leaves larger than elephant ears, with a reluctant Hawk close behind.

"You should wait and let me go ahead of you," he admonished.

"I've done my share of waiting when it comes to you," she tossed over her shoulder, "and I'm no longer game for that."

Sienna stopped abruptly when she heard what sounded like foliage being rapidly parted. It halted, in her estimation, several feet away. She looked back at Hawk when she heard the clear sound of a woman speaking.

"Girl, what you doing out here?" The woman seemed to wait for an answer, but when there was none she continued. "We look for you for long time," she declared in tones wrapped in agitation and relief. "We wake up this morning to find you gone, and Mary too, but I hear her left in the middle of the night. It a mess back at Shangri-la without her in the kitchen. And then to find you gone. Dorothy, what made you do this thing?"

Hawk and Sienna made their way a little closer to the voice. With extreme caution, Sienna parted several huge plants surrounded by blue and white orchids. She was surprised to see a woman she recognized as a worker in Paz's kitchen. Alongside her was Dorothy, the teenager who also worked there.

"I just want to get away." The younger girl began to cry again.

"Why, child? What happen?"

"Telling you won't do no good."

"How do you know that? You got to tell me first, and then we know if that is true."

Dorothy looked at the woman with swollen eyes, tears dropping steadily. "Was Mr. Paz the reason why Mary ran off last night?"

"I heard that him was, but I can't say for sure. What that got to do with you?"

Dorothy sniffled over and over again, then wiped her nose on her dress sleeve. "Him end up in my room after Mary left."

"Who? Mr. Paz?"

Dorothy nodded, her young features apprehensive.

"Oh, I see." The older woman settled back on her haunches.

"Him came looking for somebody to tell him where Mr. Selles live. Him didn't know it was my room. At first he was going to leave, but something made him change his mind. Him ask me how old I was, and I told him seventeen. Him say, 'Good,' and something about not needing Mary no more, that her was getting too old, anyway. Him made me stand up so him could take a look at me, and he touched me in ways only a husband is suppose to." Dorothy swallowed hard as a new crop of tears began to fall. "I started to cry then. I started to cry real hard after that. It seem to make him angry, and him left."

"We can thank God for that."

Dorothy's large brown eyes filled with fear. "But I know him going to come back, and I don't want to be there when him does. I hear all the talk about Mr. Paz and Mary. I don't want you all talking about me like that."

The older woman looked embarrassed as she patted her hands together. "What you mean, girl? Nobody's going to talk about you."

"What's going to stop you from doing it if Mr. Paz does the same thing to me that him was doing to Mary? What I hear make it sound like Mary's fault, and the women look to be having fun saying those awful things." She shook her head and looked down at her ashy hands.

The girl's words touched Sienna's heart, for they held such truth. She, too, had suffered harsh judgments. As a child her hurt had cut deep, and as an adult she had perfected the shield that most adults wore, coating her feelings in armor, thereby annihilating the openness of heart that a child possessed.

"I got a boyfriend back home," Dorothy announced. "I don't see him but every other weekend. We plan to get married, and I don't want to be spoiled for him because of that man. That's why I'm not going back."

"What you gone do?" The older woman's voice was laced with concern.

"I'll find some other work." Dorothy shrugged her shoulders. "I thought it was an honor to work at Shangri-la. Folks in the village build Mr. Paz up so high, just because him got money. His money don't make him better. Him worst than most people I know that don't have nearly as much." She tossed her Afro-crowned head arrogantly.

"It true," the woman admitted. "Now, money outshines everything in the eyes of most of our people. It is like an emerald green *Anansi*, a trickster that has everyone mesmerized."

"That what my younger brother, Albert, say." Dorothy's dark eyes grew large with pride. "Him always talking about a time when things will be different. I hope him is right."

Sienna's body became rigid as she heard the girl speak. She had demanded a clearer sign than the dream, and now, sitting here on the forest floor, these women, oblivious to her uncertainty, lit the way.

"You better get going before somebody else sees you, and wants to put pressure on you to change your mind." The woman stood slowly as if her joints ached from stooping. "I was on my way to *Rawa* to see if any of the women there might want to work at Shangri-la."

Dorothy showed her agreement. The two women

parted company without looking back, disappearing behind variegated shades of green and brown. Sienna watched them leave, going over their exchange in her mind.

"That Paz is a monster with two legs," she finally said, looking straight ahead. "He thinks everybody is here for his purposes, his enjoyment." She could feel Hawk studying her. "No one should be subjected to the actions of any of the Pazes of the world, especially not children. You would think by now we as a species would have learned. Money doesn't make the man, or the woman. As a matter of fact, sometimes it destroys them. Because of it, they don't have to look for the treasures within themselves. There are so many surrounding them that they are blinded by their glitter."

"You sound as if you have been hanging around me too long," Hawk chided.

"I do, don't I?" She gave him a weak smile. "I don't know, but maybe it has something to do with what happened in Martinique. A whole new world of possibilities opened up for me there. Afterward, I began to look at life a little differently. I realized we were all a part of this intricate whole." She looked at the green forest around her. "And when I say we, I don't only mean people, I mean everything. The flowers . . . that bird over there." She pointed to a black bird with yellow outer tail feathers. "The very dirt beneath our feet. And it's a wonderful feeling to really know that in your heart. Do you realize how powerful and extensive that makes us?" she asked him in earnest.

"In a way I can. I can imagine it," Hawk replied, his voice low.

"But it is not for us to imagine, Hawk. It is for us to know, to feel," she explained as she nervously realized he was standing closer to her than moments before. "Little children feel it. That's why their faces light up with such awe when they look at a butterfly or a blossom. It is a part of us when we are born, but through the years it is gradually lost. And now it even appears as if children are losing it at an earlier age than before. It is sad when I think about it."

"This innocence," he said so close to her ear that she could feel the warmth of his breath, "this oneness that you speak of, maybe it is something that should always be remembered, no matter what changes mankind goes through." He gently turned her face toward him. "There's a passion for the things you just spoke of burning in your eyes. I believe the thoughts and feelings that you are having now are connected with your purpose. Maybe it will be through your efforts that these things are remembered for all time."

She gazed into his eyes, which looked so deeply into hers. "Goodness, that sounds like it could be one helluva job." Sienna placed her hands upon her cheeks. "Why should I be worthy of such a thing? I can't imagine having such an honorable task." A husky giggle surfaced. "No matter how I look at it, I know deep down inside I'm no different from anybody else. If I am worthy of this, so is everyone else. So are you."

Hawk's eyes took on a veiled appearance. "There you are wrong. I am not worthy of it. I can only be a bystander looking on, if I am lucky."

In his hazel gaze Sienna saw a cold, unfeeling acceptance of a fate that he abhorred, and because of it a loathing of himself. The sight of it pained her, and she realized she had seen it before. It had been during the days prior to his leaving. She had caught a glimpse of it here and there when he was in deep thought, or when she approached him at solitary moments. She remembered how she had longed to take the pain away, but she had no clue how to do it. He had never let her in.

Sienna's heart went out to him, and she wanted to protect him from the evil that he saw in himself. An evil that she had never felt or seen even after he left her. "Hawk," she said, closing her eyes, then opening them slowly, "I hope that I live to see the day when you are free of what haunts you."

"That day may never come," he replied without blinking.

Sienna swallowed hard. His doubt about overcoming his predicament, whatever it was, was overwhelming. She knew at that moment how much she still loved him. It was almost like a physical blow.

At first, his words made her speechless. She was at such a loss. She hated this feeling of helplessness, and she knew it was her enemy as well as Hawk's. Somehow, though, recognizing the foe caused something to fortify inside Sienna. It would not allow her to accept her own helplessness or Hawk's. "What do you mean, it may never come?" she retorted. "Don't stand here and say that. Don't you have any faith in the future?" Her dark eyes grew wide. "I don't know what's going to happen to me in the next five minutes, the next hour, or ten years from now, but you can believe I'm going to continue to believe it's going to be great. And when things aren't looking good, and I don't know what to do, I'm going to wait for that sign that never fails to come. And you can believe," she said, poking in his chest with her finger, "when I see it, and an opportunity presents itself, I'm going to move on it. I encourage you or anybody else to do the same thing."

"You do?"

"Yes," she replied convincingly.

"So does that mean you are going to take the opportunity that's in front of you now?"

Sienna's jaw slackened just a bit. Hawk was right. She was facing an opportunity. The opportunity to go after the emerald. An opportunity she had been trying to avoid. She hadn't realized until Hawk pointed it out that she had talked herself into a corner. In her zeal to encourage Hawk not to give up on whatever it was that plagued him, she had sealed her own fate. Sienna knew she could not back down now from her own legacy. She would not allow him to see her waiver.

"Now that I've thought it through," she said, nodding and throwing her shoulders back, "it most certainly does."

"Alright." Hawk rewarded her with a lopsided smile. "I guess I'm going to have to try and be like you when I grow up." His amber eyes glowed with admiration.

"Well, I'll try my best to continue to be a good example," she replied, knowing he had her.

Hawk ran his hand down over his nose and his mouth. "So, which way are we heading?"

"I-I say . . ." she clapped her hand and pointed her finger in the direction Dorothy had gone. "Let's follow the children."

"Whatever you say." Hawk stepped back. "After you, Ma'am."

"Uh-uh-h," Sienna replied, looking up at him with her chin pointed downward. "Been there. Done that," she said, waving her hand flamboyantly, "and I've got the scratches to prove it. So from now on . . . sir" she said, fluttering her curly eyelashes demurely, "I'll allow you to lead the way."

Thirteen

With one eye closed and the other partially open, José looked at the half empty bottle of alcohol. He could barely focus on the dark liquid inside. *Maybe if I down a little rum it will improve my physical and my mental state,* he thought as he almost faded out again.

It was totally against his principles to be up so early in the morning, and he dreaded the stream of sunshine that forced its way through the curtains as much as a vampire fears the light. He swung his legs over the side of the bed, anyway. Afterward, he leaned forward and repeatedly ran his hands back over his hair. He managed to make it to the bathroom to throw some water on his face, run a comb through his dark, heavy mane, and put on a robe, before the knock came.

As he was crossing the floor, the alcohol seemed to call to him, and he grabbed the open bottle, taking several long gulps. Hastily, he replaced it, teetering, back on the night stand.

José took several deep breaths as he stood before the door. Although he knew he was sometimes considered to be obnoxious, he always appeared to be calm and collected. Maintaining that image was important to him, for he had lost so much more. His hands shook ever so slightly as he slid the bar back and opened the door. José stood behind it, waiting for the man to enter.

"I got some interesting news for you," Archie announced as his eyes searched the interior of the room.

"That's what you told me on the phone," José replied. He observed him with a distant curiosity. Although his eyes felt tired, he didn't miss a thing. He noticed how Archie's paisley shirt stretched too tightly over his built up frame, and how his pants were a little too short to be fashionable. Yes, signs like that had told him from the very beginning that Archie was in financial need, and his restless attitude convinced him he was approachable. Archie wanted more than his life was offering. "So, what did you find out?"

"May I sit down?" Archie gestured toward a comfortable looking easy chair. "I've been up just about all night and—"

"Have a seat."

Archie eased his way into the chair. "Mr. Paz says him knows the man who kidnapped his woman."

"Go ahead." José lit a cigar from a book of matches with Hotel Acon embossed on it.

"Him says him was one of the men hired to do masonry work yesterday morning."

"Is that right?" José scratched at his stubbly jaw. "So what happened? Did he find a ransom note laying around somewhere?"

"No. Nobody mentioned one." Archie's eyes were focused on José's lips as he inhaled.

José started to ignore the man's hungry eyes, then changed his mind. "Care for one?"

"Sure would."

He pushed the package of slim cigars across the small cocktail table and waited until the end of Archie's cigar turned red hot.

"So why does Paz think he kidnapped the woman?"

"I don't know. All I know is, Mr. Paz and a couple of other guys were down in a little area called *Rawa* real early this morning, looking for Mr. Selles. Him an old man that's been around for a long time, and knows everybody's business." Archie paused, looked at his cigar and inhaled again. "Supposedly, this worker came in yesterday morning with him. Mr. Paz ended up at this American's house where the man was renting a room, but him was gone when they got there."

"I see."

"After that they went back to Shangri-la, and I hear him is giving everybody *raas*. Mary, who ran his kitchen and was his *puta*, left, and I heard a younger girl who worked in the kitchen is gone, too. A friend of mine who works there full time says Mr. Paz is determined to be a part of one of the search parties. I guess because the woman was his fiancéee."

"Is that all?"

"That's it."

José rose and went over to the jacket he had worn the night before. He picked it up from the bed and touched a wad of *colones* inside the pocket. He felt uneasy about displaying such wealth in front of Archie, but when he looked over his shoulder Archie had his eyes closed as he blew smoke up toward the ceiling. José removed the cash and peeled off a couple of bills before replacing it. He didn't notice the photograph that fell out of the pocket and began to float to the floor. The small square got caught up in the current of a fan, and blew across the floor.

"Alright. If you come up with anything else let me know," he said, as he gave the paper money to Archie. "I'll be heading back to San José this afternoon. You've got the number."

"I sure do, Mr. Wong."

Archie started for the door but stopped when he saw the picture. "Hey. You must have dropped this." He looked at the faded snapshot of a dark-skinned woman and her child. They were obviously Afro-Costa Ricans. "Is that your wife and your son?" Archie asked.

José could tell from his posture he wanted to become friendly, and the picture gave him an opening to do it. Yet seeing the photograph instantly made José want a drink. "No, it's not. My wife is *Tico*, Hispanic." He took the picture from Archie. "And our child died many years ago."

"I'm sorry. I meant no offense."

"None taken."

Archie ran his hand over the bottom of a velvet painting. He held his bottom lip between his teeth as if searching for something to say. "You know, since you are a *cruzado*, half Hispanic and half Chinese, I really did not think the woman in the picture was your wife. That's one thing that has not changed in *Puerto Limon*. As much as we live and do business together, you never see the Chinese mixing with Afro-Caribbeans."

José knew Archie was trying to prolong his visit, but he was no longer in the mood for conversation. He headed straight for the door and opened it. "Call me if you hear anything else."

"Okay," Archie agreed, throwing up his hands as he went out into the hall.

José walked back to the bed, looking at the photograph. What Archie had said was right. There was practically no interracial mixing of Afro-Caribbeans and their Chinese neighbors. It was because of that very reason that he made the decision he had so long ago. Once, he had been involved with an Afro-Caribbean woman he had really cared for, but then she told him she was pregnant. He felt he had no other choice but to end the relationship. A couple of years later she had sent him the picture of her and the child, but he still denied the boy was his.

Although José was racially mixed, his father had been a Chinese, and in their culture it is through the father that the culture and lineage continued. With the lines so clearly drawn, he could not bring himself to admit to his family that he had a baby with a woman from Tortuguero.

After all these years, he wondered about the boy child. Especially now as he was getting older, and the alcohol that he consumed like water was eating away at his insides. Through his efforts he had found out that the mother had died, but he had no luck finding out what had happened to the boy.

José put the photograph back inside his pocket. Now he had other things that concerned him. The *Anansi* had given him the responsibility of keeping an eye on Paz. They didn't want him to come up with any more surprises, and they definitely wanted to know when and if he had found The Stonekeeper.

For the members of *Anansi*, ordinary life had become boring a long time ago. They needed things to fuel their zest for life, rare things. That's how and why most of them had met. They saw each other at auctions all over the world, from Sotheby's in New York to gatherings in Singapore. José thought it was rather ironic, because had they looked in the business communities in their own backyards they probably would have met years earlier. They were all natives of Central and upper South America.

In the beginning, the members had discussed their collections and where the next 'hunt' for the treasure would take place, but there came a time when owning an object of high monetary value wasn't enough. One thing had led to another, and they began to make purchases that possessed stories as well. A statue with a curse from Egypt. A necklace worn by a beheaded queen that still held her spirit. The quest for these kinds of objects had kept them quite occupied. Then they caught wind of a new collector, a man of questionable means who had an eye for truly rare things and the finances to acquire them. As time passed, they had the fortune, or ill fortune, José surmised, to meet Paz at one of the auctions. That was how he introduced himself to them. Simply Paz. A man with a single name.

Time passed, and Paz began to invite them to his functions, but each time his invitations were ignored. For, although there were well hidden skeletons in all of their family closets, this man had been no more than a beggar and a thief on the streets. The members of *Anansi* came from families of some status and means. Yet there were a couple of things they could not ignore—the collection he possessed, and that Paz was very clever, just as all the members of *Anansi* saw themselves to be.

It was because of that very attribute, cleverness, that they had chosen the name *Anansi* for the group. As children, from family and friends, they had all come to know of the folk tales of *Anansi* the Spider. In the stories, he possessed extreme cleverness which allowed him to win out over all adversaries, sometimes making fools of them. They had taken on the name, feeling that their collective successes were an example of such qualities. That's why Paz's cleverness and steadfastness could not be ignored. Everyone guessed he had built most of his empire by smuggling emeralds out of the Columbian mines where he once worked, but there was no trail. Never once had his men been caught.

José sat on the bed and downed the remainder of the rum. The potent liquor burned inside him as he recalled how Paz ended up outbidding a member of the *Anansi* in Peru for a gold mask that was purported to alter the consciousness of the wearer. After that, Paz invited them all to one of his parties to sample the mask's power. The party had been extraordinary, and the mask proved to be an enigma. From that time on, Paz had fluttered around the *Anansi* like a moth at a screen door with a light on the opposite side. He wanted to be a member. It would be his stamp of approval. His badge of respect. They all knew what he wanted, but they were determined to keep him out. It wasn't until he dangled an irresistible gem in front of them that they considered changing their minds. José turned the bottle up, allowing the last droplets to light on his tongue. Afterward, he smiled wanly at his own mental pun.

Paz had informed them that he was on the trail of a large treasure that included one of the rarest emeralds on earth, The Pirate's Emerald. But the clincher had been there was only one woman who could lead them there, a woman who in and of herself was a collectible. This woman was a Stonekeeper, a living legend. A legend that several members of *Anansi* had heard about through their travels. To say the least, all of their interests had been piqued, and they wanted to know where the woman could be found. That was when Paz made his move. He said that in the end he would present the woman to them, and they would be allowed to be a part of the treasure hunt, but his price would be a substantial sum of money and a membership in their exclusive club. The lure of legends and treasure hunts was more than they could ignore. They had taken the bait.

José took off his robe, throwing it haphazardly to the side. He lay down and pulled the sheet up around him. At least keeping watch on the scumbag Paz provided something to occupy his mind. Of late, his thoughts were too often turning toward the child he had denied, and as a result his hands too often reached for the bottle.

Perhaps, if he had acknowledged the child, things would have turned out differently. He gazed at the empty bottle, wishing it was full. Perhaps he would not have been punished with the death of his second son, twenty-six years ago.

José moved down deeper under the covers, pulling the sheet over his head. Since he couldn't drown his thoughts in liquor, he would return to the second best thing, sleep.

Fourteen

"Don't you think that we should be trying to stay out of sight?" Sienna asked, trying to yell above the cries of the howler monkeys. She looked out at the expanse of clear, blue water. It looked more like a painting than something real.

"Nope," Hawk replied as he pushed aside the branch of a large mangrove tree hanging over the water. "I believe they think we are heading for San José, a big city to get lost in. They won't be looking for us to be travelling in this direction. Of course, the real authorities are operating under that lie that Paz told them." The muscle in his jaw rose and clinched.

"That's true." Sienna sighed. She felt horrible about what it could possibly mean for Hawk. "I'm sorry that I've gotten you all tangled up in this mess. It clearly wasn't my intention."

"You haven't gotten me involved in anything that I didn't want to be in." When he turned his eyes on her, they were so full of emotion that she had to look away. "I can honestly say that this time I am here by choice."

A loving wave rushed over her, and she had to concentrate to keep herself from trembling. His words were so assuring, and the look in his eyes bore through her, touching her heart. It made her want to go to him, to wrap herself in his arms and feel the love that she felt last night. But there was a part of her that could not forget how he had abandoned her, and it had to be heard. "So, you say that we're okay travelling out in the open like this?" She had changed the subject. "I'm going to trust you on this one, although you know between us that's a real scarce commodity right through here."

"Sienna, are you going to start that again?" he said, his voice like steel. She watched him snatch the leather thong from his hair, causing the slender dreads to cascade around his face and upper back.

Now she had to take two steps to keep up with his brisk strides. "I'm not starting anything again." She pulled stiff fingers through her curly hair. "I'm always going to feel that way, as long as you hold out on me."

They rounded a bend and were greeted by two boys fishing with handheld lines from a dugout canoe. The boys gave them a curious going over before they waved energetically and went back to fishing.

Hawk reached in his pocket and pulled out a map. "According to this there are no villages or towns between here and Tortuguero. But the girl, Dorothy, has to live somewhere in between Limon and that city. I can't imagine her walking fifty miles to get home."

"Unless she plans to catch a ride on that boat," Sienna said abruptly, and started backing into the trees that lined the water. Her gaze was glued to a craft labelled The Gran Delta. Dorothy was boarding it.

"Damn, I don't know what I would do without you," Hawk said as he backed up beside her. "You called it right on time, too. Those two guys look familiar. I believe they work at Shangri-la."

Hawk and Sienna settled behind the trunk of a large tree loaded with epiphytes and climbers.

"I would think you would know exactly what you would do without me. You've had plenty of practice," Sienna threw out in clipped tones. She could feel Hawk brace himself beside her.

From the trees they watched the two men heading down a decrepit looking, narrow pier. The men stopped to talk with another man, who remained on the boat. Moments later, after various gesticulations, they retraced their steps and headed up the shore.

They tried to pick up the pace once again as they headed further inland, but there was no path to be found in the tangled mangrove forest. Sienna and Hawk picked their way carefully over gnarled roots, tangled vines, and a plethora of plants. As they travelled, the ground became a little less congested. Sienna was grateful for the patches of low growing plants, leaves, and moss that sometimes covered the forest floor.

"That was a close call," Hawk admitted. "I guess the small amount of trust that you had in me just dribbled down to nothing, huh?" The thick lashes that outlined his amber eyes made them appear that much lighter.

"I wouldn't say that," Sienna replied. "You see, I'm already on guard when it comes to you. Prepared for anything that you might come up with or dish out." She swung her hips boldly beside him.

"Is that right?" Hawk asked, his voice silky and low.

"It sure is."

"Well let's see how well you deal with this."

With both arms he grabbed her around the waist. For mere seconds her body was flush with his, suspended in the air.

"What do you think you're doing?" she squealed. Seconds later she found herself lying on her back in an expanse of leaves and moss.

Hawk covered her mouth with a heated kiss that took her breath away. "So, are you still ready for anything I dish out?"

Sienna's eyes opened wide and she started to answer, but he kissed her again before she could. This time she responded, giving back the ardor. Her hands stroked his back as she embraced him, and she could feel the tremor of his muscles beneath his shirt as Hawk continued to mold his body against hers, moving in a way she could not ignore.

Unlike before, there was no voice inside Sienna that warned against what she was doing. There was only a beckoning heat that emanated from her special place outward into her limbs. Suddenly, she wanted him to touch her, to ignite the fires that he lit so well. It was an all-consuming thought. Sienna arched her pelvis forward in invitation, closing her eyes. She waited for his next move, anticipation coursing through her, but none came. As she opened her eyes Hawk rose up on his forearms, forcing her to loosen her hold.

"You see, it's not fun to be teased and prodded, is it?" His smoldering gaze washed over her confused face.

"Huh? You mean you just . . ." Sienna could feel the heat rising to her face. "Let go of me, Hawk," she commanded, pushing him to the side only because he allowed it. She scrambled to her feet, puffing and saying, "How dare you," as she tried to walk away from him. He was right behind.

"How dare *you*." He turned the tables on her as he stopped her, catching her wrist. "You should know there must be a damned good reason why I left you." Amber eyes burned into angry brown ones. "A matter of life and death."

"But you can't tell me what it was." Sienna was angry, and hurt, and arousal still flowed in her veins.

Hawk looked at the beautiful woman that stood before him, challenge blazing in her eyes. He wanted to soothe her, to calm the jagged edges of anger that she felt.

"No, I can't. But there will come a time when I can."

Frustrated beyond belief, and embarrassed, all Sienna could do was turn away from him and take the lead, going further inland. She pushed through the greenery, wanting to put distance between them, but Hawk remained close on her heels.

"I thought you wanted me to go first," he said after they had travelled several yards.

Sienna ignored him.

"You know we can't go on like this forever. At some point you're going to have to talk to me."

"Yeah, and you can be sure it's going to be when I get good and ready," she threw over her shoulder.

A deep, rumbling growl came from above. Sienna and Hawk looked up, and over several yards away, into the open, hissing mouth of a puma perched high on a tree branch.

"Oh my God," she heard herself say. Her insides felt like a churning washing machine.

"Yep, it's a good time to call on him, I would say." Hawk put his arm slowly around her waist and started pulling her away. "But the way my luck has been during the last year, he probably is busy helping someone else."

As soon as the words were out of Hawk's mouth, the puma got down further on her haunches, as if preparing to leap, and roared again.

It was all Sienna needed. She immediately launched into a run. "I don't know about you, but I'm not staying here to find out if she's had her dinner or not."

In a matter of seconds Hawk had come up and passed her, grabbing her by the hand. The puma leapt to the forest floor and started out after them.

"What did I tell you?" he yelled as he pushed aside branches and leaves with a forceful arm.

"Look, tell me about you and your luck later. Right now I want you to save your breath and get us out of this." Sienna's head snapped back, looking behind them at the sound of quickly parting bush. Up until then, she had thought she was running as fast as she could, but as

EMERALD'S FIRE 157

she conjured up images of the puma in hot pursuit her speed increased.

Hawk cut to an angle, plunging rapidly through the flora, and Sienna felt as if her feet were barely touching the ground. Quickly, they covered a few more feet, and Sienna thought the trees had begun to thin. She prayed that would help improve their pace, but she figured it would also aid the animal. Within moments she became aware of another sound that reminded her of the puma's awesome hiss. She tried not to imagine what would happen if the cat caught up with them.

"Haw-wk! I think it's getting closer!" She screamed, her panic level reaching an all time high.

"Hold on, Baby. This is one time I hope my skills and my hearing are serving me right," he yelled.

Before Sienna knew it they were out of the bush and a fast-moving stream lay straight ahead.

"Got it," she heard Hawk say as he headed straight for the water.

"Oh no. Wait a minute," she cried as they bounded into the foaming stream. "I've taken swimming lessons twice, but I'm still not that sure about thi-i-is!" she hollered as they plunged into it.

It felt lukewarm, and was murky brown except for the white bubbles that gathered into active patches. Sienna tried to take control of her body under these new circumstances, as Hawk called to her from several feet away.

"Did you pass?"

"Oh God! What?" she yelled as she ended up on her bottom with the water swirling up around them.

"I said, did you pass the classes?" he yelled as he made his way toward her.

"It's a little late to ask, don't you think?"

Sienna was spun around by a highly spirited current, and Hawk allowed it to move him in the same direction. As the flow moved them forward, Sienna looked back at the puma who was shaking a wet paw with obvious irritation. The cat's yellow eyes met hers, then looked back down at the water. She let go of one last half-hearted roar before turning back toward the forest. All Sienna could think about was being snatched from the jaws of death only to face the possibility of drowning. But she determined that would not happen, and, like Hawk, she kept her head above the water, allowing it to be her captain.

Fifteen

Sienna and Hawk rode the current of the lively stream for yards until it dipped downward, the motion ending in a calm pool with a magical waterfall. Feeling exhausted and taxed to her limit, Sienna swam beside Hawk to the nearest bank.

"I can not believe this," she said between breaths as she pulled herself up on the plant-filled area.

"Believe it," Hawk replied as he shook out his dreads. "At least now you know your swimming skills are pretty good."

Sienna ran her hand over her hair and groaned. She could only imagine the task she had ahead of her once it dried. She noticed the shirt that she wore had turned transparent, and the jeans were a soggy mess. All she could do was run her hands down the wet material in a feeble effort to eliminate some of the moisture. Rivulets of water streamed down around her, causing a steady pitter patter sound on the leaves below. As she raised her gaze to look at Hawk with a hangdog expression on her face, he broke into gales of laughter. That was when she saw the droplets falling on his face, and realized it had begun to rain.

She shook her head and began to mumble to herself, "There is nothing else that could possibly happen." No sooner than she said the words than the bottom fell out of the sky, yielding barrelsful of rain. The rain came so fast and so hard it felt like tiny stingers on Sienna's face. She sprinted up the bank to where there was more tree coverage, and was surprised to discover an opening to the area behind the small waterfall. "Hawk, I think I've found something," she called as she climbed over a couple of boulders and carefully entered the dry but humid enclave. With hesitation she ventured further inside, then turned toward Hawk when she heard him behind her.

"Look at this," she shouted above the sound of rushing water, her dark eyes full of pride at having found the small protective space.

"You did good." He looked around the small area. "Remember, it wasn't too long after I met you that you proved you had acquired plenty of Girl Scout badges in your day. So now, I know you earned one for tying knots *and* one for camping."

Sienna looked at him and shook her head, "You need to quit," she admonished, but she couldn't help but smile.

Hawk moved further inside the cave and got down on one knee. "I think a perfect place to rest up has been delivered unto us," he said with apparent reverence. "I guess the powers that be knew we couldn't handle too much more of that last action." He removed the strap of the duffle bag over his head. "They knew our hearts might give out even if our legs didn't."

Perhaps it was because of all the stress she had been under, and the totally irrational circumstances that had been her life for the past couple of days, but for some reason Hawk's words caused her to break out in laughter. Sienna laughed so hard that tears rolled down her cheeks, and she had to sit down on the ground to control the cramping that grabbed her midriff.

"You alright over there?" he asked as he unwrapped a tied bandanna encased in plastic.

"Yes," she replied as she attempted to control her mirth, "I think so."

"Just checkin'." He spoke to her but his attention remained on the items that he was uncovering.

"What are you doing?" Sienna managed after catching her breath.

"I'm going to make us a little fire."

"With what? Everything is wet by now."

He thumped the plastic bag. "I pack certain things in plastic to insure against that."

Sienna recognized a couple of boxes of matches, but the other round flat objects were foreign to her.

"What are those?" She pointed.

"Slices of Duraflame logs. Makes it real easy and convenient to keep a fire going under any circumstances."

Sienna nodded her approval. She was really quite impressed with Hawk's preparedness for emergencies, and she wondered if he had perfected all of this during the last six months since he had been gone.

"Be right back," he announced as he slid between the rocks and the cascading waterfall. Moments later he reappeared with a forked branch that possessed a number of limbs in one hand, and a stack of small, broken pieces of wood in the other. He forced the branch down into the soft earth floor of the cave, which caused the spiky limbs to look as if they were reaching for the ceiling. Next, Sienna watched him pile up the broken branches with the Duraflame sandwiched in the middle, making sure it was accessible from the top.

"What's the branch for?" She looked at the towering, lifeless appendage.

"You'll see in a minute," he told her as he struck a match and laid it in the middle of the artificial material.

"Is any of the wood dry?"

"Uh-huh."

"Where did you find it?"

"I have my ways."

"How do you know how to do all this?"

Hawk remained silent, then he rose to his feet after the fire caught on. "You know, I had forgotten how much you could talk," he said, as he began to unbutton his shirt.

In a matter of seconds the dim area felt even smaller. Sienna knew she had been asking a lot of questions, and she realized they were a feeble tool to lessen her heightened awareness of the man before her. Each button that he undid revealed a little more of his tawny muscular chest, and Sienna couldn't help remembering how it felt to touch it, to be against it. As she watched, images surfaced of how he had tumbled her onto the leaves and moss, along with the feelings that had raged inside of her. It amazed her how it had taken so little to arouse her so much. Sienna's lips formed a circle as she started to ask why he was removing his clothes, but in light of his comment she changed her mind.

Hawk took off his shirt and jeans and hung them on the limbs that towered above the fire. His movements were smooth and uninhibited in the skimpy underwear that remained. He had no problem with nudity. His or anybody else's. As a matter of fact, she remembered him saying he thought the human body was one of the most beautiful creations on earth.

Hawk walked back over to the plastic lined duffle bag, and Sienna made a point of turning her attention toward the burgeoning flames.

"Here." He stuck out a pale, thin top.

"What's this for?" Sienna took the slightly damp object that had been buried in the middle of the bag's contents.

"I thought you might want to dry the clothes that you have on," he replied as he pulled on what had to be the matching bottoms to the top she held. "Even though it is warm, it's probably not good to keep them on." He bent over again and retrieved the foil-wrapped food Nanna had given them, setting it down beside the fire. "If you hang them up they will dry faster."

"That's probably true," Sienna replied as she sat in a wet huddle.

Hawk could tell from her expression that she knew it was true, but she was still hesitant. She simply did not want to be in a state of undress around him. He recalled how easily her body had responded to his back in the forest, and he knew his teasing had angered and embarrassed her. He vowed to himself that he would make that up to her.

Sienna stood up slowly as Hawk spread a damp blanket out on the cave floor. He watched her turn her back to him, facing the waterfall, to undress. The shape of her body seem to cut into the streaming white and clear waters like a paper doll's. She dressed quickly. Unlike his other shirt, this one rode high on her thighs, molding enticingly to the curve of her damp buttocks. When she turned to face him, their eyes met, but Hawk didn't say a word. He simply allowed his gaze to slide over the swell of her breasts and dark nipples, to the place where the damp material clung to her abdomen and the dark triangle that appeared shortly below. His gaze took in everything, thighs, knees, calves, trim ankles and polished toes, before he opened the foil, laying it on top of a tiny, well used cooking rack.

At the side of him, Sienna crossed the space to the branch. The limbs were high above her reach, and she had to stretch to hang her clothing.

"My, my, my," Hawk acknowledged in a low voice as he glimpsed the rounded globes beneath the top. But when Sienna turned to look at him he directed his attention to separating the *patacones* and *patis*. When she sat down near him, her head had a familiar tilt that he had come to know. There was something on her mind, and he was about to hear it.

"Look, Hawk. We simply can't pick up with this relationship like you were gone for a weekend or something."

"I know that."

"Well, you don't act like it."

"What do you mean?"

She looked down at her thighs, which were crossed Indian style. "You made love to me last night and this morning, and I think we need to hold off on that until we come to some kind of understanding."

Hawk came and sat down beside her. "Sienna, first I think you need to admit 'making love' is not something you can do alone." He smoothed out a wrinkle in the blanket. "But I understand what you're saying. Maybe I was a little premature with my coming on to you." He picked up an object designed like a Swiss knife that housed a hair pick, a can opener, scissors and a screwdriver. "It won't happen again until you are totally sure that's what you want." He began to untangle the ends of her hair.

Sienna held his hand to stop him. He could feel a slight tremor. Then she took the pick from him and continued the task he had begun.

"You say that, knowing how weak I am for you." The words were barely a whisper.

He was surprised by her confession, but then he didn't know why he was. From what he knew about her, Sienna had always been very truthful, almost to the point of being unintentionally abrupt.

"From the first time we made love until now, I've always been. But it was such a pleasure, then. Such a treasure," she said as she worked her way through the spongy, tight curls.

"And you don't see it that way any more?" His stomach tightened, although his tone did not reveal his feelings.

"I don't know how to see it. I've never dealt with anything like this before."

"Why must you *deal* with it?" he asked, then began to turn over the food that had started to sizzle. "Why don't you just go with how you feel? Trust that, and trust the man that you came to know during those months that we were together."

Hawk removed the food from the fire and split up the portions equally between them on the pieces of foil. He gave her a fork and he took a spoon, and they ate in a thick kind of silence that was filled with thoughts, desires, and reservations.

"You know," Sienna said, breaking the quiet, "I missed you so much during that time, and I had become so angry, that I dredged up this old song that I made up years ago." She took the dirty utensils and the foil and washed them off in the tumbling water.

"Is that right?"

"Yeah."

"I guess if I had made up any songs I would have unearthed a couple of them myself." He took the objects from her. "How does the song go?"

"Well . . . I never said I was anybody's songstress, but it went like this." She began to sing softly.

Hawk strained, but he still could barely hear her. "Hold it. Maybe I can make this a little simpler," he informed her. He came up to Sienna and wrapped his arms around her, pulling her toward him as if they were going to dance. "Alright. Let's try it again."

Before Sienna made another sound he began to move slowly as if music was playing. It was a comforting, lulling feeling, and she leaned her face above his pecs and allowed herself to go with it. Soon Hawk began to feel a tiny vibration against his chest, and he realized Sienna was humming the tune.

The notes were long and forlorn, and flowed with a

heartfelt melancholy. His body adapted to the melody she created, and so did hers. He heard her sing, in a voice that was rich though untrained, "Why am I so-o in lo-ove with you?" The question alone created a stinging feeling behind his closed eyelids. He didn't want her to question why she loved him, as if it were an unwanted prison sentence. The last thing he wanted to be was the source of the sadness he heard in her voice.

"I can't help it, but I'll tr-y. Do it or I'll di-e. How I'll really tr-y to forget you. But I really know it's impossible."

Hawk hugged her closer, and he thought about the agony she must have gone through that morning, and the weeks and months that followed his leaving. It hurt him deeply, and at that moment he would have done anything to change the past. "Oh, my Black Queen, what have I done to you?" He looked up into the darkness of the cave above them. The inky expanse appeared to have no end, reminding him of how dark and out of reach his soul had to be for him to be in the predicament he was in. He couldn't imagine what he had done in this lifetime, or even another, to deserve such a horrible fate—to find someone that he truly loved, but yet and still be unable to give all of himself because of an ungodly affliction and its unknown possibilities.

For the first time in a long time he cursed what he had become—a man, allowed to walk amongst ordinary men, but like a creature of the night, forced to hide his tainted self behind darkness, his night a black mask.

Sienna could feel a change in Hawk's body, a stiffening, and it caused her to look up. She was shocked to see pure anguish on his face, and before she knew it her hand had reached up to soothe the tragic lines and his pain. "Hawk. Don't go there, Baby. Come back, here, to me." She tried to call him away from the thoughts that haunted his mind. "I don't really want to forget you, you know that," she said, retracting the words of the song, although her intuition told her it was not the song alone that had brought him to such an emotional depth. "I love you." The words flowed with all of her feelings—joy, pain, uncertainty. Sienna tightened her arms around him, and she could feel him crushing her against him in response.

"Tell me again, Sienna," his raspy voice beseeched. "Let me hear you say it again."

"I love you, my sweet man." She reached up and bent his face toward hers. "I love you," she repeated, seeking out his lips, but they did not respond to her ardor. "Hawk, Baby, don't do this." Sienna murmured the words against his mouth, and she began to suck and nibble at the lips that she had known to set her on fire. But when Sienna looked up into his eyes she became frightened, because there was a distant look in them that she had never seen before.

"You don't know what I am, Sienna."

"Yes, I do. You're just a human being like all the rest of us. We all have faults, and whatever they may be, it doesn't make us of any less value in the overall scheme of things." She planted kisses on his eyelids, forgetting that it was she who had said there should be no lovemaking between them.

"I've got to find a way out of this. Maybe if I could reconcile it within myself it would all be different." He looked over at the cascading water. "But it was like waking up one day and knowing exactly how you perceive the world, other people . . . yourself, but by nightfall just about all of your belief systems lay scattered at your feet. No longer was anything the same. No longer are you the same."

"I've experienced some of that." She pulled open the top and revealed the mark between her breasts. "For as long as I could remember it had been here, just a part of me no different from the rest, and then one day I came to realize because of it there was a whole different definition of me. One that changed everything. So you see, we are alike in that." She examined the mark that had done so much. "The difference is, you and I both can see how my being a Stonekeeper is something amazing and good, but whatever your gift is you perceive it as something dark and evil. You won't even allow me a glimpse of it, to give my true assessment of the situation." Once again, Sienna looked into Hawk's face, but she found his eyes were fastened to the crystal-shaped mark between her breasts.

"I recall someone else who spoke of gifts." Slowly he went down on his knees in front of her, his body heavy with some unspoken burden. "His name was K'in." Hawk rested his forehead between Sienna's breasts as he wrapped his arms around her waist. He could feel Sienna gently pressing his head against her. Suddenly the words that were a catalyst for his present predicament sounded in his head. *Take not these crystals into your hands lightly, for they hold the power of sight. Cast them away from you if you can not bear this worldly burden. Hold them near to your heart if you claim it as your own. But remember, in the end, justice can only be found with the Stonekeeper.* Hawk squeezed Sienna even tighter.

K'in's healing words reached out to him, and he loosened his grip.

"I think this woman that you speak of can help you heal . . . if you let her." Hawk recalled his response had been. "Obviously she can. I told you, she is The Stonekeeper." But K'in had replied, "As a Stonekeeper, she can only heal one part of you. As a woman, I believe, she can heal all of you. It be all a part of the whole."

Hawk lifted his gaze to Sienna's face. At the same time, he lifted his hand and cupped what made Sienna a woman. That special place that made him ache with longing for her, that consumed him in every way possible.

She froze with the intimate contact, and sighed as he began to knead it with his palm ever so gently. His eyes devoured her face as he said, "I'll stop if you want me to," but he prayed she would not stop him, for now he knew for sure it was only in her arms that he could find peace.

The blazing look in Hawk's eyes initiated a feverish wave inside Sienna. She could not make herself stop him, for she did not want him to, and her response was to rub herself against his palm in active invitation. After that it was as if she had opened a flood gate of passion, for they both touched, and felt and kissed all they could of one another. One position led to another as they sought the limit in physical intimacy without rewarding themselves with the ultimate that a man and a woman can bestow upon each other.

Sienna was panting profusely above him as Hawk lay waiting on his back, and they knew the final moment was at hand. Their need for one another had built up to immeasurable proportions, but he told her he would not take her as he had done so many times before. "You always know how much I want you." She could barely recognize the deep, breathy tone of his voice. "This time I need you to show me how much you want me." He ran his hands over her breasts and her abdomen, and lightly touched her there. "I am all yours, Sienna. Do whatever you feel. Take whatever you want. I give my power to you."

Sienna was surprised at how empowered she felt by his docility. It was different, freeing. For as long as she had known Hawk he had always been the aggressor, urging her on with his body, and words that fired her consciousness. Now she would play that role. This time their joining together would be of her doing. She would engulf him with her love and steer them on to the peaks of ecstasy.

Sienna looked down at the symbol of his love, and she

wanted to show Hawk there was no part of him that was not lovable, no part of him that she could not embrace over and over again, thereby opening the way for him to accept and love himself.

With her passion at its height, and a need to make him whole in her heart, Sienna easily engulfed him with her softness. She was instantly rewarded as Hawk began to writhe and moan beneath her. The sight inflamed Sienna, and she became a woman mentally and physically on fire, her body revealing that she loved him with an intensity she had never felt before. It was as if all her inhibitions and fears had been washed away in the cascading waterfall, and she filled herself with his maleness at a maddening rate. Hot sensuous words spilled from her lips, and for the first time she claimed all that it meant to be a sexual, female being. It was a joyous, exhilarating union.

Sienna overflowed with the burgeoning, sensuous energy that engulfed her, and she felt compelled to bathe Hawk in a stream of verbal passion. "No matter what has happened before, no matter how many women you have known, this you will never forget." She bent forward and sampled his lips, her breath hot upon his face. "I open myself to you like this moist cave, willingly, eagerly, taking you in. You will never forget me or the love I give to you now for as long as you live," she charged him.

As Sienna breathed the last words her head flung back, and she arched her spine as she rode the wave of pleasure to its apex, where she hung for an indescribable moment before letting go. Her moment launched his, and this time both of their cries filled the space around them before she sank down on Hawk's chest, into the peaceful floating that always followed ecstasy. Moments later, as they cuddled together with the soothing sound of the waterfall embracing them, Sienna's eyelids became heavy, and she drifted off into a needed sleep.

Sixteen

"This is well-tended farmland," Sienna observed. "I guess that means we're on private property."

"Could be," Hawk answered quietly as he looked at the rows of corn plants that surrounded them.

Sienna didn't know what to think of Hawk's attitude since they had left the cave. He was more silent than before, and she caught him studying her at times when he thought she was not aware. She contemplated the change in him as they climbed a shallow hill.

Once they reached the top, the sight of a tiny woman executing slow, graceful movements in the middle of an expanse of flat grass surprised her.

She was dressed in mint green, which in Sienna's mind gave her the appearance of being a part of the abundance of nature around her. Her top was shortsleeved and stopped at midthigh, and she wore matching, near ankle-length pants. Sienna noticed how her completely grey, paper-thin braid waved like a reed in the wind as she moved with her back turned toward them, exhibiting fluid arm, hand and leg motions.

"What in the world do you think she's doing?" Sienna asked.

"She's performing tai chi."

"It's beautiful."

"Yes, it is. Especially when you have a large group of

people doing it early in the morning right after sunrise. I've seen that in China."

"You've been there? To China?" Thoughts of all the travelling he had done flashed through her mind, and she wondered how he had weathered it and managed it financially.

"Yes, I have. That's where tai chi started, in the Taoist monasteries of old China. It's believed to promote health and longevity."

"It is not a belief," a gravelly but thin voice said. "A belief is something that has not been proven. The virtues of tai chi are real. I, and many others like me, are proof of that."

Sienna could not believe the woman had heard their low volume words from so far away, but when she turned to face them Sienna knew it was true.

"I am ninety-one years old," she announced, her slanted eyes looking like mere slits in her flat, high cheekboned face.

"You are?" Sienna responded, truly awed. "I never would have believed it." She was so taken by the woman's pronouncement she had given little thought to the circumstances under which it was said.

"What are you doing on this land?" Sienna saw the wrinkled, heart-shaped lips barely move.

Hawk started to speak, but Sienna cut him off.

"We've come this way by accident. We didn't mean to trespass on your land."

"There are no accidents," the woman called out strongly, although her posture was humble. "And man can not own the land. He can only use it for the time he is here." She began to advance toward them.

The woman's strange words of wisdom struck a familiar chord in Sienna. She had heard her great-great Aunt Jessi express a similar belief. She assumed with reasonable certainty that they had never met. This Asian woman lived in Costa Rica, while Aunt Jessi was United States born and bred, the child of an Ibo and a Cherokee. But still she wondered how could it be that two people from different cultures could have embraced such similar beliefs.

"Why are you on this land?" The woman repeated.

Sienna looked at Hawk as if it would be futile to try to explain, but he decided to take his chances, anyway. "We're on our way north."

"You are foreigners here."

"Yes," he replied.

"It has been a long time since my eyes have beheld such."

Sienna didn't know what to make of the woman's words, but nevertheless she felt uncomfortable. They had broken the woman's ritual and were cutting across the land where she obviously lived. They were the ones in the wrong. "We're sorry," she apologized as she tugged at Hawk's sleeve. "We'll leave you alone now, so that you can get back to your exercising. Your tai chi." She turned to walk away with Hawk in tow, but the woman spoke again, halting them.

"Wait. What is your name?" she asked, pointing a straw thin finger at Sienna. "There is something about you that reminds me of a woman that I once met in the House of the Seventh Moon."

"The House of the Seventh Moon." Sienna repeated the words that sounded like something out of a black and white romance movie before she looked up at Hawk and back at the Chinese woman.

"Yes. It was one of several homes for the old here in Costa Rica. A place where the elderly from my culture would go before they made the great transition."

"I see."

"This woman, she was a foreigner, too. Like me, she had come to provide entertainment for those living in the House of the Seventh Moon. That was many years ago." Her voice faded as if she had gone back in time. "We never really spoke, but I could feel her spirit. It was restless." She stepped up and stood directly in front of Sienna. "Her name reflected that. She was called Just Sea. Like the water that touches the east side of this country, sometimes calm, at other times restless."

"Just Sea. It is a unique name," Sienna replied.

"She pronounced it as one. Just-sea," the woman corrected her.

"Just-sea. Jus-sea." Sienna's dark eyes filled with disbelief as she looked into the narrow black ones of the woman she had just met. "Jessi!"

"Yes," The woman nodded her head up and down very slowly. "It is so."

"I had an aunt whose name was Jessi." She shook her head in a negative fashion. "But it couldn't possibly be the same person that you are talking about." Sienna went and stood closer to Hawk. He allowed her to slide her hand into his.

"How can you be so sure?" the woman responded. "This life is a place of oneness. Like kernels of corn, one event leads to another. You may choose to see them otherwise, but it doesn't make your perception the truth."

"You say Sienna reminds you of this woman."

"Yes, very much. Back then, I would say she was not much older than you are now." She looked at Sienna. "And the physical resemblance is strong. There is also a sameness in their carriage, in the way their bodies talk to the world."

"I don't know what to say," Sienna replied. "It's just hard to fathom how you would have met *my* Aunt Jessi, at all." Sienna watched the woman make several small puckering motions with her lips.

"Come. I will show you what I have." The woman began to walk ahead of them, but stopped when she realized they were not following her. "Come," she repeated.

Sienna didn't know why she was so reluctant to follow her. Perhaps it was because she was afraid, and at the same time anxious. What if this woman had really met Aunt Jessi, the only relative that she actually remembered who had played a part in her life? She was so young when her parents died that she did not remember them. It blew Sienna's mind to consider it. Was this woman some kind of preplanned connection between them, since Aunt Jessi had been The Stonekeeper before her?

Sienna could feel the gentle pressure of Hawk's hand pulling her forward. "I think we should go and see what she has to show us," he advised as the woman looked on.

Sienna licked her lips nervously. "What is your name?" she finally said.

"It is Shau Lo." She bowed slightly before turning and walking at a steady pace across the grass.

It was a short walk to the house, which was set on the opposite side of a grove of mahogany trees. It looked as modern and Western as any that Sienna had seen so far. That surprised her, for she had expected a building of Oriental design.

"This is my son's home," Shau Lo informed them. "It was built several years ago, many years after my parents and relatives arrived here to labor on the banana plantations."

"I didn't know there had been Chinese laborers in Costa Rica," Sienna said as she entered a side door behind Shau Lo. "To be honest, I didn't know there were any Chinese in this country at all."

"Yes, we came with many West Indians and Italians to do manual labor. Since then we have created communities and businesses." She led them into an area that was self-sustaining. "Costa Rica, which means rich coast, has been that for many of us here."

Sienna watched her remove her shoes, and she and Hawk did the same. On bare and sock covered feet they entered another door. As barren as the exterior had been of Oriental features, Sienna discovered that the interior was just the opposite in Shau Lo's private apartment.

Beautiful silk scrolls of craggy mountain ranges with peaks lost in cloud filled skies dominated the room. The handdrawn panoramas seem to glorify nature with their exquisite, towering waterfalls, streams and gorges. Paper lanterns were frequent eye-catchers, hanging above low tables accentuated by vases and sculptures.

Shau Lo motioned toward two decorative wooden stools whose tops were curved and carved, offering them to her guests. Sienna sat down, feeling as if the placement of everything in the room had been thought over very carefully. There was an open, systematic flow of the furniture and the objects around them. Finally, she turned her attention back to Shau Lo, who was looking inside a hinged, wooden chest. Her clothes hung against her spine-dotted back like material on a *papier-mâche* doll. She used extreme care in disturbing the organized papers and articles in it, until she came across what she was looking for. She placed the object in the palm of her hand. Sienna reached out to take the brittle, wax paper envelope Shau Lo offered.

For a moment she studied the waxy cover that protected what looked like an old postcard. Carefully, Sienna slid the object out of its cocoon. Across the top it read, in faded but bold letters, *Jessi Thompson's Magic Act*. Afterward, it listed several brief titles of the feats Jessi could perform, and at the bottom there was a small, drawn likeness of her.

"Hawk," she said, turning to him shocked and misty eyed, "this was Aunt Jessi's."

"It sure looks that way," he responded, his eyes hooded.

"It is." Then she read the words out loud as if to verify them. "Jessi Thompson's Magic Act." She examined the card further, turning it over. "Aunt Jessi never said anything about what she did before she went back to Campbell, Alabama. And now I know . . . she was a magician."

"She was a special woman," Shau Lo announced. "I knew it from the way she captured all eyes in the room and kept them there until she was ready to let them go." She spoke from her kneeling position on the floor. "I was a singer, older than she, singing songs that were very familiar to those who stayed at The House of the Seventh Moon, but Just Sea commanded more respect from them than I did."

"I wonder why she was in Costa Rica," Sienna said, almost to herself. "It is not one of the countries that was listed before the last three." She looked at the bracelet and then at Hawk. He shook his head in a negative fashion.

"She wore a bracelet like the one you wear now." Shau Lo tapped her own thin wrist. "I remember it well, because each time she would make the stones and shells disappear, bringing them back with a flourish of her hand, the bracelet would glitter in the sunlight." Her slanted eyes glanced at the shiny orb through a window. "While she performed, she filled the room with scents of myrrh and lavender, and it seemed to soothe everyone. The old ones who had nervous quirks in their bodies became still." Her awe from the past was rekindled on her wrinkled face. "At the end of her act, she gave each and every one of us tiny red and dark grey feathers that she said came from a bird called a cardinal. She said it would bring us all blessings, and it did."

"Why do you say that?" Sienna asked, enthralled by the story, not wanting it to end.

"Because when I came back to The House of The Seventh Moon, I was told for days the people talked of nothing else but the woman, Just Sea. With her simple actions she seemed to have brought many of them a peacefulness about whatever the days ahead might hold. For now I know, it is when you are old, young ones, that all your fears are able to come alive in a way they have never done before." She smoothed the paper-thin skin on her hand. "You are at a certain closeness to the end of this life as you have known it, and if you have regrets over the life you have lived, or uncertainties as to whether the darkness of death is no more than darkness, it is a frightening place to be." Shau Lo looked deep into their eyes. "Maybe it was the way she used the sunlight and the sky as her backdrop that drew us all in, and the green fire. It appeared as if she would hold a sea shell up in front of a drifting cloud and mimic its movement, or a colorful stone held just so against the ray of the sun, and then it would disappear, causing our fears and anxieties to disappear as well. Whatever she did was spellbinding, and for those moments you were one with the clouds, the sun. You felt as though, like them, you, too, could shift shapes and rise and fall, and live on." Her voice had risen with her vigor, so when Shau Lo stopped speaking, the silence was tangible.

Sienna looked back down at the drawing on the postcard.

"This woman, Just Sea, is your aunt?" Shau Lo inquired.

"Yes, she is."

"So you were on this land to learn more about her, and therefore yourself," Shau Lo informed her.

Sienna looked up at Shau Lo and back down at the postcard. "As farfetched as it seems, I believe you are right."

"Now I have been able to pass on to both of you peace about your future, such as she gave to those of us at The House of the Seventh Moon. It was her gift to us, and now it is my gift to you."

This time when Sienna glanced up, Shau Lo was looking directly at Hawk. She reached out and touched his hand.

"Young man, by now you must know, you can not walk in the sunshine," she said, lifting both hands toward Sienna, "without having its light spill over you and inside you. Secretly it enters the openings of your body, your eyes, ears, and nose, and it starts an internal flame. So, although you may think there is nothing but darkness, it is not so. The light is always there with you, for the light and love are the same." Shau Lo unfolded herself and stood up. "Now it is time for you to go, and I know why I was allowed to sleep the sleep of death, only to perform my tai chi in the later morning hours. I would not have met you any other way." She bowed toward them.

Sienna and Hawk returned the courtesy before all three started for the door.

"Shau Lo," Hawk said softly, "when you were explaining Aunt Jessi's acts of magic you mentioned the green fire."

"Yes." She held her tiny hands folded close against her body. "It is only at certain times that you can see it. It is a pale green light that shines like a rainbow in the sky. When Just Sea performed for The House of the Seventh Moon, the glow could be seen in the sky."

"Where does it come from?" Sienna asked, excited now that she had picked up on Hawk's train of thought.

"I have never seen its place of origin, but they say it starts in a swamp palm forest far north of here, in *Barra del Colorado,* near Tortuguero. That is why it is so miraculous for us to see the glow here."

"Thank you, Shau Lo. You don't realize how helpful you have been. I shall never forget this," Sienna confessed as she attempted to return the postcard.

"No," Shau Lo replied. "It is yours now, and I believe it has served its purpose well. I wish you happiness and prosperity." She bowed once again.

Seventeen

Sienna clung to the side of the oxcart as the solid wheels rolled in and out of the trench-ensconced road. Her nostrils constantly inhaled the scent of green bananas that were piled high between her and Hawk, but a ride was a ride, and she was thankful to the Tico who provided it. For miles they had ridden between fields of banana plants and coffee, with an occasional forest in between, and although she was grateful not to have to walk, her backside had formed another opinion.

"I wonder how much further we have to go before we get to Tortuguero," she said, lifting up one hip and then the other to ease the discomfort.

"Why don't you ask him?" Hawk said, looking comfortable wedged between the side of the cart and a voluminous banana stalk.

His lackadaisical reply made Sienna reflect on the change she had seen in him since their stay in the cave. She could not say that he was cold toward her or even distant. It was more of a cautious acceptance of her and the things they were going through. Sienna got the feeling he was waiting and watching for the perfect opportunity. To do what, she wasn't quite sure. It peeved her, to say the least, because she had no idea what had caused this change, and she believed it would be a waste of her time to ask. Most of all, Sienna couldn't help feeling that now that she had poured her soul and body out to him, this was the thanks she got.

Determined to prove she could manage without him, she pulled herself to a standing position on the rickety cart and shouted up to the driver. "Not meaning to rush you or anything like that," she began, "but I was wondering how much longer will it take to get to Tortuguero."

"Not long." The man looked back over his shoulder as the oxen plodded on. "Soon you will see a grove of cocoa trees on this side of the road." He pointed to her left. "We will be entering Tortuguero shortly after that."

"Thanks. Who-oa!" She fell over a stalk of bananas as the cart hit another furrow. Sienna straightened up quickly, feeling somewhat embarrassed under Hawk's quiet, watchful eyes. When she was able to gracefully make her way back over to her space, Sienna settled herself in again, actually grateful for the short respite.

About a half an hour later the landscape changed, and she began to notice a grove of trees that appeared to be infected by a prolific growth. Large pods were growing in great quantities from the trunks of the trees, and although the profusion of leaves above looked quite healthy, she could not imagine that the trees' overall health was not being affected. Sienna wondered why the owners had allowed the infection to get so bad. She started to mention it to Hawk, in her usual, talkative way, but she changed her mind, considering his present attitude.

"There is the cocoa grove," the driver called from behind her. She turned just in time to see him pointing at what she had assumed were infected trees. "I can tell from the look of the pods, the cocoa is ripe and ready to be dried in the sun." He paused before adding, "Soon we will be in Tortuguero."

Sienna realized that what she had thought were infectious growths were the cocoa pods, and she was glad she had not spoken out, revealing her ignorance. She remembered that during the months she and Hawk had spent together there were times when the difference in their educational backgrounds had been so apparent. Although she was far from illiterate, and had loved to read books all her life, her high school education sometimes paled in comparison to the numerous degrees he had obtained. She had felt uncomfortable at the times when she believed it showed, no matter how Hawk tried to reassure her.

Sienna glanced over at Hawk's strong, stoic profile as he studied the nearby fields, and her insecurity mounted. Heat rose to her face when she thought about how wild she had been while they made love in the cave. Perhaps that had played a part in his newfound attitude. Perhaps he had found the woman who had made love to him with such abandon too crude and free, and not refined enough for his academic taste. Sienna crossed her arms protectively in front of her, and her chin tilted up slightly. At the time he had appeared to like it, but now she believed he was having second thoughts.

The recurring images of how carnal she had become behind the waterfall singed her pride, but instead of covering her face in shame as her feelings called for, Sienna stiffened her back against a bothersome banana stalk. She had nothing to be ashamed of, she told herself. She could only be who she was, and if that wasn't good enough for Hawk, then there was very little that she was willing to do about it. Maybe his reason for leaving her had been along a similar vein, and now, for his own reasons, he was once again in need of The Stonekeeper, not in need of Sienna the woman.

The sun had begun to sink in the western sky, and Sienna had retreated deep into her thoughts when she saw the first stilt-raised house nestled between a pair of tall coconut palms. It proved to be the prototype of the houses of Tortuguero. There was no rhyme or rhythm to how they were placed amongst the trees, and sometimes an unpainted, rustic gray color made them appear to be a part of the natural habitat. The exceptions were the painted houses, and the homes with corrugated roofs. Most of the houses she saw were topped with palm thatch.

The driver evidently felt they had officially arrived inside the village, for the wooden cart came to a slow, rumbling halt.

"If you go up that way," he said, gesturing, "you will come to the center of the village There is a store there, and they have hotels, too."

"Thank you," Sienna called as Hawk handed the man some *colones*. Still feeling the adverse affects of her thoughts about Hawk, Sienna wished she had her own money to pay her own way. "Thank you," she said curtly to Hawk, "I'll reimburse you when I get the chance."

His amber eyes narrowed as he watched her turn and start heading toward the center of the village, but he kept his silence and simply fell in step beside her.

Sienna felt uncomfortable walking down the middle of the road for all to see. At least during their ride on the oxcart they could have easily hidden behind the large stalks of bananas if it had become necessary. They had come across only one other oxcart during the entire trip, and it had been driven by a man who had shown little interest in them or their driver. Here, on the main street of Tortuguero, there was no place to hide. Luck seemed to be with them, though, for the street was virtually empty.

An interesting, aromatic combination of food scents slowly filtered in around her, and Sienna's stomach responded loud and clear to their call. She realized that a small restaurant was the origin of the smells, and she longed to walk right over, pull up a chair, and ask for a menu, but once again money was an issue. She secretly hoped that Hawk was as hungry as she was, but she wasn't about to ask him to feed her. She had determined she would eat wild seagrapes and cocoplums before she resorted to that.

"I think we should stop here and get something to eat," he said.

Sienna had to restrain her sigh of relief. "If that's what you want," she replied cooly.

"Aren't you hungry?" A slight smile curved his lips as Sienna's stomach responded audibly.

She cleared her throat in an effort to mask the sound, although she knew it was too late. Embarrassed again, she looked him dead in the eye as if challenging him to make fun of her. "Yes, I could definitely eat."

They entered the clapboard building and saw a woman rapidly wiping down a table. She stopped in midstroke when she saw them.

"Wa'apin. You want to eat?" she called, her dark eyes missing nothing.

"That's what we had in mind." Hawk's glance skimmed over the chairs that were placed on top of several tables as if the place was closing.

"It's good," she replied. "All I got left of the big meal is rundown." She motioned to the table that she had just cleaned. "I think I have a few johnnycakes and some yucca pudding, if you want." She placed the rag back in the plastic container and headed for a side door.

Hawk looked at Sienna.

"Whatever you have is good," she confirmed.

"Good thing," the woman replied, wiping her hands on her apron. "I have it on the table in a minute."

She was as quick as her word, and she brought out two large bowls of hot rundown at the same time. Sienna studied the soupy contents of her bowl, which had chunks of vegetables in it and some kind of fish or meat. She watched Hawk dive in greedily as the woman returned with the johnnycakes and two healthy servings of yucca pudding.

"Is something wrong?" the woman asked, seeing that Sienna had not begun to eat.

"No," she quickly replied. "I've just never had rundown before, and I was wondering what is in it."

"Oh." The woman sat back comfortably. "You use coconut milk, cassava, potato, plantains, banana, any of that" she advised, "plus your fish or meat. Today you have snook and a little turtle. You cook it all together with pepper, and onion, and salt and thyme. English sauce is also good, and tomatoes."

Sienna placed a spoonful in her mouth, chewed, then nodded appreciatively. "It *is* good."

"You think it would not be?" the woman asked, but she was smiling and Sienna realized she was only teasing.

"I appreciate your feeding us. I can see that you were in the middle of closing up," Sienna acknowledged.

"Yes, but it's alright. Tonight is Nine Night. Miss Melba died over a week ago, and we had the Set Up for her that night. I, myself, help put the four pieces of board under her house to help with her passing, and I think we did a good job washing her and dressing her for viewing." She tapped her foot as she appeared to mull over the completed task.

Sienna looked over at Hawk, who had sat back listening to the woman's account. All she could think to say was, "Sorry to hear that."

"No need to be sorry. It our way of honoring the dead and giving comfort to her family," the woman assured. "All in all, the Set Up went well. The next day the wood boards were cleaned up and the coffin was made, and the reverend conducted the funeral. There was plenty of singing from the Sankey, our hymnbook," she explained. "Miss Melba had been around a long time, and a lot of people love her."

Sienna and Hawk continued to eat as the woman talked, as she encouraged them to. It was obvious she liked company and that she loved to talk.

"So that is what is going on around here," she concluded after digressing on a variety of subjects. "Everybody is getting ready for Nine Night."

"We were told that you had some hotels," Hawk said.

"Yes we do, but the cabin that is empty is owned by Miss Melba's niece, and I'm sure she is already over to the house getting ready for Nine Night."

"So the hotels are full as well." Sienna looked out the window. She couldn't imagine the hotels being full of tourists in the quiet, remote village.

"Yes, that what I said. The cabins are full, and the only one left is owned by Miss Melba's niece," the woman explained again, as if talking to a child.

"I see," Sienna replied, realizing the cabins were the hotels.

"The best thing for you to do is to come to the Nine Night with me. They call me Amanda." She patted her bountiful chest. "And I will introduce you to her when the time is right." She rose from the chair that she had seated herself in. "It won't take me long to finish up in the kitchen." She started back across the floor.

With the woman gone, Sienna concentrated on her food, making a concerted effort not to make eye contact with Hawk. They ate in stilted silence until he said in a matter-of-fact fashion, "They have the same custom in Jamaica." Afterward, he spooned a creamy combination of fish and bananas into his mouth.

Sienna looked over at him questioningly.

"Set Ups and Nine Nights," he informed her.

Any other time she would have bombarded him with questions, showing how curious she was to know more. But this time Sienna decided to keep her curiosity to herself. She simply would not give him the pleasure.

"Um-mmm," she said as she continued to eat. She could feel his probing amber eyes upon her.

"You got something new on your mind," Hawk said, peering around the dreadlocks that hung against the side of his face.

"No more than usual," Sienna replied as she looked into his eyes, then quickly looked away. To her dismay, her breasts began to rise and fall quickly, betraying the effect he had on her.

"You've turned real quiet over the last few hours."

"I could say the same for you. You got something new on *your* mind?" She had turned the tables on him.

"To be honest, I'd have to say, yes," Hawk admitted.

Sienna had expected that he would say no and continue to hide his feelings of rejection toward her, but his positive answer made her heart beat even faster. It was a moment when she would have preferred to hear an alibi or even a lie, not the truth she thought he was about to reveal.

"I forgot to bring you something to drink," Amanda said, breaking into their repartee as she reentered the room. Sienna's apprehensive eyes fastened on her, grateful for the interruption.

"Here. This is some sorrel that I made for the Nine Night. It made out of the red petals of the sorrel flower boiled with ginger," Amanda explained as she sat the plastic tumblers down and headed back out of the room.

As soon as Amanda left, Hawk leaned back in his seat, watching Sienna. "Do you want to hear about it?"

"Hear what?" Sienna asked, her words breathy, her eyes narrowed.

"What I've been thinking about ever since our stay in the cave."

"If you want to tell me, yes." Sienna held her breath as she waited for his answer.

She watched Hawk study her face for a prolonged moment. Then his eyes hooded over and he said, "No. This is not the time or the place."

She looked at him, not knowing if she wanted to kiss him or slap his face. Her insides screamed, "You torturous son of a biscuit," but Sienna verbally responded over her tumbler of sorrel, "Suit yourself." She nearly choked on the snappy drink as her constricted throat attempted to swallow, with her mind in chaos and her heart beating erratically.

"Who did you say them were?" Dorothy's stepmother stood on her porch looking through the dimly lit trees.

"I don't know who the man is, but the woman is Mr. Paz's fiancée. She ran away from him too, just like me," Dorothy replied defensively. "Him looking for her, probably not because him love her. Him think she something special cause of this mark she got between her breasts. I'm glad him looking for her and not for me."

"Raas, maybe she got money back wherever she live to make it okay for her to run away, but you don't."

"Money not everything," Dorothy threw back at her, "and I'm not going back there for him to feel me up, and do whatever else him want to me."

"Well, you not going to stay here, either. Your father been sick, and I got two other children that are younger than you that I got to take care of. I don't need no other grown person tugging on my purse strings. Now you don't have a job, that even less money for the house."

"That alright." Dorothy began to put the few belongings she had in a brown paper bag. "I'll go live with Johnny now. We gone get married soon, anyway. I don't have to stay here," she proclaimed, her already swollen eyes glistening with tears.

"You go and stay with Johnny, with your no money self. But if things ain't what you thought they were gone be,

don't think you can come back here unless you working."
Her stepmother followed her to the door and out onto
the porch.

She watched Dorothy jump off the wooden structure
and head off into the woods. *Young people so ungrateful
these days,* she thought. *The girl had a job at Shangri-la, and
she quit! She know the situation here. If it wasn't for the garden,
and the turtles the turtle man kill on the beach every week or
so, we might starve.* The woman went and sat on the
straight-backed chair. She swiped aggravatedly at a loose
palm that had come undone from the handwoven seat.
Now what we gone do, she thought as she looked over at
the curtainless window where her sick husband lay. *We
needed that money that Dorothy was sending home every week.*

The woman ran her hand over her bushy hair, which
was parted down the middle and braided into two plaits,
concern for her remaining children and her sick husband
uppermost in her mind. Distraught, she walked down the
porch stairs and strolled out from her house. She headed
down the road that led into the center of town. She was
unaware of the two young pairs of eyes that watched her
progress.

Dusk was approaching as her worried eyes searched
the familiar surroundings. Then she saw three people
heading out of the restaurant. One of them was Amanda,
the owner. The other two, a man and a woman, were
strangers. She looked at the nice jeans and blouse the
woman wore, and then looked down at her own worn
dress. Then she looked up suddenly, realization setting
in.

"I bet that is Mr. Paz's fiancée, and that him would
pay pretty good to know where her be," she said into the
partial light, a spark of hope igniting. "Yes. I bet him
would." She stood for a moment with part of her dress
balled in her fists as her mind turned over the possibilities.

She was out of breath by the time she ran back up to the house and found the slip of paper Dorothy had given her long ago with the number of one of the public phones in Limon on it. There were no private phones in Limon, so whoever answered the public phone would relay the message to the proper person, or bring them to the booth if possible. Before now, she had never had a reason to call the town.

Eagerly, but with care, her shaking finger traced the numbers around the rotary at the only public telephone in the village of Tortuguero. She dialed it by the blossoming moonlight, the hope inside her mirroring its intensity as the phone on the other end began to ring.

Eighteen

Archie left the bar feeling the full effects of the beers he had consumed. Although the brew had helped him to become physically relaxed, his mind had not bought into the program. He looked across the street, his youthful face lifting into a slow scowl as he recalled the events of the day.

He had left José's hotel room in high spirits, and he was determined to come up with more information to feed the wealthy *cruzado*. It was an easy way to make money, much easier than busting his butt doing physical labor with the others like Selles, who knew nothing else.

As he rode down in the elevator, he knew what his next move would be. He would go to Shangri-la and offer a different kind of service to The Paz. With all the hunting he had done as a child, he was good at tracking, and he wanted to join in with The Paz's personal search for his fiancée. That way, he could ingratiate himself with the man while keeping a close eye on him for José at the same time.

Archie leaned against a wooden beam identical to the others that helped hold up a large veranda, running above his head. He reached into his pocket and pulled out his last cigarette. To his dismay he found that it had broken in half, and most of the tobacco had spilled out. He let go an expletive, then made do with the piece that remained, inhaling deeply as he mulled over what had happened once he arrived on the estate.

From the way he saw it, he had presented himself decently enough at the kitchen door, but that was as far as he was allowed to go. The old woman Tina played guard, and told him The Paz had all the men he wanted working on the search. Then, as she was closing the door she advised him if he was still in need of work tomorrow, to meet out front with the other laborers early in the morning, and *maybe* he would be hired then.

Archie shoved off of the beam, stepped down off the sidewalk, and entered the street, his thick, muscular body moving heavily. He had left no stone unturned in his quest for money in the coastal area. He had dabbled in the sale of drugs, collected numbers for the Chinese-owned Chance numbers racket, and had also tried to work his way into The Paz's emerald mining force, which was a very select group. He had stopped his previous dealings because of the constant emotional protestations of his mother. He had never been able to infiltrate the mining ring, whose smuggling work was kept very quiet, and only a small number of men, who could be trusted even if threatened with death, were chosen.

Archie threw his head back as competing tunes with African rhythms blasted on the street from well-lit bars. Through it all he tried to concentrate, contemplating his next destination. Irritated, he gave the side of a telephone booth a dissatisfied slap as he went by, which seemed to cause the phone to ring. Archie stopped and looked back when it continued to do so, realizing his act of rebellion had nothing to do with the aggravating sound. Perturbed, he picked up the bothersome receiver.

"Wa'apin."

"Is this one of the phones in Limon?" a hesitant female voice called over the line.

"It is."

"I need to talk to Mr. Paz."

"Raas," Archie cussed beneath his breath. "We all need to talk to him," he replied sarcastically. "You think him gone to come all the way from Shangri-la and talk to you on this phone? Never happen. Who is this?"

"I got something important to tell him," the woman insisted. "It is about him fiancée."

Everything but Archie's eyes went stiff at the woman's words. "You say, you know about him fiancée?"

"Yes."

"Tell me about her. I work close with The Paz." He leaned in close between the plastic panels, raising his hand up to cover his ear.

There was a pause.

"No. What I got to say I need to tell him myself," she finally replied.

"Where are you, woman?" Archie asked as he tried to think of how to handle the situation.

"In Tortuguero."

"So, what s'pose to happen? If Mr. Paz have to come to this telephone from Shangri-la him might as well go all the way to Tortuguero to see you in person. Like I said, never happen. You tell me what you know, or I hang up now and somebody else will call us with the same information."

"No," the panicked woman called. "Wait. Wait. Hello?"

Archie held the receiver a few seconds longer before he replied, "Speak quickly, woman. I got better things to do than stand here talking to someone who probably don't know nothing, anyway."

"Do you think the information is worth something to Mr. Paz?" Her voice was a little less confident.

"If it lead to his fiancée. Yes."

"Well, I want you to take down where I live, so him can send me whatever him gone pay. You hear?"

"Sure," Archie replied, digging in his pocket for the pencil stub and slip of paper he had felt earlier. He knew he didn't have to honor his word, but the woman's voice reminded him of his mother's. "Go ahead."

"The Moises. On the east side of town, west of the lagoon. Got that?"

"Yes. Now, what you know?" Archie asked, getting impatient.

"I saw the woman with a man, coming out of one of the restaurants in the center of the village. They were with the owner, Amanda. They probably heading for the Nine Night at Miss Melba house. Everybody in town gone be there."

"You sure it is her?"

"Sure I'm sure," she answered quickly. "My stepdaughter Dorothy said it is. She used to work at Shangri-la, and will be back some time next week," she lied. "She just left because her was not feeling good. That all."

"Alright. I will tell Mr. Paz what you told me. And if you right, you get paid something for your trouble." He mashed the few bills that were left in his pocket.

"Don't forget where I live. It is The Moi—." Archie hung up while the woman was repeating herself.

He stood looking at the receiver, then a large smile spread across his face. Archie patted the inanimate object, then blew it a kiss. If the woman was telling the truth, like he thought she was, in a matter of minutes his luck had changed drastically.

He crossed the street in brisk strides. Suddenly, he felt lighter, and his outlook was extremely bright. This time when he showed up at Shangri-la, he knew he would get past the kitchen. Not only that, before he was through he would be able to command an audience with the man himself.

A self-satisfied expression rested on Archie's face as a burst of loud, pompous laughter emanated from a small bar to his right. He recognized the source, a brother of one of The Paz's right-hand men. Archie thought about how he had always been a gambler, and he reached down and pulled out the thin crop of *colones* he had in his pocket. He had no proof the woman was telling the truth, but his hunch told him her word was as good as gold, and he could take it all the way to the bank. Archie stopped in mid-stride. Perhaps he should direct his energy in another, more immediately profitable direction.

As quickly as he had headed across the street, he retraced his steps back to the phone booth. There was one thing he had to do first, and perhaps the right words dropped in the proper manner would motivate the man across the street to carry his message to Shangri-la. Right now, as always, his foremost concern was cash.

Pursing his dark brown lips, he whistled a catchy tune as he dialed the number. This one he had memorized by heart. Archie knew the *cruzado*, José, would be pleased to hear what he had to say. After this phone call he would be well on his way to yielding a nice cash crop.

"You see the horseshoe?" Amanda asked.

"Yes," Sienna replied as she looked up at the object nailed above the doorway.

"That is to get Miss Melba spirit out of the house." Amanda leaned closer to her ear. "Now, of course, I don't believe in all that, but some of the older people do, so we let them have their way."

Sienna nodded appreciatively as she looked at the horseshoe with newfound interest.

"Some of them take keeping the spirits happy real serious." Amanda sat back as she prepared for a good talk. "They believe nine nights after the person dies their ghost rises out of the grave and returns to places it knew during life. Like their home. So, before the night is through one of our older citizens will take a bottle of whiskey and sprinkle it into the four corners of this house. They believe it will make the spirit go away from here, and it will never return."

"I guess anything is possible," Sienna replied, looking at the horseshoe again.

"Her right." Amanda looked at Sienna with a new-found respect, then at Hawk, who stood almost behind her.

"On our way here an old Chinese woman told us about something she called the green fire," Sienna said, taking advantage of the moment. "She said from time to time it appears, like a green rainbow in the sky." She hoped her reference to the interesting phenomena would cause Amanda to tell what she knew, if she knew anything at all. She was not disappointed.

"Her telling the truth," Amanda quickly chimed in. "I've seen it myself many times."

"You have?"

"Yes." She nodded emphatically. "It seem to have started long time ago, but it gotten brighter within the last few years."

"What do people around here think it is?" Sienna pressed for an answer.

"We don't know. The older people think it is a sign of the times. That us younger folks have gotten so far away from the way things use to be. They say it is a sign that we have made money our God. It kind of funny, but my youngest boy, Obed, him ten years old, him kind of agree with them, and him don't agree or talk about much at all."

"Shau Lo, the Chinese woman, said she had heard it originates in a swamp palm forest in the *Barra Del Colorado*."

"Her might be right. But it hard travelling up that way. You can only get to it by boat or by plane." Suddenly

Amanda's attention was across the room. "Look like Miss Melba's niece, right over there," she said, pointing, "need some cheering up. I'm going to put the sorrel and johnnycakes with the rest of the food and go talk to her," Amanda said before she made her way across the room.

Sienna looked around the medium sized space that was booming with activity. No one seemed to mind her and Hawk being there. There were a few curious glances, but after a moment or two the inquisitive parties soon got caught up in their own doings.

Sienna appraised the mixed group of men, women and children. All of them appeared to be quite comfortable at the traditional gathering. She hadn't known what to expect, but from the overall appearance of things Nine Nights was going to be a gay event, despite the sad faces of a few.

"Look out, we coming through," two men carrying a card table warned. Sienna and Hawk were forced to back up against the wall as they made room for them to pass. Inadvertently she settled her buttocks just below Hawk's groin, and before she knew it he had wrapped both of his arms just below her breasts.

"Be done in a minute," one of the men reassured them.

"Take your time," was Hawk's husky response, while Sienna tried her best to put a little space between them. "What's your hurry?" He bent down and crooned into her nearly twitching ear.

"I don't like to be where I'm not appreciated," she replied, disengaging herself from his possessive embrace.

"Why don't you find a seat?" Amanda called, waving her arm around inclusively. "Anywhere you like would be fine, except for Miss Melba's bed. It is not to be soiled until after tonight."

Sienna was acutely aware of the twin size mattress and box spring covered with an impeccably white sheet as she and Hawk settled into two chairs not far away. Her gaze travelled back and forth between the bed and an animated group of Dominoes players, who were chiding the men with the newly acquired card table. A heavyset woman with a friendly smile came over and offered them a drink. "Care for some *chicha?*" She held a chipped cup out to Hawk.

"Sure." He gave her a half smile before taking it.

"How about you?" She turned to Sienna, "You want *chicha* or ginger beer?"

"I think you might be better off with the ginger beer," Hawk suggested. "It's nonalcoholic. The *chicha* is cane liquor. It can be quite strong."

"*Chicha*, please," Sienna said without blinking an eye.

The woman's smile broadened as she looked from Sienna to Hawk. Quickly, she handed her a cup, then covered her mouth, giggled, and walked away.

"I guess I should have suggested that you drink the ginger beer. That way, I could be sure you would drink the *chicha*," he said, taking a swig of the brew.

"Has it ever occurred to you to not suggest anything at all?" Sienna retorted as the smell of the liquid in her cup tickled her nose.

"It's occurred to me, but that's just not my style. I like to warn people when I think they may be getting into something over their heads."

"Is that right?" Sienna took a swig of the *chicha* and fought hard not to shut her eyes against the sting of the potent brew.

"Um-mmm. That's right."

Sienna thought she saw Hawk's lips trembling as if he were trying not to laugh, and her eyes began to water. To prove him wrong, she took several more swallows. It amazed her how quickly the *chicha* took effect.

"Well, since you're such a helpful fellow, maybe you should have warned me in the beginning, before I got involved with you." She looked him straight in the eyes, her dark, curly lashes batting languidly.

"And why should I have done that?"

"You could have saved yourself, and me, a lot of trouble." She felt the warmth of the drink trickling through her veins.

Sienna watched him turn up his cup before he spoke again.

"I guess we have had our share of trouble, but if you ask me, it has all been worth it." His eyes melted into a soft gold as she watched, and a small whimper vibrated in her throat before she could stop it.

Sienna realized the conversation was not taking the turn that she thought it would, and a warm, inviting feeling had her floating in her seat. She hated to admit it, but Hawk had been right. The *chicha* had gone straight to her head.

"Wallace," a female voice called, "why you don't play us some music on your guitar? I know you bring it."

Sienna noticed a man who looked to be in his seventies sitting against the opposite wall. He had looked over at the woman as she called his name. In response he waved his hand as if to say, *not yet,* but she wasn't alone in her desire, and her request prompted others to ask the same thing. Before long the request had become a chant. "Play, Wallace. Play, Wallace."

A younger man, grinning from ear to ear, with a congo drum in tow, pulled up a stool in front of him. "I know how to get Wallace started." Instantly, his hands began to slap the skin-covered instrument rhythmically as he continued to smile and stare into Wallace's face.

For a minute or so Wallace just rocked to the beat, then the rhythm became too much for him and he was forced to pull out his guitar. He began to strum a lively tune.

Shortly afterward, one of the card players shouted, "I

like the music well enough, but I can't hear my partner call above the noise. Why don't you take it outside beneath the large palm? That way we still can hear it, but we can hear each other, too." The men around the table laughed.

"I think it a good idea," a smooth, dark, voluptuous young woman agreed. "Out there, there is more room for dancing."

Sienna could tell a little nudge was all they needed. She watched a group of young people follow the musicians out the open door to a palm several yards away. No sooner had the music picked up again than the young woman who had spoken up earlier grabbed a tall, slender man for her dance partner. From her chair Sienna had a pretty good view of the action outside. As the dancers got deeper into their craft, the more intrigued she became.

Already the *chicha* had fired her blood, and the sensuous movements of the dancers fueled it even more. As the music progressed, their actions became more erotic as they joined together, each one obviously enjoying the other's antics.

Sienna was very aware of Hawk sitting beside her, his hard, muscular thigh nearly brushing her own. She longed to close the gap between them, to feel the heat of his body, if only subtly. She looked down at her palms, which had begun to sweat, and she wiped one hand slowly across the other. Nervously, her tongue ran across her bottom lip, and the silky feel of it made her want to offer her tongue and her mouth to the man beside her. Although she didn't dare look, she knew that Hawk's eyes were on her.

Sienna sat there for as long as she could, but in the end she felt compelled to take some kind of action. Finally, she rose to her feet and headed out of the door, into the yard outside. By then two more couples had joined the original pair, and Sienna's new position gave her an even better view of their lithe body movements. The thin dress of the voluptuous woman clung to her curves as rivulets of perspiration deemed proper, causing her partner's eyes to glow with passionate fire. It was easy for Sienna's mind to substitute the man's nearly black eyes for an amber pair as she conjured up memories of how Hawk had looked at her in the cave and in the bedroom the night before.

She allowed her foot to tap out the arousing beat because there was no way she could stand there and not acknowledge it. Sienna realized that standing still in and of itself was quite a task, for the *chicha* had created a rhythm of its own inside her. As the minutes passed, one song connected with the other, and the musicians seemed to never tire. Lone dancers began to join the frenzied couples, all of them becoming caught up in the driving beat. Sienna had contained herself from breaking loose and joining the enticing scene, but then the music dove into a primal beat that not even a saint could ignore. Her body responded. She moved in place, yet it wasn't enough. She wanted to fully experience the African subrhythms.

Sienna made up her mind with the help of the *chicha*, and she began to march forward to the beat. She advanced with both arms raised high above her head, her wrists bending back and forth limply, which caused her hands to wave like tan handkerchiefs in the air. Her hips began to rise, naturally, as she swayed from one side to the other, and she closed her eyes and allowed her body to dance to the beats. It was easy for the deepest core of her to respond, and like the others she began to answer a heritage call. Sienna had leaned back, her hair swaying in a cohesive mass, when suddenly she encountered a rock hard chest behind her. Without turning around she moved from side to side, allowing herself a glimpse of her partner. The sight of him caused her heart to flutter, for it was Hawk who had come to join her.

The only time she had ever seen him dance was in Martinique, for during the time they had spent together they never went to a club or a party.

She turned to face him, stumbling as her feet got wrapped up in the process. "So you finally decided to act like the rest of us and join the party, huh?" she said as they were face to face. "I didn't think you had it in you, Hawk. From what I remember you've always been the hard, silent type. What's the old saying?" She paused, and looked up into the branches of the huge palm. "That's it. Treat 'em bad and make 'em love you." Her words ran together as if she couldn't say them fast enough. "Sometimes a woman needs to know what a man is really thinking, how he really feels." Her eyes opened and closed languidly from the *chicha*. "So tell me Hawk, tell me exactly how you feel about me."

He just stared at her for a moment before he started pointing down to the ground between them. Sienna studied his actions, totally confused.

"This is how I feel, Sienna, like my life and my feelings are in your control." He paused as his hungry eyes scanned her face. "Do you want me down there? Always on my knees?"

She received his words through a *chicha*-and-music filtered haze. They seemed so strange. She simply did not understand. "What are you talking about?"

"You don't know, do you?" Slowly he pulled her against him. "You can't even imagine how I feel." They swayed together momentarily before he led her into a labumba type of step that was all his own. "That makes it even worse."

While Sienna's head attempted to keep up with the things Hawk was saying, her body had no problem at all following his. It appeared they were so well in tune that even the most complex dips and sensual movements were done as if they were one. The *chicha* had made it hard enough for her to think, but Hawk's overwhelming closeness made it nearly impossible.

"Just tell me what you mean," she implored.

"Why do you think I've been acting the way I have ever since we made love in the cave?" Instead of answering her question he had fielded it with another.

"I thought perhaps you'd discovered something about me that you didn't like." Her words were hesitant, breathy.

"Didn't *like*." He made the term sound incredible. "Oh, no, my sweet thing." He clasped her even tighter to him. "It was just the opposite. I loved it too much," he announced in raspy tones above her ear. "I was like putty in your hands. Anything you would have asked me to do, I would have done it. No matter when, no matter where. You took me inside of you and I became lost to everything, including myself. At the time it was wonderful, but afterward it nearly scared me to death."

Sienna's body tingled as she listened, her nipples became rock hard and the nectar between her legs flowed. Although she hadn't told Hawk how his words had aroused her, it was evident he knew, from the hardness that now pressed against her.

"Hawk . . ." His name seemed to tremble as she said it. "I thought you had come to believe I was too loose, too bold. That you wouldn't want a woman like me at your side, only in your bed."

"No Baby, I want you by my side. That is for sure. But you were right in thinking every time I make love, I want that woman who was in the cave in my bed. She has spoiled me for everyone else," he confessed. "My fear is that she has spoiled me for life. Some men believe you can come across something that's so good that it's bad for you."

"Was it that good?" Sienna looked deep into his eyes.
"That good, and more."
"Oh God, if we weren't right here in the middle of all these people, I would show you good." She sighed, reveling in the knowledge that it wasn't that he felt she wasn't good enough it was his fear, resulting from their experience surpassing any that he had ever known.

"I'm going to hold you to that promise," Hawk declared. "While you were out here, Amanda introduced me to Miss Melba's niece, and I have a key to one of the cabins."

"Then what are we waiting for?" she asked as they danced nearer to the brush.

As soon as it was convenient, Sienna and Hawk entered the woods, a monstrous anticipation leading the way. They weren't the only ones who were full of anticipation. Several others marked their leaving, all for different reasons.

Nineteen

"It's midnight," an elderly woman announced. "Time to serve the chocolate, black coffee and tea."

"We got enough styrofoam cups for everybody?" Amanda asked as she surveyed the room. Then she dropped the cup she had in her hand as her gaze focused on the doorway. "Who is that?" she asked under her breath. "Is it who I think it is?"

"Lord," Miss Melba's niece replied. "I think that Mr. Paz, although I haven't seen him in years. Has him come all the way from Shangri-la for my aunt's Nine Night?"

"You better able to answer that than me," Amanda replied.

Paz entered the small house with three men at his back, along with Tina. Quickly, he looked around the room, just as he had searched the yard outside, but there was no sign of Sienna or Hawk. His eyes narrowed with anger, before he consciously softened the lines of his face. "Good evening, everybody. Or maybe I should say goodnight." He did his best to conceal a belch that reeked with liquor.

A low chorus of *"wa-apin"* and other greetings sounded.

"I'll have a cup of coffee, if you don't mind?" he said to Amanda as he crossed the room.

"Don't mind at all, Mr. Paz," she replied as she prepared another styrofoam cup.

He took it, extremely aware of its inexpensive nature. "And who is this Nine Night for?"

"It for my aunt, Melba Bryan."

Paz looked over at the woman who had spoken, "Glad I could be here to honor her passing," he said, lifting the white cup into the air, "and her safe and permanent journey."

Everyone in the room agreed and partook of the appropriate fare of the hour.

"But I must admit, there is something else that has brought me here tonight."

"We thought so," a very elderly man commented, to the agreeing grunts of others. "It been a long time since we seen you in Tortuguero."

"Yes, it has been a long time," Paz agreed. "Much too long," he said, lifting his nose a tad into the air, "but I'm here now. And I'm looking for someone. As a matter of fact, I'm looking for two people. A man and a woman. They are strangers to Tortuguero. I have reason to believe they were here tonight."

"You wouldn't be talking about your fiancée, and that man that her was making a spectacle of herself with out there in the yard no more than thirty minutes ago?"

Once again, anger surfaced on Paz's handsome but marred features as he searched for the familiar purveyor of the disrespectful words. He watched Mary slowly make her way to the center of the room. Paz studied the woman that he had dealt with for so many years. He felt the urge to slap her as he had done so many times before, but he restrained himself, aware of the people around him and, most of all, of the refined image he had struggled to build.

"Hello, Mary," he said, smiling slightly. "I wondered where you had gone. You know you left a very good job at Shangri-la. One that I'm sure many of these good people would love to have had." He held out his palms as if he had nothing to do with her leaving. "It's sad that things did not work out for you."

"*Raas,* you know why I left, and I wouldn't wish that job on anybody I know. Find yourself another *puta* outside of Tortuguero."

All of the eyes in the room went from Mary to Paz, and back to Mary, as if they were watching a ping pong game.

Paz's face trembled with controlled anger, but he still managed to say, "I'm sorry, I didn't know that you felt that way about me. Like everyone else, I find it flattering when I realize I have a secret admirer." He displayed the perfect amount of humility. "Perhaps if you had told me your feelings you wouldn't be saying the awful things you are making up now." He stuck his trembling hands into his tailor-made pockets. "Now," he said, beginning to speak to the crowd again, "if anyone really has information about my fiancée I would have you know that she is very sick. She is not herself," he announced to the room. "The man she is with kidnapped her, but because of an injury she sustained to the head she is confused, and has a hard time knowing what is real and what is not. It is very important that I find her and take her back to Shangri-la, where she can get help."

"There was a man and a woman here earlier," Miss Melba's niece explained, "them came with Amanda."

"Yes, them did, but I didn't know—"

"Of course you didn't," Paz reassured her. "Where are they now?"

"The man paid me for one of my hotels." She pointed to Mary. "She say they left over thirty minutes ago. I guess that where them went."

"Which cabin is it?" Paz's voice became dangerously flat.

"It the one closest to town, about a ten minute walk from here."

* * *

Hawk went down to kiss Sienna for the last time, her mouth still puffed and trembling from the previous kiss. Their hungry lips clung together as they savored every part of the other. He raised up above her as amber eyes locked with soft dark ones. "Oh, Baby, this is so good. So good, I don't ever want it to end."

"Don't let it end, then, Hawk. Don't let it end," she pleaded. "You can love me forever, any time and any place."

By now their bodies' momentum was beyond the point of no return. Over and over again steel wrapped itself in velvet, and although their mouths and minds tried to prolong the inevitable, their feverish bodies played their own tunes, ending with a crescendo that vibrated out into the universe. They did not hear their own cries, so overpowered were they by the intensity of their love.

Sienna clung to Hawk as her body's heightened senses spiraled downward, leaving her fulfilled and complete. She lay with her head on his chest, associating his departure from the peak with the declining beat of his heart.

Suddenly, they were both startled by someone beating on the door. Sienna sat up, pulling the sheet up around her. Immediately, Hawk's bare feet were on the wooden floor. In a flash he pulled on his jeans and went over to the gunnysack-covered window. The few moments between shock and reality allowed Sienna to collect her wits, and she, too, hastily put on her jeans. Tense, she watched Hawk try to see through the opening between the coarse material and the window frame. She could tell from his expression he couldn't see a thing.

The pounding started again, and below it Sienna thought she heard a child's voice saying, "You must open the door."

Hawk and Sienna looked at one another as she buttoned her blouse. Sienna crossed the floor and placed her ear against the door. "Who is it?" she called.

"Please open the door. Hurry!"

Responding to instinct, Sienna struggled with the old fashion slide bar, and it finally gave way. She opened the door, and there stood a young girl about ten years old. Her face was wet with perspiration, and her eyes were round with fear. Deep inside them, Sienna could also see sheer determination.

"You must leave here now," she advised. "The Paz and his men are on their way."

Sienna looked behind her and she could see that Hawk was already taking the girl's words to heart. Without delay he grabbed the duffle bag and his walking stick.

"But who are you?" Sienna asked the child.

"I am Junie," she announced boldly. She lifted Sienna's wrist surrounded by the bracelet and held it before her. "And you are The Stonekeeper."

"Yes," Sienna acknowledged with heartwarming conviction as she saw the glow of hope in Junie's eyes.

"Hurry. Follow me."

All three bounded off of the stoop and into the yard, with Junie leading the way. Behind them a male voice shouted, "There they are!" as they attempted to round the corner of the cabin.

Sienna turned to see Paz and three other men running toward them. Her first inclination was to switch gears into a high sprint, but she could see Hawk had other things in mind.

"Get back, Sienna," he shouted. She could not follow his instruction, for she was petrified with fear as two of the men lunged toward him.

Hawk was ready, and he wielded the walking stick with accurate and masterful strokes. The carved end of the object hit the first man in the temple, causing him to fall back. Immediately, with the opposite end of the stick, he whacked the other across the bridge of his nose. It startled him, but he did not stop.

Sienna was the target of the third assailant, who grabbed her as Hawk dealt with his partner. His sudden moves jolted her out of her paralysis, and Sienna screamed out of fear, also using the sound as a call to fight. She writhed and squirmed as he attempted to pick her up, and she pummeled him with her fists in his face and about his head. "Get away from me. Let me go!" she insisted.

Sienna's dilemma appeared to give Hawk a new sense of purpose. Although his assailant had recouped and was now brandishing a knife, he wasted no time in disarming him with a kick to his solar plexus and a chop to his wrist. Hawk quickly finished it, by striking the man in the throat.

Sienna had managed to keep her adversary from carrying her off, and his eye had begun to swell as a result of her prowess, but now she was on the losing side of the struggle as he grabbed her from behind. All of a sudden, she felt a jolt. She realized Hawk was behind them, and had caused the man's knees to buckle. Sienna heard him sputter and choke as he loosened his grip around her waist, then finally let her go before he dropped to the ground.

Hawk grabbed Sienna around the waist, "Let's go," he ordered, but they heard an opposing command. "Hold it right there," Paz called from somewhere behind them.

Sienna turned to see him pointing a pistol in their direction. Her insides immediately turned to jelly.

"This is for you," he said, his eyes focusing on Hawk, "for cuckolding me, in my own house." He pointed the barrel straight at him and squeezed the trigger.

"No-o-o!" Sienna shouted. The only thing she could think of was saving Hawk's life and she flung herself in front of him as the gun went off. She did not realize it at the time, but another "no" had resounded with her own as Tina had grabbed Paz's hand and declared, "You will kill The Stonekeeper!"

The chaotic moment seemed to manipulate time, and Sienna did not know if she had been shot or not, but when she looked into Hawk's stunned features and saw the love and relief that was shining there she knew that they both had survived.

It was all the chance they needed, and Hawk put his arm around her as they turned and bounded into the forest.

"Where should we go?" Sienna asked out of sheer frustration.

"This way," an excited voice called, and Junie stepped out from behind a tree, motioning as fast as she could. "We must head for the river."

Sienna was amazed at how agilely the young girl maneuvered in the dark forest. It was as if she had done it many times before. As Sienna ran behind her she looked up into the dark, navy sky and thanked the moon for her fullness that night. Without her, their flight would have been impossible.

"Hurry," Junie called over her thin shoulder, "it is not far," and she jumped over an exceptionally large root. Moments later she slowed down as they came to the edge of a river. She motioned again for them to follow her as she called into the semi-darkness in an audible but hushed voice, "Albert and Obed, are you there?"

"Yes, we're over here," another childlike voice answered, and they turned to follow the sound, which was heading down river.

Sienna's eyes kept searching the grey, muggy currents. Finally, a boat similar to a canoe floated into sight.

"There they are," Junie cried, and she ran toward the craft, which was maneuvering closer to the shore.

"You made it!" she exclaimed to her two friends.

"So did you," one of them replied.

Then all three of them turned their bright eyes toward Sienna. "Is this her?" the youngest boy asked, looking from Junie to Sienna.

"Yes, this is The Stonekeeper," she replied with obvious pride before quickly adding, "but we must hurry. Soon they be coming after us."

The children maneuvered the boat, which was about thirty feet in length, so that Sienna and Hawk could board.

"My name is Albert, and I think you should sit on that end," the oldest boy commanded as he looked at Hawk. "And you sit there." He pointed to the opposite end of the boat for Sienna. "We will distribute our weight in the middle, so it will not turn over. *Cayucas* are usually built for two people, but we built this one ourselves, and hoped that we would soon use it for this very purpose."

Sienna examined their intent faces. "You knew that we were coming?" Sienna asked as they pushed off into the water.

"We had been promised that The Stonekeeper would come. We did not know when, but we were told to be prepared," the other girl answered.

"Told by who?" Sienna enquired.

"Told by The Mother, who resides in the forest."

"A woman who lives in a nearby forest told you about me? About The Stonekeeper?"

"She is not a woman," Junie replied, her eyes bright with an intense light. "She is The Earth Mother."

Twenty

"What in the hell did you just do?" Paz shoved Tina away from him, her thin arm feeling like a doll's appendage beneath his hand.

Tina remained in the spot where she had landed, massaging her bruised forearms and quietly watching his livid features.

"Do you realize what you just did?" His flustered state caused him to repeat himself. "Do you?"

"If she doesn't, I do." José stepped into the clearing, followed by Archie. "She just stopped you from killing a man and adding that to your disreputable reputation."

Paz spun around to face the voice that was becoming irritatingly familiar. He was in no mood for José's wisecracks. Long ago the man had begun to get on his nerves. Now he was treading in even more dangerous waters. "What are *you* doing here?"

"The same thing that you're doing, in a matter of speaking. I'm protecting my investment. The *Anansi's* investment."

"I'm here to take my fiancée back to Shangri-la." Paz spewed out the half truth.

"Oh. Is that all?" José displayed a cool kind of haughty surprise. "My sources say otherwise. I heard that you planned to make this trip a little more worth your while." He advanced closer, so that they stood no more than two feet apart, which brought their eyes on the exact same level.

"What are you talking about?"

"I heard that once you caught up with your *fiancée*, you were going to take her to the area where you felt The Pirate's Emerald would be found."

The muscle in Paz's jaw jerked in his smooth face as he cast a distrustful eye toward his injured men. He noticed the guilty expression on one's face as they looked at Archie. "Well, you heard wrong."

"I'm glad to hear that." José put on a plastic smile. "I simply figured with all of the excitement, and with the urgency of the moment, that you did not have time to inform any of the *Anansi* members that the treasure hunt was on. It was an emotional issue, I'm sure. You were too caught up in pursuing the woman that you love." He paced a couple of steps away and adjusted his sports coat. "So in the same vein, it was my good fortune to learn about your . . . plans." He looked at him pointedly. "But now everything is fine." He raised his arms, then allowed them to drop to his side. One of his hands struck the silver flask he always carried with him. "As a result of my being here your reputation won't be tarnished any further, and so the *Anansi's* investment will be protected."

Paz was silent as he summed up the situation. Some kind of way, José had gotten wind of what he had planned. There had always been something about José that got under his skin. Of all the *Anansi* he appeared to be the most self-righteous and pleased with the easy life that money had afforded him. He made no apologies for it. *Although,* Paz thought, *from the way he drinks you would think he was trying to drown some unforgivable sin.*

Paz knew he did not handle liquor well himself. His mouth had a tendency to operate on automatic when he drank. Perhaps, he admitted to himself, in his excitement and thirst for vengeance he had said more than he should have in front of his men. But his pride had been greatly injured when he thought of Sienna deserting him for Hawk, and he had felt a need to boast and brag of his impending conquest. He vaguely recalled loudly claiming not only would he bring her back, but he would also bring back one of the rarest emeralds the entire world had ever seen.

Paz looked at José. He knew he could not afford to upset the *Anansi*. They were well connected in Central and South America, and if they put their minds to it they could do him great financial harm.

"I must admit I am glad that you are here. My relationship with the *Anansi* and my reputation are very important to me, as you well know." They locked eyes again. "But I must tell you, your sources were wrong. I would never have gone after the emerald without informing the group. My position amongst you means that much." He plied José in the same patronizing manner the man had bestowed on him. "But I must say things do work out for the best, because now that you are here we can go after my beloved *and* launch the search for The Pirate's Emerald."

Paz's eyes gleamed with his pronouncement. He knew it was well after midnight, and although José was not an old man his penchant for liquor was visibly taking its toll. For him to join in the search this time of night would call for a great amount of strength.

"Sounds good," José replied. "But I do believe that with neither one of them knowing these parts, and your fiancée not being well, they can not travel far in the dark. My suggestion is that we bunk down for the night, and start on their trail early in the morning."

Paz placed his hand dramatically over his heart. "My emotional involvement won't allow me to do that. It hurts me to know that she is in danger and she doesn't even realize it." Paz shook his head. "I can't stand being this close but yet so far away. So I can't afford not to go on tonight, but I can understand if you choose not to do so. A man of your *background* and *status* is probably not accustomed to coping under these kinds of conditions."

"Your men don't seem to be doing too well, either, from what I can see." José looked at the bloodstained group who stood not far away.

"Oh. By all means, don't be misled," Paz retorted. "We have all been through the school of hard knocks. As ironic as it may seem, sometimes it comes in quite handy." Paz played up the differences in their backgrounds, as José tended to do. "So, will you be taking the night off? Or heading out with us?"

Paz recognized the clumsily veiled disdain that crossed José's face. He knew José did not like the idea that a man like him, one he considered a nothing from the streets, would challenge his abilities under any circumstances.

"Need you ask?" José countered. "I'm as ready as you will ever be."

Several of the villagers from the Nine Night, including Amanda, were now standing in the clearing. Paz could tell they wondered what his next move would be, and their unsolicited curiosity irked him. He knew most of them looked up to him because of the financial gains he had made, but there were a few who resented him because they believed he felt he was better than they were. They were right.

"They could not have gone far without coming to the river," Paz stated, relying on his childhood explorations. "Let's spread out and check the area from here to the bank."

"It do you no good," a woman exclaimed.

Paz focused on her gaunt features, and the frightened face of the child she held roughly by the arm. "How do you know that?"

"My Thomasa told me so," Dorothy's stepmother announced.

"What does the child know about this?" Paz's eyes narrowed with confusion.

"Tell him. Tell him what you told me when I caught you sneaking out of the house with them johnnycakes."

The little girl refused, shaking her head adamantly.

"I said *tell* him." The woman boxed her ear, which caused the child to start to cry, but she still said nothing.

"I tell myself." She looked down, giving the child another shake. "I caught her running out back of our place. I know I scared her, and from the way her acting here that probably the only reason she told me what she did."

"What did she tell you?" Paz demanded impatiently.

"Her said her running to take the food to her brother, Albert. Him and Obed, Amanda's son, were waiting at a *cayuca* they had all built together," she announced, looking at Amanda's stunned features.

"Obed!" Amanda repeated. "Where them going this time of night?"

"She say where them were going was a secret. But I told her if her wanted to eat tomorrow her would tell me, and tell me right then."

The woman's ramblings set off Paz's fuse. "What does that have to do with any of this?" he demanded.

She appeared frightened for a moment, but then she straightened her shoulders as if she had had enough. "It got plenty to do with it. Here I am trying to help you when I need help myself. What am I doing it for? What in it for me and my family beside your shouting at me like I some child?" The woman's face trembled as if she was about to cry.

Thomasa's tear-stained face turned up and looked at her mother. She reached out and gently touched her hand. "That's alright, Mama. I'll tell him." Her wary eyes focused on Paz. "They were going to help the one with the mark. The Stonekeeper."

Thomasa's words caused quite a stir amongst the villagers. It appeared the adults knew nothing about such a person, but the expressions on Paz, José and Tina's face showed pure surprise.

"What do you know about The Stonekeeper, child?" There was a tenderness in José's voice that surprised Paz.

"Only that she is special, and that her coming here will make a difference." The young girl's eyes seemed to look through him as she answered. "It was Junie and Obed who had told us that she was coming. Coming from far away."

"Us?" José queried.

"Albert and me." She looked around at the attentive faces of the adults staring at her who seldom gave her any attention at all. "And she did come, just as they said she would," she announced proudly. "I overheard Dorothy tell Mama that she was here in Costa Rica. And that she had run away because she was unhappy, like Dorothy." Thomasa pointed at her stepsister, who had joined the crowd. "They both had run away from Mr. Paz."

"Run away?" Paz repeated the incriminating words and began to protest before José cut him off.

"Your protestations are of little importance now." José knelt down in front of Thomasa, who was near the age his son was when he died. "Where were they taking her?"

"Somewhere in *Barra del Colorado*. A place that has something to do with the green fire. I have never been there, but Obed and Junie have. They used the *cayuca* to get there."

"Oh God," Amanda wailed. "Those children don't know what them doing out there. It is still a wild place in many ways." She expressed her greatest fear. "What them know about finding the place of the green glow?"

She shook her head with worry. "But I remember Mr. Paz's fiancée did seem to be really curious about it. Her asked me lots of questions. Of course, I didn't have much to tell her."

José remained kneeling until Amanda had finished, then he patted Thomasa's hand, rose, and crossed over to Paz. "It sure is a strange way for a woman who was kidnapped and confused to be acting. To me, she's playing a vital role in the escape." His dark eyebrows lifted in unison. "Now I understand why the foreigner, who you said kidnapped her, didn't head for a big city, or try to get out of the country. It sounds like they're on a mission to me. One that they are participating in together," he said, his eyes full of distrust.

"You can think whatever you want to think, José," Paz retorted, although he admitted to himself he was quite impressed with the man's deductive abilities. "At this point, as you have so aptly expressed, your main concern is protecting the *Anansi's* investment. I've already fulfilled the first part of our deal, which was presenting my fiancée, The Stonekeeper, to you. You just need to concern yourself with the latter half."

They locked eyes again, each one feeling an unusual kind of emotional charge from the other.

"Alright, Mr. Paz." José was the first to speak. "I guess that means we are headed for the wildlife refuge tonight."

"I guess it does," Paz replied, thinking of how Amanda had said it was a wild place. He knew for a fact the western portion had never been explored, and it was not going to be easy. "We will need at least three *cayucas* to get there." He started to demand them from the gathering crowd, but when he looked into their distrustful faces the words caught in his throat.

"Feeling a little uneasy, Mr. Paz?" José teased, a knowing gleam in his eye. "I'll ask them." He turned to the group. "We will need to ask you good people for three *cayucas* to make the journey. I give you *my* word that we will return them in good shape, and we will bring back the children."

There was silence as the villagers looked at one another.

"No," Wallace replied. "The only way we will allow you to use our boats will be if some of us are with you. Our children are our responsibility." Sounds of agreement followed.

"I understand," José replied.

"Three of you," Wallace said, counting on his fingers, "and three of us."

José looked at Paz. "At least I did better than you would have done. You've just about lost their trust and their respect." He ran his hand through his thick mane. "They are no fools. They recognize a man of honor when they see one."

Paz came up on him, his temper once again at its breaking point. "You think you are so much better than I am because of who you are, who your parents were, how you were raised, and the money that you acquired as a result of it. But in truth I'm beginning to think I'm better off than you are. Now you're asking yourself, 'Why does this peasant feel that way?' I'll tell you why." They were so close they could feel each other's breath. "I know where I come from and what I am. And I will do anything to make life what I want it to be. I wasn't fortunate like you to have parents who loved me, and took care of me. They hated me so much they abandoned me to the streets, and I had to make my life there any way I could. And I did. But you," Paz said, looking at José as if he were filth beneath his feet, "you have had all the advantages, and you're still not satisfied. You've got to have more. The stranger the better." He tapped the metal flask hanging at José's side. "Now I think *that* is someone who is weak, and unworthy. As a matter of fact, I'm beginning to think the *Anansi* are a group of perverts, and in trying to be like you I have become one as well."

Paz walked away, falling in behind the villagers, who had started to disperse. For some reason he felt extremely tired. He had been forced to look at himself and his life under a microscope more than he cared to during the last couple of days, and he wasn't sure he liked what he saw. He looked beside him and saw Tina, who had always tried to protect him and who had stopped him from killing a man over his pride. He looked behind him at José, who was shakily taking a swig from the metal flask. He thought of the tearstained face of the child, and the distrustful eyes of the villagers. All he had craved throughout his adult life was respect, and he believed money could buy that. For a long time he thought he was right, but now everything seemed to be falling apart right before his eyes.

A tiny thread of compassion began to weave itself inside of Paz, compassion for the children, like the little girl, that he had promised to protect once he became an adult, and compassion for himself, for he realized he had lost his way long ago. He had gotten swept away in the inner rage that dominated his life.

All of a sudden, Paz could feel the sting of tears behind his eyes, and he hated the self-pity that filled him. To him it was a debilitating emotion, and he could not afford to be weak. With practiced precision Paz allowed the familiar rage to edge out the softer feelings. It had served him well all of his life, and he would allow it to continue, no matter what the cost.

Twenty-one

"Let us take over," Sienna declared as she looked at the children, who had been rowing for quite some time.

"No," Albert insisted, "we can handle it. We have done it many times before."

"I believe you have, but it is late, and you should try and get some sleep." She began to remove the oar from his hand as Hawk was relieving Obed of his.

"But you don't know where you are going," he persisted, his eyelids heavy.

"Tell me, and I will follow your instructions to the letter." Sienna noticed his tired features. He looked pleased with the compromise.

"Albert just wants to be the leader," Junie said sleepily. "There is nothing for you to do now but follow the river until it forks. Then you should go to the right."

"Is there no place for us to pull off to the side and set up for the remainder of the night?" Hawk spoke for the first time.

"Yes, there is," Albert added hastily. "After you go to the right you travel for a short distance and there is a place right there."

"How do you know?" Obed asked, his mouth cocked to the side.

"I just do," Albert replied.

"Yes, you do, because Junie and I told you," he said,

asserting his rank. "He's never been before. He has only heard us talk about it."

Albert's round face took on a deflated appearance.

"It really isn't important," Sienna intervened, wanting to end the discussion. "I just want to tell you we can't thank you enough for what you have done." She warmed even more at the broad, sheepish smiles that bloomed on their faces. "All of you. Now, you three get some rest, and Hawk and I will take it from here."

Although they protested in the beginning, minutes later all three children lay in cramped positions, asleep in the bottom of the *cayuca*.

"Boy, this is another first for me." Sienna gazed up into the star-filled sky, needing to hear her own voice. Everything around her had a surreal quality. It was hard to believe she was really there.

"What's that?" Hawk replied, watching her.

"Paddling a boat." She looked over and gave him a tired smile. "I've never paddled a boat before."

"Oh," he exclaimed, then became quiet. "That's not what I thought you were going to say."

"It wasn't?" She rolled her aching shoulders.

"No," he said softly. "I thought you were going to say today was the first time you ever tried to save somebody else's life by giving your own."

Sienna continued to look at him, but the smile disappeared from her strained features.

"Yeah." She finally looked away. "That was a first, as well."

"Why did you do that, Sienna?" Hawk's voice was dry. "You could have been killed."

"I could have," she said, looking at him with a smile that was forced, "but I wasn't. I guess it just wasn't my time to go." She attempted to sound nonchalant despite the tremor that surfaced as she thought about what had taken place.

She and Hawk had been reunited for less than two days. In that short time she had experienced all kinds of emotion from extreme anger to heartstopping passion, but what she had done naturally, no more than an hour ago, said it all. She loved this man more than life itself. Somehow that was more frightening than death. Death was a given. You knew that at some point and time it would come. But to deeply love someone didn't adhere to any absolutes. It might or might not be returned. If it was, it was a living heaven. If not, life could be a living hell.

"I would not have been able to live with that," he said in slow measured tones.

"Well, I didn't get killed and you don't have to," Sienna said with finality. "Besides, maybe one day you'll return the favor."

"I hope one day that you will be so far away from this kind of thing that it won't be an issue." His angular face appeared harsh as the result of shadows from towering trees along the banks.

"I hope the same for *both* of us," she replied pointedly. "And if this bracelet is as accurate a gauge as it has proven to be so far, once we have found the emerald there is only one other gem left. A diamond." She lifted one eyebrow and pushed out her breasts. "And as one sexy woman was known to say to the most famous of undercover agents, 'Diamonds are forever'." Her antics did not draw the amused response from Hawk that she had expected. Instead, his amber eyes were sober and unrelentingly steady, as if, in some way, he was seeing her for the first time.

Sienna wondered if she would ever have a diamond on her hand, a gift and a symbol of love from the man who sat on the opposite end of the *cayuca*. She hoped so, but there was no way she could be sure.

They rowed in silence. The river appeared to be a molten, lead-colored ribbon that stretched endlessly ahead. Sienna was extremely glad to come to the place where the waters forked, for her shoulders ached more than ever, and she longed to lie down and sleep, if just for a little while. Nearly exhausted, she let her gaze search the bank for the spot Albert had said would be there. She believed she saw it about a quarter of a mile down.

"I think that's the spot Albert was talking about." She pointed ahead.

Hawk nodded. "Yes, that must be it. But I think we need to continue until we find a place that's a little less conspicuous. That probably would be the first place Paz would look," he added.

Sienna moaned softly to herself, and closed her eyes just for a moment's respite. She must have dozed off instantly. When she opened them again, Hawk was sitting in the middle of the craft and the children had been placed as comfortably as possible at the other end.

"You know what?" he said softly.

"What?"

"I've picked out a name for you." His eyes were gentle.

"A name." Sienna yawned. "Don't I have enough names already?" she chided. "Let's see, what were some of the names you called me earlier tonight? Um-m-m, Brown Sugar, and oh, I really liked Sweet Dark Honey." She looked at him through eyes yearning for sleep. "Actually, you're quite good with names." Her finger touched the end of his nose.

"Yeah, but I had a different kind of inspiration then." His comment was deliberately husky. "This is different. It calls for a little background information." Hawk acted as if it were a complicated issue he was about to address. "You've got the name your parents gave you, Sienna Russell. And you've got the title that you were born to, The Last of the Stonekeepers, but you don't have a spirit name," he announced. "It's a beautiful Native American custom. And of course, now you know that with all the travelling I've done, I've gathered all kinds of interesting tidbits and wisdom from one side of the globe to the other."

Sienna's hands lay still on the paddle. She was enamored with what she saw. This Hawk was a calm, sharing soul, who had so much to give, so much to offer. She wanted to hear more. "Go on."

"I think it is time that you were given a spirit name, and I'd like to be the one to do it." He placed both hands upon her face. They felt slightly rough against her tender skin. "I name you Always Antelope." He leaned forward and kissed her softly. "For you are always taking action, no matter what the consequences might be. You are a survivor, and you encourage those around you to survive and fight the odds, no matter how many. Because your medicine is powerful, whatever you do is done with great strength of mind and heart. Never fear, Always Antelope, for you will always accomplish your goals."

Sienna looked at his sincere features and returned his gentle kiss. She could feel his intent to honor her, and it was one of the greatest gifts she had ever received. Yet the imp inside her could not pass up such a delectable opportunity.

"You better not let the brothers back home hear you talking like this or you'll be kicked out of the M.A.N. club."

"M.A.N. What's that?"

"Men Against Nonsense." She tried to keep a straight face as she made the comment.

Secretly, Sienna believed the things he said allowed her to see how he saw her, and it was overwhelming. She wanted to throw her arms around his neck, hold him close, and have a good cry. But she decided those were not the proper actions for someone who had just been named Always Antelope. She didn't want to wreck the esteemed image he had of her. At least, not yet.

Hawk gave her one of his rare smiles before he said in a chastising manner, "You must be tired. You go back to sleep. I'll," he said, pointing to his chest, "do the rest of the rowing."

Sienna didn't need any convincing. She angled her knees across the thin bar that had served as a seat, and lay her head on the irreplaceable duffle bag. It felt good allowing Hawk to take over, if only for a little while. From behind heavy eyelids she watched the stars and the moon, finding comfort in the repetitious sound of Hawk's paddle parting the water.

Later, she awakened groggily as Hawk put her down on a bed of leaves. A small fire danced merrily close by, built in the hollow base of a tree. She watched him bring the children one by one out of the boat. He held them like a man who naturally knew how to hold children, and not one of them awakened under his tender care. When Hawk was through he looked over and winked at her, the orange glow of the firelight turning his hair and his skin to a burnished gold, a color that Sienna had always associated with dreams and magic. Finally, Sienna saw him settle at the edge of their tiny clearing with his knees raised, and his arms circled around them.

"Aren't you going to get some sleep?" she called tenderly.

"No, I think I'd better keep a lookout, just in case Paz and his friends get inspired tonight. I have a woman and children to look after now." He looked at her meaningfully.

"Is that something that you want? Children?" she concentrated on a leaf that she was turning over on the ground, not wanting him to see how important the question was to her.

"Yes, I'd love to see myself in some little face," Hawk

replied, speaking over his shoulder. "But not before I have a wife." He turned completely away from her. "And not before my life has been put back into some kind of order."

Sienna could see his shoulders stiffen, and she was so pleased to know that if the circumstances were right he would want a family that she didn't want to break the spell.

"Hawk." she said his name just to say it.

"Yes, Always Antelope?" He kept his back turned.

"What do you think the children meant, saying The Earth Mother told them about me?"

"I don't know what to think about that." He shook his dreadlocks back away from his face. "Kids can have such active imaginations. It's hard to guess."

"That's true." She contemplated what he said. "But . . . they found out about the legend of The Stonekeeper somehow." She stared at his broad back. "And I don't think it is a coincidence that the place of the green fire, the *Barra del Colorado*, is the same place where the children were told to take me. It's almost like my dream, except that in it I was leading the children, they weren't leading me." She paused. "But yet and still, something inside tells me we are in the right place, and we will find the emerald at the end of our search."

"It won't be long before we find out," he replied.

Several times while they were on the run he had longed for the gift of sight that had come so easily to him many times before. He wanted to know what lay ahead in their futures. Would it be triumph or failure? And in what manner would that be judged? Would he and Sienna be together in the end, when all of this was over? Once again, the powers that be seemed to be calling the shots, in a fashion that only they could. They would not allow him even that slight comfort. No, the sight would only come when they felt it was appropriate, not when the vessel they worked through deemed it to be so. He had been told the sight could never be used for his own means without dire consequences.

A vaguely familiar feeling passed through him, and when he recognized it the blood seemed to drain from his golden brown face. It had been months since the pulsing energy of the sight had made itself known in such a way, and he wondered what it meant. Automatically, his hand went up and touched the side of his face, and his shoulders slumped with relief when all he felt was the familiar stubble of several days without a razor. Comforted, he gazed up into the sky.

Hawk could count the times on his hand that he had felt so at peace. It was strange that it would come in the midst of such outer turmoil, but he knew it was the result of the love that he felt for Sienna, coupled with the love he received from her, that made the difference. At that moment Hawk knew with all of his being there was nothing that could overpower the power of love.

It is strange how things work out, he thought as he listened to the fire crackle and the sounds of the animals of the night. In the beginning he had looked for The Stonekeeper all around the world just to relieve his physical suffering, but in finding Sienna the woman, he had been given the closest thing to mental bliss he had ever known.

Hawk attempted to ignore the surge of energy that escalated inside him once again. He would not allow it to shatter his peace. Not yet.

Twenty-two

"Told you," Albert cried as he ran toward them with another fish on his line.

"My goodness, we won't be able to eat all the fish you and Obed are catching." Sienna played into boosting his ego. "What kind is this one?"

"It's a bobo," Junie said, jumping in.

"Ah-h, come on. That can't be it. You guys are pulling my leg," Sienna declared.

"Um-mmm." "Yes it is," Junie and Albert replied.

"So we got wahoo," she said, adjusting the fish that was already cooking on the rack, "and now we've got bobo. I wonder who came up with these names."

"It's not stranger than his name—Hawk," Obed said, defending the names of the fish he had eaten all of his life. "Or your being called a Stonekeeper."

She looked at his stoic features. "Well, when you put it that way, I guess you're right."

"Don't tell him that," Albert declared, rolling his eyes at his younger friend. "I will never hear the end of it."

"I am right," Obed insisted. "Just like I was right about The Mother's message."

"Tell me about that." Sienna's expression turned serious.

"Actually it was Junie and me who figured it out," Obed admitted. "Sometimes it is hard to understand what The Mother is saying, and we had to guess. I was the one who guessed right the last time." He stuck his round chin up in the air. "Although Junie is the one who usually understands."

"How does The Mother talk to you?" Sienna asked as Hawk looked on.

"It is hard to say," Junie said as she held out a leaf for her hunk of fish. "All I know is her breathing is so heavy it makes it hard to make out her words."

Sienna threw Hawk a questioning look.

"We will have to show you," Obed declared. "Then you will see," he said with finality. "But now we need to hurry and eat. We slept much too long. It is already after noon." He looked at the position of the sun in the sky. "We must get there before it turns dark." He gave Hawk an admonishing look.

"Don't worry, I did the right thing by letting you sleep." He patted the boy's coarse hair. "You needed that rest. You all have been working very hard," he added as Obed and Albert dipped eager fingers into their flaky white hunks of meat.

"We did kind of overdo the sleeping, didn't we?" Sienna asked as she settled down beside Hawk after placing the bobo on the cooking rack.

"Like I told Obed, we did the right thing," he replied under his breath. "I saw a group of *cayucas* pass by not too long ago. I guessed it was Paz and his *entourage*. They will be expecting to find us somewhere ahead of them, but we won't be there."

"Oh. I see." Sienna looked over at the children. "I bet their parents are worried sick about them." Her forehead folded with concern.

"Probably." He chewed carefully. "But it is clear to me from the way they are taking care of business they believe they are obeying an authority that is even higher than their parents." He turned his attention toward Junie.

"And if they are right, their parents will never be prouder."

Sienna's mouth turned up slightly as she thought about what Hawk was saying. She knew he was right. Still, she thought it was such a heavy duty for ones so young.

"But in the meantime, we'll take good care of them," he reassured her. "Hey, remember, we're on a mission here," he reminded her, "and you're The Last of the Stonekeepers."

Hawk made the title sound impressive before he paused, and a cloak descended over his rugged features. "And only God knows who and what I am," he added softly, looking down at the chunks of fish, popping one into his mouth with finality.

Sienna did not like the way he had said that, and she started to challenge his assessment of himself. If it had not been for the children, she would have.

They all hurried and finished their food, but Sienna's mood was heavy as she helped clean up the campsite. She was the last one to linger in the woods, standing between the trees as the children waited in the *cayuca*. She knew they had to go, but she needed a moment of solitude to fortify herself.

"Sienna," Hawk called as he approached, "it's time to go." He saw her looking up into the boughs of a mighty tree before her dark, thickly lashed eyes feasted on him. They were full of worry not for herself, the children, or the mission, but for him.

"I know. I'll be there in a moment," her lips replied, but her eyes said she was not ready, that her heart was heavy and he was the cause of it.

Hawk felt angry at himself for being the one who had brought this down on her, brought it at a time when she would need all the mental and physical strength she possessed, to deal with things that he felt were much more important than he could ever be.

With deliberate strides he walked up to her and took her in his arms. "Look, Baby. You don't have to worry about me," he declared as he held her tight. "Remember who I am?" He looked down into her uncertain features. "I'm the Hawk, and that is a mighty powerful bird. I'm known for my ability to maneuver quickly with grace, and my impeccable sight allows me to see exactly what I'm doing, and where I'm going." He ran his hand over the spongy curls that surrounded her face. "So there's no problem here. I'm going to do what I have to do, and so will you."

Once again images of K'in surfaced in his mind, and from the words of encouragement Hawk gave to Sienna he drew strength. Then another kind of realization hit him. "And you know what else?"

"No, what?" she replied, her eyes too shiny.

"When things get a little too far out there for us, and we have to deal with things we hardly understand, we can always pull on the tried and true." He kissed her forehead. "It's our heritage. We come from a long line of fighters and survivors." He watched a heartfelt understanding rise in her eyes, and he knew he had accomplished what he tried to do.

"So did I do good? Are you ready now?" he challenged, pulling out his most devastating, masculine charm.

Hawk watched Sienna's mouth set in a determined line, and her eyes began to beam with intensity before she replied, "After a speech like that," she said, giving his face an affectionate pat, "you can add another name to my list. Just call me Sojourner Truth."

She walked around him, heading for the river. Feeling satisfied, Hawk joined her at her side.

* * *

"I knew we should have left last night," Paz complained, his eyes searching the empty river ahead.

"There's nothing we can do about that now." José licked his dry lips as he dipped the paddle into the water again. "They didn't want to leave until they had done a thorough search for the children. You can't blame them for that." His eyes involuntarily went to the lump his flask made under his jacket, which lay in the bottom of the *cayuca*.

"I don't give a damn about those children," Paz retorted. "Nobody gave a damn about me when I was a child." Then he looked at the woman riding in the craft slightly behind them. "Except for Tina," the sight of her forced him to acknowledge.

"So that's how it is," José exclaimed. "At long last I get to see the real Paz. Because life dealt you a raw deal, let's make sure nobody else gets a fair one." He swiped at the sweat that matted his hair to his head and rolled down his face. "I thought you were nothing but scum from the beginning, and now I know it."

"Save your preaching for somebody else, and go ahead and take a drink out of that container that's calling your name," Paz responded condescendingly. "I'm tired of listening to you."

José wanted to do just that, but he wouldn't give Paz the pleasure of being right. With trembling fingers he unbuttoned a few more buttons of his tailor-made shirt. His heart was beating faster than he could ever remember, but he wouldn't let the low-life Paz outrow him, even though he was younger. "Crawl back into the hole that you came out of," he countered with all the venom he could muster.

A sudden rapid splashing of water erupted at the side of the *cayuca*, and José jumped, rocking the boat so much that it nearly turned over. The shaking and quaking was followed by Paz's devilish mocking laughter.

EMERALD'S FIRE

"Did that scare you, old man?" he teased.

José looked at the animated group of caimans that had created the uproar. Their gaping mouths and flapping tails continued to create a white foam. He realized it had been a long time since he had been out in untamed territory like this. It had never really been an integral part of his life. Even as a child he had stayed close to the city. Close to San José.

The pounding of José's heart seemed to enter his ears, and his hands started to shake uncontrollably. Before he knew it he had reached down, grabbed the flask, and was guzzling the soothing alcohol. He closed his eyes as temporary relief flooded through his trembling body.

Once again, Paz's laughter accosted his ears. For a moment José hung his head in shame, then he lifted it higher. Even if he was an alcoholic he was still better than that lowlife bastard Paz. José had bent over to replace the flask inside his coat pocket when he heard the excited voice of one of the men from the other *cayuca*.

"Look! Look up there!"

José raised red-veined eyes to the sky, where an arch of vivid green soared and fell. "My God, look at that," he heard himself say, excitement edging his voice.

"Yes, look at it," Paz repeated.

José's eyes traced the phenomenon across the sky. "The left side disappears somewhere to the far southwest of here, but the right side," he said, stopping to study the situation, "it seems to go right down into the trees on the top of that hill. It looks so strange. I've never seen anything like it," José confessed.

"That's because there *is* nothing like it," Paz replied with ill-concealed exuberance.

José watched him hurriedly put down his paddle. With anxious fingers Paz searched inside one of his pockets, producing a folded piece of yellow paper. He read the contents to himself as José strained to hear.

"When you are near it seems to be
The emerald disappears inside the trees.
How vivid the green! How unique the place!
Who dares to touch The Mother's face?"

Paz's eyes gleamed in a fashion that José did not know was humanly possible. The strange sight frightened him, but the thrill of the hunt was just as powerful.

"That's it," Paz declared. "It's got to be. That's where we need to go." He pointed to the top of the mountainous hill. "That's where we will find the emerald."

Jose looked at the group of trees that seemed to be so far away. "Are you sure?"

Paz never answered him, at least not in a verbal way, but José knew from the way his paddle was striking the surface of the river with renewed determination that he *was* sure. José noted how he hadn't said a word about his fiancée, The Stonekeeper, because possessing The Pirate's Emerald was paramount in his mind.

José knew the gem had been Paz's main interest all along, that he wanted it for himself, and that greed propelled his every action. Here was a man who had been able to drag himself out of the filthy streets, obtain riches beyond his wildest dreams, and it still wasn't enough. He wanted more, and he always would.

Once again, José looked at the green that streaked above him. Suddenly, it seemed to reflect his thoughts about Paz back in the form of self-examination. At that moment it was very clear that Paz's becoming a member of the *Anansi* was perfect. They all possessed the same weakness that he had, extreme greed. José knew that when he searched his own heart, like the hearts of the other *Anansi* members, there would never be enough, no matter what they owned, no matter the price. They, like Paz, would always want more.

Twenty-three

"Look, she is showing us the way," Junie exclaimed excitedly as she pointed to the green ribbon in the sky. "The Mother knows we are coming, and she is showing us the way!"

Sienna looked up and a chill vibrated her insides at the sight of the green fire. She reached out and touched Hawk's back, which had gone still like the paddle that lay across his lap. "Can you believe it?" Her voice was full of awe.

"You're asking a fellow who can believe just about anything," he replied. "But yes, I can most certainly believe what all our eyes can see."

"You see how it seems to disappear into those trees," Obed explained, loudly.

Sienna nodded, then finally said, "Yes."

"That's where we must go."

"It seems so far away," Albert surmised, forgetting at that moment that he was the older boy in his fascination.

"It looks farther away than it really is," Obed explained eagerly. "Once we go around the next bend in the river we should go on shore. There we will find a path that is not too steep to climb. It is steady, although you can tell it is not used a lot. At least, not now."

"I'm surprised to hear it's been used at all," Hawk said as he looked at the virgin land.

"Maybe it was used a long time ago," Junie suggested,

her dark eyes focused overhead, "long before our people came to this land. Even before the Caribs and the Miskito Indians came here. Maybe it was used when The Earth Mother was first born."

Silence fell over the *cayuca* as they all thought about what Junie had said. Then Sienna re-examined the vivid green rainbow that spanned the Costa Rican sky, and there was very little that remained in the realm of impossibilities.

"Can I paddle now?" Albert asked Obed with newfound respect. In silent honor, the younger boy handed his friend the oar and sat down beside Junie.

Hawk and Albert propelled the boat to the bend, and it was Hawk who was the first to see the three *cayucas* in the distance. "We've got company up ahead," he reported. "How much further do we go before we pull over to the side?"

"There it is right there," Junie instructed, indicating a small indentation in the bank which transformed into a thick shore lined with swamp palm trees.

Sienna watched as Hawk quickly put his muscles into high gear. Albert did the best he could to assist him as he made a rapid beeline for the shore, but an excited shout reached them from one of the *cayucas* ahead. Sienna could barely see the pencil-thin figure standing up in the narrow boat, waving its arms above its head. "They've spotted us," she announced, although she was sure they were all aware of that fact. "That must be one of the children's parents," she surmised, feeling a twinge of guilt.

"It will be okay." Junie touched her hand, understanding showing in her eyes. "Sometimes it takes something like this to wake parents up. They never listen to us, or we're not really important until something happens, or we're gone," she stated with wisdom beyond her years.

Although Sienna hated to admit it, she knew what Junie said was sometimes true. Still, she found herself defending them. "I know sometimes it seems that way, Junie, but there is no book or straightforward explanation that truly prepares a person for being an adult. It's not easy, just like it isn't easy being a child. We're all learning and evolving, and as long as we never forget that, we won't judge each other too harshly."

"It will take them a little while to double back," Hawk declared as he maneuvered the boat into even murkier water.

Sienna looked at the spongy wetlands and the insects that appeared to creep and glide along the surface between them. "It doesn't look like we can walk out there to me." Her hesitant features produced a scowl.

"We usually go as far as we can that way," Obed revealed. "The land becomes much drier after a while."

Carefully they maneuvered the *cayuca* through the trees until they could go no further. Hawk grabbed onto a supple palm trunk, and tied a rope connecting the boat and the plant.

Sienna and the children clamored out. Immediately, brown, runny mud closed in around her sandaled feet. She tried to ignore the clammy moistness as she picked her way across soil that gave in with every step. They had gone a short distance when Junie proclaimed, "The path should start somewhere around here."

The group continued to progress in an eerie silence, and Sienna realized that the forest had been full of calls from macaws, parrots and herons only moments ago.

"There's a path over there," Albert shouted. "Is that it?" He looked at his friends for confirmation.

No confirmation was needed, for a swarm of colorful butterflies launched themselves simultaneously into the air at the sound of Albert's voice. Sienna watched their iridescent blue wings blend with the green tree tops, turning the air above them greenish blue, very similar to the one that arched across the sky.

"I guess that's our answer," Sienna said, her voice a whisper among the whir of tiny wings.

They started on the narrow path that was barely a path at all. With all the proof around her, Sienna's heart was confident that whatever lay at the end would be like finding the pot of gold at the end of a rainbow.

"What are you doing?" Paz shouted at Wallace as he began to turn his *cayuca* around.

"I'm going back to get my grandchild, Junie. I saw their boat back there," he declared as he dipped the paddle back into the water.

"You're not going anywhere but where I tell you," he ordered, producing the pistol. "We're going a little further downriver so we can be closer to that hill over there. The big one that looks like it is the source of the green fire." Paz watched Wallace's eyes narrow in disbelief.

"And you would shoot me, wouldn't you, if I disobeyed you?" The older man looked into Paz's determined eyes.

For a second the man's disbelieving look made Paz falter, but only for a second. "If that is the only thing that will make you listen. Yes."

Wallace became silent, and Paz noticed a dimming in his wise eyes. Finally, he said, "We, the older people of the Caribbean coast, have tried so hard to keep the spirit of our ancestors alive. The one thing they believed in was unity, but I know for sure today that we have failed." He shifted his gaze away from Paz, as if he no longer existed. "A saying that has been with us for years no longer has a meaning, because we are no longer all one people," he proclaimed as he turned the boat around that transported him and Tina. Slowly, it began to move in the direction Paz had designated.

Amanda, who was in the *cayuca* with her husband, Eduardo, turned accusatory eyes on Paz, and Tina's gaze was full of remorse when she looked down from the green above her.

Paz's handsome features hardened. He had heard the statement so many times before, "We are one people," but it meant nothing to him. If it had meant so much to the people of the Caribbean coast, they would have cared more about the boy who was left to fend for himself on the streets. He had never felt like he belonged, and back then he needed so much to feel acceptance. He swallowed hard when he recalled how they just quietly accepted his suffering. Now they must quietly accept their own.

"If you didn't want them to go after their children, why didn't you threaten them with the gun last night and just take the *cayucas*?" José asked, openly drinking from the flask. "Or were there just too many of them then?"

"Mind your own business, old man, before I take my frustration out on you," Paz retorted as he made his boat fall in behind the other two.

What had been a persistent mist turned into a heavy fog around them, and Sienna could barely see four feet in front of her face. Even before then, the intermittent cry of a jaguar or a howler monkey had caused her to start, but now, as they walked through the white vapor that created its own unique version of night, the animal cries sounded much more unnerving.

"Are you okay?" Sienna called to Junie and Albert, who walked just ahead of her.

"Everything's fine," they replied almost in unison.

"What about up there, Hawk?" she called even louder. She waited for the immediate response that always came, but this time there was silence. "Hawk and Obed, do you hear me?" she demanded, a slight panic in her voice. After what seemed to be an unbearable amount of time, Obed finally replied.

"We're okay, but something's wrong."

"Wrong?" Sienna echoed. "Just stand right where you are" she immediately instructed. "We'll be there in a moment. It shouldn't be very difficult, because we're right behind you," she tried to reassure herself, Junie and Albert. Her words proved to be correct. They nearly collided with the boy.

"Where's Hawk?" Sienna asked, beginning to feel ill at ease.

"I'm right here," he replied. His voice sounded as if he were only a short distance away.

Sienna became irritated, wondering why he had not answered before. "Why didn't you say something earlier?" she chastised, trying to peer through the fog that had become even thicker.

Obed was the one to answer in an uncertain voice. "Something's wrong. I don't remember the fog ever being this thick."

"I don't either," Junie confirmed.

Sienna tried to supply a logical explanation. "Maybe the clouds have come down further on the hilltop today than they did on the other days when you came here."

"But that's not all," Junie declared, "I don't remember there ever being so much open space around us until we had reached the top."

It was only then that Sienna realized the absence of trees on both sides of her. Unprepared for it, she felt the slow grip of a hand around her upper arm. It felt extremely large and held her tightly. "Hawk?" she said, fear edging up inside her.

"Yes. It's me," the familiar voice replied.

Sienna breathed a deep sigh of relief.

"Albert, Obed and Junie," Hawk called, "take each

other's hands. Sienna, you take Junie's hand and I'll hold yours."

The fog had thickened to the point that she could not see Junie standing beside her, so Sienna felt around in the moist whiteness until their hands met blindly. She grasped the child's small fingers eagerly, and Hawk let his hand slide down her arm, taking hers into his once they met. Again, he began to lead them forward.

It was uncanny, walking with them so near but unable to see their faces. Sienna had lost all sense of direction, and it amazed her that Hawk had not. "How can you see where we're going?" she asked as she moved along with him.

"It's hard to explain," he replied, his voice sounding different to her ears, "but I know that the fog will begin to lighten as we travel in this direction."

They walked a little further, and his words proved to be on target. After several moments the fog did begin to thin, and she could vaguely see his outline before her, and Junie's little form behind. All of a sudden, in the middle of the milky mist, what appeared to be a massive wall came into view several feet away.

"Hawk, do you see that?" The sound of her own voice sounded strange to her ears.

"I sure do," he remarked as he continued to travel toward it.

"It looks like a building of some sort. But how can that be, way up here?" she questioned, attempting to merge what she thought was impossible with the wall that grew larger with each step. Finally, it was so close she could touch it. In some places the surface was cool and smooth, but most of it was covered by grass, plants and lichen. The smell reminded her of the leaves that she had slept on the night before.

"What is it?" Obed asked as he and the other children

gathered close around Sienna. She could barely make out Hawk's form as he continued to explore several feet away.

"It seems like some kind of mound," Hawk replied. "There were many cultures in the past that built mounds like this for their homes, places of worship, and for burials."

"This was somebody's house?" Albert questioned, his tone revealing his disbelief.

"I didn't say that," Hawk countered. "I simply said there's a chance that it was, or something close to that." His voice sounded even further away. "And usually they built more than one."

"Hawk, wait for us. We don't want to become separated out here," Sienna warned, but there was no reassuring reply. Then, she heard him say somewhere in the distance, "I've come across an opening of some kind. A door."

"Where are you?" she called, beginning to feel confused because of the circular shape of the object.

"Just stay where you are," Hawk advised. "I'm going to go inside and see if this is a place where you can rest, and get your bearings."

Sienna would have continued, but as she tried to see through the fog in the direction that Hawk's voice was coming from, the mist seem to collect and disperse, forming images that were more than disconcerting. She knew it was her nerves, but she decided to stay put all the same. She had to maintain her cool, if only for the children's sake.

Several minutes passed before they heard Hawk's voice again.

"I was right. It is a mound," he announced. "Sienna, continue to your right. At one point you're going to feel the shape of it change, as if another round wall were being connected to the larger one," Hawk instructed through the fog. "That is exactly what was done. Continue alongside it, and you will be at the opening. There are several steps that lead down inside, and you must descend them carefully. From the way the mist is moving, it should be lifting very soon."

Sienna followed Hawk's instructions to the letter. The opening came quicker than she thought it would, and she could tell Hawk had cleared away climbers and other vines that had made their home there, weaving a thick web.

"Alright, I'm going down first just to navigate," she explained to the children. As she placed her foot upon the first step, she could see the glow of a tiny light. It shifted like a candle flame meeting the breath of a child, and Sienna realized Hawk had started a fire to guide their way.

"This is going to be easier than I thought," she called back up to the kids. "Hawk already has a fire going. It's alright to start down behind me."

She was at the bottom, and had to bend her head to enter a larger space. Sienna lifted it as she said, "That fog was something else, wasn't it? I felt like I was in The Twilight . . . Zone." The last words died on her lips as she looked around the empty space. Hawk was not there.

Twenty-four

Hawk grabbed the trunk of the palm with both hands, leaning his forehead against it. He could feel the horrible rash growing, bubbling over the left side of his face, encasing the side of his neck.

It was different this time, far different from the previous attacks that had racked his entire body with pain. The only physical discomfort, this time, was the stinging growth of the burgeoning outbreak as he continued to cling to the tree.

It had been months since he had experienced it at all. Hawk had come to believe, at least hope, the outbreaks were over, because he was fulfilling his mission. Over time, he had come to understand that the pain and the rashes were the ways the power that be forced him to acknowledge his ability, his gift of the sight. For the last six months he had lived alone because of it. *So why have they returned now,* he beseeched in mental anguish. Now that he had reunited with Sienna after leaving her because of it. Had he not done what he was supposed to do?

Hawk pushed away from the tree, readjusted the duffle bag and the walking stick on his back. Aimlessly, he walked through the fog, his mind and his heart in turmoil. All he could think of was Sienna and the children going inside the mound and finding he was not there. He could imagine their confused faces because they would not understand, and he feared Sienna would believe he had abandoned her without a reason once again.

Still, Hawk knew he had done the right thing. How could he have explained the blatant, blistering growth to the children who had come to trust him? He had seen his abominable face in such a condition more than he cared to remember, and there was no doubt in his mind his looks alone would have frightened them. With his new appearance he might have caused them to panic and run off into the confusing fog. Although they had been fortunate up until now, this *was* untamed country with jaguars, ocelots, and other predators.

He replaced a dreadlock that had fallen against the tender side of his face back inside the leather string.

Then there was Sienna. What would he have said to her? How could he have explained the atrocity into which he had turned? Perhaps if he had a complete understanding of what this thing meant in his life, it would have been easier to tell her about it, before this occurred. But he lacked that understanding, and he had no idea when, or if, he ever would have it.

In desperation, Hawk progressed with his head thrown back, finding the clammy mist to be an unlikely, soothing balm for his rash-ravaged face. Reluctantly, he recalled how he had felt the familiar bursts of energy the night before, but he had hoped it was not the precursor of what he was experiencing now. It was only after they entered the fog as they climbed the path that he had begun to worry, and he had no idea that the outbreak would surface so quickly. In the past it had always come right after dusk, but here it was late afternoon and it had already taken its terrible toll.

As Hawk continued to walk, feeling anger more than self-pity, he realized why the rash had come so early. Although it was still daytime, the fog had turned the surrounding area into an early dusk, and his body had reacted accordingly.

The sound of a scurrying animal caused him to peer to the side of him, and he discovered that what he had told Albert was true. The mound in which he hoped they were resting safely was not the only one. There was another that he could barely see a couple of feet away. Feeling desperate, Hawk made his way toward it. Inside the mound, alone, he could collect his thoughts, and nurse the mental wounds that never had an opportunity to heal.

"We've got to take a rest," José demanded as they approached the nearest thing to a clearing they had come across. "Look." He pointed at Tina, who was trudging along silently. Her thin face looked exhausted and drawn, and the lines in her forehead and around her mouth had deepened. "Fifteen to twenty minutes is not going to make that big a difference," he insisted, wiping the sweat that ran down his face.

Paz started to ignore José's cries, but when he looked at Tina's weathered features he admitted to himself that resting for a short while was not a bad idea.

"Alright, we can stop for a little while." He looked up at the remainder of the trail and noticed that a fog had set in near the top. He could see it moving, lifting, and he surmised waiting until it was totally gone would be in their best interests.

Paz settled down away from the others. He felt safer that way, and it also made it much easier to keep an eye on his disgruntled companions. He watched them unwrap the snacks they had prepared the night before. In silence they offered some of the food to José and Tina. They accepted, expressing their gratitude softly.

A few feet away, he adjusted his body against a tree. The inside of his abdomen felt like a contracting accordion, his hunger was so great, but he would not let them know of his need. He told himself he was no stranger to hunger, and although it was an uncomfortable bedfellow it was a familiar one.

Paz allowed his head to settle back, and his eyes nearly closed as the minutes passed, but the subtle movement of someone much closer than he remembered caused him to jump. His immediate reaction was to point the pistol in their direction. It was Tina's surprised yet understanding gaze that he found himself looking into. Paz realized she had come to offer him a piece of her johnnycake. Feeling ashamed, he lowered the weapon and turned his head away, ignoring the food he so much wanted.

"Take it," she coaxed softly. "I know you must be hungry."

He shook his head, refusing to look at her again.

Tina moved closer, finally placing the bread on his thigh.

"You were always a stubborn child, and now you are a stubborn man. I should have tried to curb your extremely selfish nature, but at the time I knew it was the only thing that was keeping you alive."

With his peripheral vision, he could see her examining the landscape.

"You know, I always wanted children of my own, a husband and a family, but it was not to be. The few times that I became pregnant I lost the baby." She sat down right beside him. "Maybe it was for the best, because I didn't really know their fathers. The babies had simply been the result of my bargaining for a meal and a few *colones.*" She paused, dusting her hands. "It is best when a child knows their father, then they can have some idea what to look for in themselves. Even though it is not always that way, it is something that should not be ignored. And you, my Paz," she said even more softly to ensure she was not overheard, "you had no clues at all. No mother. No father. At least, none that you remember. So, being the adult, I should have been wiser than I was." She covered her eyes with a thin hand. "Now, when I look at you, and I truly see the man you have become, I fault myself for backing up the mad things you did. At the time, it was the only way I knew to keep you happy, and as you became older, you would not take no for an answer." She drew a deep breath. "But now I know it was not the right thing to do. Through the years I tried to close my eyes against some of the things you have done. Why? I don't know. Maybe I didn't want to believe that you were capable of some of them, or maybe I was just afraid to speak out. But I do know this, my Paz, the way you are treating the people of your own Tortuguero is not right. Perhaps if you open your heart to their children, you will release some of the pain from your own childhood."

Paz couldn't bring himself to look at her, even as she rose and returned to the others. Tina's words had touched him in a way that he had not been touched since he was a little boy. They tugged at atrophied heartstrings. It confused him, and once again made him feel weak.

He forced his thoughts back to the mountainous hilltop. All these years he had yearned to own The Pirate's Emerald, and now it was no more than a mile and a half away. He would not let Tina's sentimental words take away the momentum of his victory. If he was lucky, he would not only return with the emerald, but with Sienna, The Stonekeeper, as well.

Paz wanted to eat the bread that Tina had laid on his thigh, but his pride would not let him. By now he knew the people here had no respect for him, but that no longer mattered. In the end he would show them all, including José, that what they considered to be unacceptable behavior was a sign of strength, and the compassion they longed for him to show was nothing more than weakness. He was their better, each and every one of them. He did not need a people. He did not need a family or a friend. All he needed was The Pirate's Emerald, and he would be able to buy the rest.

"Where's Hawk?" Albert asked, trying to stifle the distress on his face and in his voice.

"I don't know," Sienna answered honestly, reeling from the shock of finding him gone. She looked at the dark, potholed walls of the partially underground room and shivered. Even with the fire it felt like some kind of tomb without Hawk there. The moment provoked an unwanted feeling of *déjà vu*, and she tried to conceal her distraught reaction from the children.

"He is probably outside scouting around for something to cook," Obed volunteered as he ventured farther into the medium sized space.

"Yes, that's why he started the fire," Albert said, kneeling down to nurture the infant flame. "He wouldn't just leave us alone without saying so."

Sienna could feel Junie's uncertain eyes upon her face.

"Is that right, Sienna?" she questioned softly.

For a moment she was at a loss for words. Finally, she managed, "I'm sure whatever the reason is that Hawk is not here, it is a very good one."

Suddenly, Albert looked up from the fire and their eyes met. She knew that he could tell that she was not sure about Hawk's return, and he swallowed hard as he continued to build up the fire. Sienna didn't realize how tired she was until she sat down against the packed dirt walls. The children joined her in anxious silence as the time ticked away.

"I'm hungry," Obed complained as he glanced at the opening to the mound for the umpteenth time, only to look away with disappointment. He began to dig agitatedly in the hard dirt floor with a sharp rock he had discovered.

Albert was quick to try to comfort his friend, who was showing his age with Hawk's absence. "I've got one more johnnycake left." He pulled the mushed bread out of his pocket, showed it to Obed, and began to divide it up. "We can all have a little piece."

Sienna accepted the food Albert offered, but her throat was thick with emotion as she tried to swallow the heavy bread. Like Obed's, her gaze kept straying to the opening as she silently prayed for Hawk's return. Where had he gone? And why had he left them alone after his fervent promises to take care of them? It made no sense at all. Part of Sienna wanted to be angry with him, but another part was concerned for his safety. The man she knew would not have left them without a damn good reason.

Many of the things that he had said about himself formed a writhing ball of thoughts in her mind. *Only God knows who and what I am. That is where you are wrong. I am not worthy.* Could he have been forced to come face-to-face with the one thing he dreaded most about himself? Sienna felt as if she were reaching for straws. It was so hard for her to conceive, let alone grasp, what might have happened.

She felt Junie's small hand on her arm, and knew she, too, could feel her turmoil. Sienna gave what she hoped was a reassuring smile as the young girl snuggled up against her.

Their moment of comfort was jarred by a sudden noise coming from the direction of the entrance.

"Hawk," Obed called as he jumped to his feet and crossed the floor. "Hawk," he called even louder. He was already on the stairs before Sienna could stop him.

"Wait, Obed," she instructed. She rose swiftly, and

when she got to the stairs, she could see the boy had stopped midway on the stairwell.

"What is it?" Sienna inquired, her senses on alert.

"I don't know," he replied hesitantly. "I don't see anyone. But I know I heard something."

"We all did," she replied, "but you come down here, right now, and let *me* see what it is."

Reluctantly, he began to back down. Sienna and Obed met on the bottom step, with Junie and Albert not far behind.

"Just hold on," she advised as she looked back into their anxious faces. Slowly, she began to mount the earthen stairs.

"Hawk?" she called hopefully. There was no answer, and her intuition warned it was not him, but she ignored the small voice, in her anxiousness. "Hawk, is that you?"

Sienna was almost at the top and there was still no reply. She began to think that perhaps an animal had come out of the forest and had ventured near the opening. Drawing up all the resolve she had, Sienna made her way to the entrance. Carefully, she stepped outside. The fog had just about cleared, as Hawk had predicted, and she was about to dismiss the sound when a voice that she had no desire to ever hear again said, "So your bodyguard has deserted you, has he, my dear fiancée?"

Twenty-five

Sienna froze at the sound of Paz's voice. It came from the side of the entrance to the mound, and she knew he had been waiting for this very moment. She could just picture him standing there, listening to her call Hawk's name, waiting for her to emerge.

She did not turn to face him right away. Instead, her mind tumbled through the possibility of escape. She could have tried to run, but the thought came and went like a flash. To run would mean leaving the children, and there was no way she was going to do that. They had put themselves out for her, and she would definitely not leave them now. The truth was, there were no options for escape on the obscure hillside. Had Hawk been there she might have put up a good fight, but he wasn't, she admitted regretfully, so she was on her own.

"I said, so he abandoned you, did he?" Paz said.

He was right behind her, and the truth behind his words struck home. Yet Sienna wasn't about to let Paz talk down to her, considering what he had done, and she wasn't about to let him trash Hawk, either.

"Fiancée?" She turned, plastering a look of derision on her face as she threw the false term of endearment at Paz. "I'm no more your fiancée than I am that tree's fiancée." She pointed to the nearest palm. "So you can come off of that, and all the other lies you and Tina strung together to put on that elaborate hoax."

She hoped she had responded in a way he had not expected, and she was right. Sienna watched surprise surface and cool in his dark, heavily lashed eyes, soon replaced by a fervent appreciation.

"So, my little dove is really an eagle behind those smooth brown feathers." Paz reached out and stroked the front of her neck, allowing his hand to trail down over her breasts.

Sienna stiffened at his touch, but she did not waver, nor did she remove her challenging gaze from his. "You don't know what I am, because you don't know me," she corrected him. "You had me kidnapped and brought all the way over here against my will, for your own bizarre purpose. Yes, I'm the one you were looking for. I'm The Last of the Stonekeepers, so you'd better watch yourself around me." She donned what she knew was a mighty attitude, hoping it would help protect her.

Sienna could see from the uncertain look in Paz's eyes that she had him going, and she knew it wasn't time to stop. "And another thing, where do you come off thinking you can collect another human being like a statue or a book?" She placed her flat palm in front of his face. "No-ot. It's not going to happen here." She paused for effect. "You see, you're so wrapped up in trying to own everything and everybody around you that you don't even know what your problem is. So I'm going to school you on that." She leaned back slightly. "You do all of that to justify your own worth, because you know the person, Paz, isn't worth a cent."

By now the children had come to the entrance of the mound. Amanda, Eduardo and Wallace were embracing Obed and Junie, while Albert had come to stand protectively at her side. All of them listened intently as she spoke.

Sienna watched the side of Paz's mouth tremble slightly. She could tell she had touched a nerve with her performance, and she hoped he believed she had some special ability to back up all her talk.

"You think you're smart, don't you?" he replied, his eyes narrowing. "Well, you're going to get your chance to prove just how smart you are, and just how powerful you are." He paused. "Yes, we're going to find out if your being The Last of the Stonekeepers is fact or fairy tale," he challenged, looking at the position of the sun in the sky. "We only have a couple of hours before dusk begins to set in, and I want to have The Pirate's Emerald in my hand before it does. And guess what?" he said, forming a villainous smile, "you're going to help me find it."

Paz pulled her away from the group, forcefully disengaging Albert's hand from her own. It was only then that Sienna saw the gun. She looked down at the cold metal, and into the cold, calculating features of the man who stood beside her.

"So, Ms. Stonekeeper," he said, his tone making mockery of the word, "you can do it any kind of way you want. You can use your . . . magic . . ." he said, smiling enticingly, "or you can buy more time by using whatever else you might have to offer." He deliberately allowed a lascivious look to come across his face. "My intention is to get to enjoy the latter, no matter what happens. So," he said, squeezing her arm painfully, "there you have it. Oh, and by the way, if I don't have the gem by the appointed time," he said, brandishing the gun in the direction of the stunned group gathered near the opening of the mound, "one of them will be real sorry."

Sienna looked at the array of frightened faces. Her heart went out to them all, especially the children. She was painfully aware of Albert trying to pretend he wasn't afraid, but his pretense was weak.

"You don't have to threaten them in order for me to help you find what you're looking for," she retorted between gritted teeth.

"I know that," Paz replied lightly, "but it makes it that much more interesting, and it makes the hunt that much more exciting. Doesn't it, José?"

She saw his gaze flicker briefly in the direction of the man she had seen the night of the party, but José didn't answer.

"Doesn't it, José?" Paz demanded again.

José tilted his nose slightly in the air. "You are a very sick man, Paz, even sicker than I thought you were. Just look at you." His lined eyes were full of disdain. "In the beginning you pretended you were using the gun to protect your fiancée." He forced a chuckle. "That was all a lie. Then you threatened Wallace and me in the boats. And now you are even threatening the lives of innocent women and children. Not only are you a low, worthless bastard, you are a coward as well," José declared.

Paz had fired the gun before Sienna realized what was happening. The single shot sounded on the hillside like a blast from a rocket ship.

"Now the *Anansi* will never know that I found The Pirate's Emerald. I'm sure no one here is going to tell."

Hawk sprang to his feet when he heard the shot, like he was the one who had been shot. Instantly, he broke out into a sweat, which caused the black suit to cling to his face and his body even more. His amber eyes shone through the slits of the mask like a cat's eyes in the dark.

Psychologically the outbreak had set him back. He had entered the mound like a man in a daze and automatically put on the attire that was synonymous with the pain and the shame, a whir of collective thoughts and voices in his head. The communication was loud but jumbled, like a radio program that was not quite clear. Afterward, he sat there in the dark, feeling it was where he belonged, buried away from the light, away from the others.

The gunshot, a familiar noise from his days in the 'hood, jolted him out of his altered state. The foreign explosion amongst the natural sounds forced his thoughts toward Sienna and the children. Immediately, he felt a debilitating guilt about leaving them, and his mind conjured up all kinds of horrible images. In the midst of this mental torture, Hawk knew he had to do something, and do it fast.

He didn't know how he got to the mouth of the mound, but he was there, and he could hear women and children shouting and crying in the distance. With his heart in his throat he ran toward it, a black streak amongst the green, his mind going faster than his feet could carry him.

Hawk's heart compelled him to rush into the midst of the scene no matter what the consequence, but his head screamed against it. Sienna and the children were in danger, and they would be better served by a cool head with a steady hand than an emotional one.

Concealing himself as best he could, Hawk worked his way in. He could see them near the mound in the forest-encroached clearing. He hid himself behind a thick line of growth not too far from where Paz and Sienna stood.

"He's dead!" Junie screamed, and Hawk peered over the oversized leaf to see a man slumped down beside the mound, blood all over the front of his shirt. Although he felt compassion, Hawk thought his chest would burst with relief when he saw it was this man who had been shot, and not Sienna or the children.

"That's what happens when you talk too much," Paz retorted, pulling Sienna closer to him. "Now that you all know that I won't hesitate to use this gun, I suggest you do exactly what I tell you." He gave them a visual going-over.

Hawk could see that the children were backing even

closer to the adults, and the men who remained standing looked as if they were trying to decide what to do.

"I can tell you now, unless you want to end up like José I suggest you don't get any new, brave ideas." His gaze seemed to focus on Wallace and Eduardo. "But already I can tell I might have to help you out," Paz announced, "because you're getting a little edgy after my demonstration. And since there are so many of you, and only one of me, I'm going to have to even the odds."

Junie turned her face into Tina's skirt, and the older woman placed a shaky hand around her small shoulders. Hawk didn't know how to describe the expression he saw on Tina's face. It was as if some light had gone out inside her as she watched the man she had raised from a child. He knew they all wondered, as he did, what Paz meant by evening the odds.

"So you," Paz said, pointing to Eduardo, "I know you have a small pocket knife. I can see the print." The barrel of the gun pointed toward the man's leg, then over toward a section of the encroaching forest. "I want you to cut loose a couple of the longest vines you can find, right there at the edge. I think I'm going to have you all tied up. Everyone except for Tina and The Stonekeeper, that is." He rubbed the side of Sienna's cheek with the barrel.

Hawk cringed as he watched. He could tell Paz was trying to elicit fear from Sienna, but she stood her ground, her eyes looking down at the shiny metal, never uttering a sound.

The way Sienna did not react seemed to amuse Paz, and he continued to look at her as he spoke. "And I have a special job for the old man, even in his present condition."

Amanda and the children looked from Paz to José's inanimate body, disbelief plastered on their stricken faces.

"Once Eduardo gets through cutting off those vines, this is what you're going to do. I want everybody to line up. Then I want the adults to tie up the children, one behind the other with the same piece of vine, starting from one end. And I don't want any funny business, either," he warned, donning an inappropriate smile. "It will be like the chain gangs I've seen in some of your American movies," Paz said close to Sienna's ear before continuing. "The adults will be next. Eduardo, you're going to have to help with the last one, and then I have a special job for you."

Live anger bent Eduardo's average features as he turned and looked at Paz. Hawk could see that if he could get his hands around Paz's throat it would be all over.

"So you want to know, why you?" Paz asked. "Because you appear to be the strongest," he said in a pleasing voice before his tone changed to stone. "Now turn around and finish what you're doing."

Hawk watched Eduardo cut the plants and drag the tough, rope-like vines over toward the group. He let them drop down in a heap in front of him.

"Now I want everybody to do exactly what I said," Paz reiterated.

Hesitantly, Wallace and Amanda followed their instructions. The children stood still while their hands were tied. Obed's bottom lip extended out during the process, and it became even more distended as he watched Wallace tie his mother's hands. Hawk guessed the sight of it was too much for him.

"Who do you think you are, doing this to us?" he said. "You're not going to get away with it. You can't get away with hurting people for no reason."

"Sh-sh," Amanda said, trying to protect her child. "It's alright, son. Everything going to be alright."

"Yes, you better talk to him," Paz retorted. Then he looked at Obed, "All I have to say is, grow up, kid. I had to, long before I was your age."

Hawk could see Paz's reference to Obed's immaturity affected the young boy greatly.

"You won't be talking like that when Hawk comes back. He's going to put an end to all this craziness."

"Is that what you think, *little* boy?" Paz had also recognized Obed's soft spot. "Yes, I'm concerned about Hawk, but it's not because I think he's going to come back and protect you. I think the yellow-eyed bastard wants the emerald for himself. That's why he came to Costa Rica and wormed his way into Shangri-la in the first place, and made such good friends with you, sweetheart." He kissed the side of Sienna's mouth. "You see how he had you bring him all this way, and now he's gone." He lowered his voice as he spoke directly to Sienna. Hawk could barely hear his words. "I heard you calling his name from inside the mound. It was so full of, what should I call it, expectation. In it I could hear the way you probably said his name while you allowed him to take you in my house." Sienna's lips brushed against the tip of the gun as she turned her face away from his. "And I'm going to make sure you call my name the same way, when the time is right."

It took all the willpower Hawk had to not attack Paz at that moment, but he knew the surprise could result in him pulling the trigger, injuring, if not killing, Sienna.

"So, Hawk's got the jump on the situation," Paz continued, "and I don't want him to get too far ahead." Paz turned his full attention over to the trussed up group. "Excellent!" he exclaimed as he examined their work. "Now, Sienna, if you will do the honors for Eduardo."

Tina stood watching silently as Paz repositioned himself closer to the mound, allowing Sienna to walk forward. Hawk saw her tie Eduardo's hands slowly as she looked up into the faces of the children.

"That's good enough. You don't have to take all day," Paz interrupted. "Now, last but not least, tie the end of the vine around José's waist. And that's where you come in again, Eduardo." He smiled in the larger man's direction. "When she's done, you're going to get down and allow her to lean José's body across your shoulder, and then you all are going down into the mound. That way, if you get any bright ideas about escaping you will have to take the dead body with you. Now, of course, like I said, Eduardo, you look pretty strong. But I do believe if you decide to try to escape, the scent of José's fresh blood will call every jaguar and puma for miles. When I think about it, you better pray that it doesn't happen anyway." His eyes turned hard, and calculating. "Now do it." He stepped back, waving the pistol toward the opening.

Hawk watched Eduardo stumble on the stairs under José's dead weight but not before his angry but frightened eyes turned towards Paz and the gun for the last time. The rest of the group disappeared behind him, with Albert bringing up the rear. Afterward, Paz took what appeared to be a cleansing breath.

"So, Tina, I guess it's you, me and The Stonekeeper." His dark eyes feasted on Sienna, the excitement of the hunt clear.

Wearily Tina responded, "You forgot someone else, my Paz."

"Who?"

"The Protective Spirit of The Earth Mother."

Paz looked at Tina, then Sienna. Hawk thought he recognized a tinge of fear on his features before he said abruptly, "Not now, Tina," and took Sienna by the arm.

From Hawk's point of view Tina was right. Paz *had* forgotten someone, and *he* would be waiting for the proper moment to take action.

Twenty-six

"I wish you hadn't said that back there." Paz spoke for the first time since they had started to climb. "I could do without thinking about your mumbo jumbo at the moment," he continued as he looked around at the thickening fog.

"I only say what I believe to be true," Tina replied. "And somewhere deep inside, you also believe, or you would not be here with your gun threatening The Stonekeeper. You must believe in her power, or you would not think she would be able to lead you to The Pirate's Emerald."

"Yes, there are some things that I believe," he admitted grudgingly, "but the truth is, I don't know if her magical powers are on that list. One of my main reasons for bringing her to Shangri-la was so I could boast before the *Anansi*. I knew there had been much talk about her, rumors about her performing unbelievable acts in the Caribbean. She was my ticket into the group, along with the jewels." He leaned forward to see through the mist. "Plus, I am not a man to pass up any opportunity. It's possible her powers are real. In that case, I come out on top either way. She simply will help me find The Pirate's Emerald quicker than I would have alone. But find it I will before I leave *Barra de Colorado*." He looked over at Sienna, who had been quiet through the entire exchange.

"What do you have to say about this, Stonekeeper? he asked, pulling her along beside him.

Sienna did not answer his question right away, because her mind was elsewhere. An underlying sound had garnered her attention. It was unfamiliar, and unlike the animal sounds of the rain forest. She knew Paz was waiting for an answer, and she inhaled to control the rapid beat of her heart as she considered her predicament. The scent of green leaves, moss, flowers, and the wild filled her nostrils, verifying how far she was away from home and the norm.

Sienna looked at the percolating fog, how it rose into the sky, blending with the blue and the green of the glow. There was an air of mystery as they drew closer to the top, and her mind conjured up memories of what happened with The Passion Ruby in Martinique. The memory of the final moment was vivid as she answered in solid tones.

"I know that the power of the gems is real. Like you and I, they have a life force within them. It all comes from the same source. We have a choice about how we use that force, but the gems, their purpose is pure and clear."

Paz threw his head back and laughed. "Is this the same woman that spoke back near the mound? She sounded like a woman who was familiar with the streets, but you, you sound so different, my dear. So . . . what's the word for it, deep."

Sienna remained silent, keeping her eyes straight ahead. Back at the mound she had reacted out of fear, and now, heading toward the hilltop, she was forced to rely on the most powerful of sources.

She thought of the people tied up in the mound . . . the children, and how their frightened faces had looked as they entered the underground cavern attached to the body of a dead man. All of that, the result of Paz's greed for The Pirate's Emerald. *Or was it?* a voice inside her questioned.

Was all of this about one man's greed, or was there a more powerful, deeper source acting through human beings who were blind to their mission? Sienna thought about how she had arrived in Costa Rica, and how Hawk had mentioned her being there was no coincidence. Slowly, there was a dawning of how the negative might have had a positive reason behind its birth.

With conventional reason fighting her every step of the way, Sienna realized that except for Paz and Tina she might not have ever come to Costa Rica. If Paz and the *Anansi* had not coveted each other's belongings, seeing her as a Stonekeeper to be collected instead of a human being to be respected, she would not have run away with Hawk and met Shau Lo and the children, and begun her quest for the emerald. If it had not been for all these negative things forcing her in the direction of her life's mission, would she have willingly gone into the wild rain forest of Costa Rica to fulfill it? Sienna had to answer the question truthfully. The answer was no. Even without Hawk, life had been comfortable and familiar back in Atlanta with The Stonekeeper shop on Blossom Street, her apartment, and her friend, Dawn. She would not have willingly ventured away from its safety to face danger for an uncertain, lofty goal.

The noise had become louder under the chatter of countless birds, and she could tell there was a pacing to the sound. Paz and Tina were aware of it as well, and she could see Paz looking curiously into the fog for the source.

"What is that noise?" he asked, somewhat irritated, as Sienna felt the earth move subtly beneath their feet.

"I did not know before now, my Paz," Tina said slowly, "but I can see the answer lies before us."

Sienna realized they had come to the end of the forest

canopy and were at the top of the hill. Not knowing what to expect, she stepped from underneath the tall trees into direct sunshine. None of them said a word as they surveyed the scene. It was breathtaking beyond measure, and the source of the fog and the sound was clear.

Stretched out slightly below them was an immense sparkling green lake with a white fog-like cover floating above its depths. Sienna did not know what to make of it, for it did not appear to be an ordinary lake with its vapors drifting into the surrounding forest. As she studied the liquid she began to hear the sound again, ever so softly. Slowly, it swelled with each passing second, and the earth began to move. When the rasping sound was at its height the lake appeared to lower, as if it were being sucked into the ground. Then, slowly, as the noise began to dissipate, the green liquid rose and the earth became still.

"It is the breath of The Earth Mother," Tina said in reverent tones. "It is her breathing that we hear."

Tina's words were fitting, and Sienna recalled how Junie and Obed had spoken of The Mother's breath.

"This is the mouth of a volcano," Paz stated with amazement, "but there are no records of a volcano being in *Barra de Colorado*."

"What does it matter, my Paz? Now you know the truth. You see it with your own eyes. It is the mouth of The Earth Mother," Tina announced with respect. "We stand upon her face."

Hawk stepped down into the dark mound, and turned on the flashlight. The small light in the medium-size space did very little to illuminate it, but it provided enough light for him to see the huddled forms lined against the wall.

"Obed, Junie and Albert, it's Hawk," he declared, anxious to help them but aware of his bizarre appearance.

"Hawk." Obed responded immediately to his voice. "I knew you'd come back. I knew Paz was lying," he continued in his excitement. "But I can not see you."

Hawk scanned the light on his anxious face as he came closer. He watched a smile spread across the small familiar features, soon replaced by bewilderment. "Oh, there you are," Obed proclaimed, "but why are you dressed like that?"

"Don't worry about that right now," Hawk said quickly. "I need to untie all of you before Paz gets too far away." He looked at the relieved but cautious group. "I'll untie you first," he said, approaching Amanda, "and that way you can undo the others."

Automatically, she moved closer to the wall. "Obed. You sure you know this man? How you know who is underneath that mask?" she questioned, scrutinizing his black form.

Hawk's jaw jumped spasmodically against the black material, which caused the rash to itch. Amanda's apprehension rekindled his insecurities about his true appearance.

"I just know, Mama. It's Hawk," he spoke up quickly. "He helped take care of us on our way here."

With clear reluctance Amanda bent toward him, and he took a knife and cut her loose. "Now here," he passed the blade to her, "free the others."

"Wait for us, Hawk, we want to come with you," Obed yelled as he returned to the stairs.

Hawk turned toward them just as the floor of the mound began to shake so violently that he was thrown up against the hard-packed earthen stairs. Sparks of pain shot through his shoulder on impact. He used his legs to brace himself against the quaking side of the stairwell. Injured but determined to go on, Hawk balanced himself as the rumblings began to subside. "No, you stay with your family," he yelled above the grating noise. "I'm going after Sienna."

* * *

It was as if someone had flipped a switch, turning off the sounds of the forest. Sienna looked behind her, listening for the overwhelming chatter of birds. There was none. Then the earth began to move again, and this time it was much more forceful. The tremors escalated with such power that it forced them to stumble backward, and Sienna, Paz and Tina tumbled to the ground, scattered like seeds in a garden, clutching at anything that would give them stability.

"Raas," Paz yelled above the noise as the gun flew out of his hand. At that moment he could do no more than reach for a climbing vine, swinging from the shaking canopy. The effort did him little good. His body was thrown farther into the brush.

Sienna's eyes opened wide when she saw the weapon fly into the air, but there was no way she could go after it as she struggled against the earth's rocky motion. The ground felt as if it could tear apart beneath her, and a portion of the land did rise up and buckle beside her, creating a shallow opening. She clung to a convenient bank of dirt, riding out the earth's show of displeasure until it finally came to an end.

It took a few moments for Sienna to recover, and when she did she discovered the wedge of earth she was clinging to was no wedge at all. Feeling bruised and disoriented, she looked down at the large brown object beneath her. She was astonished to see an old wooden chest stuck deep in the soil. She reached out and touched the lid, her hand sliding down to a ring that protruded from the middle. Sienna tested the lock, giving it a rapid tug; the lid responded eagerly. She got up on her knees, pushing the heavy top open with both hands. Immediately, her gaze was captivated by a deep, vibrant green that danced and sparkled joyously, making mockery of her fear of only moments before.

It was hard for Sienna to believe her eyes. An emerald carved in the form of a bird, with inlaid pearls for eyes, rested inside a compartment of the chest. Awestruck, she reached down and drew it out.

A splintering cry pierced her ears.

At first she did not know if the source was human or animal. Her startled eyes turned in the direction of the noise, and she recognized the voice.

"Tina-a! Tina-a!" Paz yelled in anguish.

Slowly, Sienna pushed herself away from the chest and began to walk towards Paz's outcry. Moments later she spotted them, several yards away. Paz held Tina's thin, dead figure in his arms, and he yelled to the sky once again before burying his face in her shallow breasts.

Sienna stood silently with The Pirate's Emerald in her hand, and although they had done much to harm her her heart went out to Paz and the only mother he had ever known.

He turned his anguished eyes in her direction, and for a second they held in silent understanding, until his gaze travelled downward, landing on the gem.

"You've found it." His mouth moved like that of a wooden puppet.

Sienna nodded slowly, and she watched his lifeless eyes slowly ignite to a raging fire. "You've found it," he repeated as he became full of rage.

Still disoriented and now shocked by Tina's death, Sienna watched Paz allow her body to slip lifelessly to the earth. He was standing several feet away from her, like a raging bull, before she came to her senses.

"You and your stones. I should have listened to Tina," he accused as he began to walk quickly toward her. "She said that the earth would protect her own, and she did. So, because I threatened you, one of her chosen ones, in return she took the life of the only person who has ever really cared about me," Paz accused her, with vengeance in his eyes. "But she won't be able to protect you now." He lunged for Sienna's throat.

Twenty-seven

The gem flew out of her grasp as Sienna was knocked to the ground, but instead of feeling Paz's hands around her throat, she found herself gazing at the blue sky. There was a slight throbbing in the back of her head, and she thought it was responsible for the bumping she heard, but in short order she realized that wasn't so. Sienna recognized the sound of thrashing about, and grunts and groans not far away. She sat up quickly, and was shocked to see Paz battling on the ground with a mysterious figure in black.

In total confusion Sienna watched them roll over and over in a test of strength until the figure in black achieved the upper hand. Masterfully, he straddled Paz's struggling figure, and he raised his arm to strike a subduing blow. It was at that moment that Sienna recognized the familiar mask and jumpsuit. To her horror, instead of Hawk completing his action, he was the one who was struck down.

Sienna screamed at the top of her lungs as she saw him tumble over and Paz rise up on his side with The Pirate's Emerald in his hand. He stared down at the gem that he had sought for so long, examining it like a man would examine his own heart if he were able to hold it.

"Yes, you'd better look at it, you lowlife bastard," a voice called from inside the forest, "because it is going to be the last thing you ever see." José walked forward with the pistol in his hand. Sienna could see Obed, Junie and Albert breathing hard behind him, forming an anxious cluster. Sienna's terrified gaze travelled from Hawk to José, and finally to Paz, who was looking at the blood-soaked figure as if seeing a ghost.

"You thought I was dead, and it made no difference at all, did it? You even decided to use me like a human weight." He laughed deep down in his throat. "No matter what happens, huh? You're just the same old Paz, seeing people as objects to be used to your advantage. Take a human life just like that." He snapped his finger, then grimaced from the flesh wound in his shoulder, "Feeling no remorse. So in light of that, it shouldn't matter to you, Paz, when I take your life."

Sienna watched in dread as he extended his arm and aimed. Amanda, Wallace and Eduardo stood dumbstruck nearby.

"Would the father kill his only son?" a thick resonant voice called out.

José jerked visibly, and his eyes widened as he continued to look at Paz. Then, like everyone else, he turned his gaze toward the person who had spoken the unlikely words.

"What?" José demanded as he looked at the black figure rising slowly up from the ground, turning his back to all of them.

"Would you kill the son that has been in your mind and in your heart for the last twenty years?" The nuances of Hawk's voice wove through the sound of the visionary. "If you would, then aim and fire."

"What kind of lie is this?" This time it was Paz who spoke, with incredulity lacing every word.

"It is no lie. It is the truth." Hawk spoke in paced intonations, as the gift of sight descended upon him full force. "Paz Peters, born to Dorling Peters on May twenty-sixth, nineteen sixty-one, was the seed of José Wong. He loved her, but because of social and racial pressure they parted ways before your birth. When you were two years old, she sent a picture to José, who had married and had a child a year younger than you. Your mother died shortly after that. José's child died ten years later. That is when José's search began, but there was no trail to follow. The photograph, the proof, remains in José's wallet to this day."

"My God," José declared, dropping to his knees with the pistol hanging limply at his side.

"It can't be," Paz mumbled, shaking his head. "It can't."

"He's telling the truth," José replied softly as he extracted his wallet. "This is the picture." He gazed down at the familiar faces.

Exhausted, Paz went and stood above José, looking down at his trembling hands as they held the small square. Overwhelmed, he fell to his knees in front of him, tears streaming down his broken face.

Everything and everyone seemed to stand still as they watched the amazing reunion.

Sienna's shock at Hawk's words was beyond measure. How did he know that Paz was José's son? And why hadn't he told her before now? She looked at his broad back, held stiffly as he continued to look straight ahead. It was impossible for her to understand his actions. He had disappeared with no explanation at all, only to return when she needed him most, wearing the familiar mask and jumpsuit.

Suddenly, the children ran across the grassy area. Sienna put her arms around them as they eagerly reached out to her, but her eyes remained on Hawk, who continued to look out over the green lake. He had not looked her way once since he had begun to speak in a tone she had never heard before.

"Look!" Junie exclaimed as she pulled away. She ran over and picked up the emerald from the place where

Paz had left it. "Look, Obed! It is the seed of transformation of which The Mother spoke. She said it would be delivered in the form of a bird with pearl-like eyes!"

Obed and Albert went to touch the emerald as Amanda and Wallace looked on with amazement.

"How did the earth speak to you?" Wallace asked. His elderly features showed immense strain, but as he looked at his granddaughter a youthful seeking seemed to transform the weary lines.

"I don't know, Granddaddy," she replied as she sought the answer to his question. "I could hear her in my head, but I could also feel her in my heart." Her girlish voice spoke with all the truth she knew.

"And so should be the way of the children." Hawk's booming voice rang out again. "In innocence and love should they be raised, honoring their connections with a source that most adults have long forgotten. The children can be a brilliant light illuminating the future or, without loving guidance, they can be a force of rage hurtling forward the downfall of humankind."

Sienna watched Junie's slim back straighten as Hawk spoke. Then, with an air of expectation and honor, Junie drew back from her friends and relatives and walked over to Sienna.

"The Earth Mother said it would be up to The Stonekeeper to plant the seed." She spoke softly, offering her The Pirate's Emerald.

Solemnly, Sienna took the gem from her small hands, and she looked from the expectant features of the children to the awestruck faces of the adults. It was on Paz and José that her gaze concentrated the longest, for she realized Paz was a prime example of a child raised without loving guidance who had turned into an adult full of rage. When she finally looked back down into the green depths of the emerald, she was at a loss for what to do next.

"And so it has been the way of The Stonekeeper since

the beginning of the ancestors to return to Mother Earth the thoughts and feelings of her children, humankind," she heard Hawk say. "It is not for The Mother that this is done, for she will always remember. It is for humankind, for, like children they will only grow through remembering their mistakes, and never revisiting them."

Sienna found herself being drawn to Hawk's side as he spoke. She looked up into his black, masked face as the mystical words continued to tumble through the slit, under which she knew his firm lips lay.

"And so it is within the emerald that the wrong and the right choices of action will be kept, to teach discernment, for through its green vibration the hearts of all humankind will be stimulated toward love, and the quieting of hatred will be magnified."

She closed her eyes as his words flowed over her, and she pressed the emerald against her mark as he spoke of the heart. In what felt like the twinkling of an eye, Sienna experienced all of the thoughts and emotions of the people she had come in contact with since the day she was forcefully taken from the store. In that moment she automatically reached out and touched Hawk's hand. When she removed the gem from between her breasts, she knew intuitively that she was to cast it into the lake.

The dying rays of the sun appeared to highlight all of the facets of the emerald as it tumbled through the air, creating tiny, colorful prisms of floating light. Her gaze followed the spiralling motion until it cut into the smooth, placid, green surface. She watched the ripples from the impact move outward, enhancing the shade of green until the lake gleamed as brightly as the emerald itself.

"Wow!" Obed exclaimed. "Look! The green rainbow is getting darker."

Sienna raised her face to the sky and saw that Obed

spoke the truth. The green ribbon appeared to brighten, as did the trees and foliage around them, and as she looked out over the countryside even the forests that were miles away seem to glimmer and gleam.

"This will be a story that will be told many a Nine Night in Tortuguero," Amanda declared.

"You are right," Wallace agreed. "I am glad that at my age I was blessed to be a part of this day." He took Junie's hand in his.

Sienna watched as Amanda, Wallace, Eduardo, and the children started to head back toward the path, but Paz and José were near the entrance, blocking their way.

Paz was the first to rise to his feet. He looked over at the place where Tina lay. "I will be back for you, my Tinatico, when I can transport you properly. I will be back to give you a proper burial and a Nine Night." He looked at Amanda and Wallace as if seeking their cooperation in the tradition. They showed their agreement.

In silence Paz bent down and put his arm around José, helping him to his feet. The father draped his arm around his son's shoulder, and they walked together into the woods.

"Now I am encouraged," Wallace said loudly, "because I know we *all* one people."

"Sienna and Hawk, are you coming?" Obed called.

Sienna looked over at Hawk, whose body appeared much more tired than moments before.

"Shall we go?" she asked quietly.

He shook his head and continued to gaze out at the sun, which was well into its descent.

Sienna did not know what to say. She only knew that she was not going to leave him.

She turned to the group and replied, "No, we are going to remain here." She could tell from Obed's slumped shoulders those were not the words he wanted to hear.

"We're going to leave you the *cayuca* that we made so you can get back," Junie yelled.

"Thank you," Sienna replied, her voice trembling with emotion. "Thank you, and go in peace and love."

She watched them disappear into the forest.

Twenty-eight

In a pregnant silence, Sienna followed Hawk back to the mound. She waited in darkness until the first sparks of the fire he was building provided a limited amount of light. She didn't realize until then that this was not the same mound where she and the children had found shelter. Hawk's carved walking stick and the familiar duffle bag told her this was the place where he had gone when he left them alone. She watched him work, building the blaze to a comfortable level.

"There's one thing I'm certain of," Sienna said, breaking the silence.

"And what is that?"

"You can't run away from me now." She spoke to him across the flames, where he had settled. "Not unless you intend to leave me alone in the middle of a wild, Costa Rican rain forest," she said softly.

"No," Hawk replied. "I don't intend to do that."

"What do *we* intend to do?" She emphasized the plural.

"We . . ." He repeated the word as if hearing it for the first time. "Such an interesting concept."

"I guess you could say that," Sienna said, her brow furrowing at the strange remark. "I prefer to think it is a good concept."

"For some people I guess it is," Hawk replied.

"But you're saying it's not for you." The words hurt as she said them.

He lifted his head and looked directly at her for the first time since his return. The flames reflected inside his amber eyes, turning them into yellow diamonds in a sea of black. "It's not that I don't want it to be."

"Then just let it be, Hawk," she beseeched.

She saw his chest rise and fall as he sighed audibly.

"It's not that simple." He spaced out each word.

"It is," Sienna insisted. "You only have to want it bad enough. Believe in it strong enough. That's all."

"Not for me, it isn't," he confessed. "There is more. Much more."

"Well, the only way you're going to make me understand is through telling me what makes you do the things you do." She stared at the uncanny figure he made in the black suit and mask. "What makes you say things that my heart tells me are not what you want to say, but what you feel you must say."

"It's a strange story, Sienna."

"Alright," she said, and began to nod, "you *know* you are talking to a woman who believes in and knows about strange." She attempted to lighten his mood.

"That's true," Hawk agreed. "And once there was a man who told me that because you are special, you of all people would understand if I told you my story. His name is K'in. He is the only person on the planet that I've ever told the reason behind my wearing this mask." He looked into the flames. "It was hard for me then, and it would be even harder for me now," Hawk confessed. "Telling you would be like facing one of my greatest fears."

Sienna looked down at her hands. She knew it had taken a lot for him to tell her that he was afraid, and she wanted to reassure him that he need not be. Quietly, she got up and sat beside him. "Do you mind?"

He was silent for a moment. "I think the question should be do *you* mind?"

She heard the pain behind his words and quickly answered. "It's obvious I don't. I just want to be near you, that's all." She reached out to touch his masked face.

Immediately, he turned away. "Please, don't do that."

Hurt by his reproach, but wanting to respect his wishes, Sienna replied, "Alright, I won't."

Hawk placed his hand on hers, which had settled nervously in her lap. "I'm sorry." The words were raspy. "But once I tell you, maybe you'll be able to understand how I feel."

"Then tell me, Hawk," she coaxed. "I need to know."

Sienna realized it was the first time he had ever told her the complete story of his life. Yes, she had heard bits and pieces, but never the complete tale of Hennessy "Hawk" Jackson. She guessed he had started from the time he was a little boy to buy more time, and so she listened.

A stick turned to ashes and collapsed into the flames, symbolizing the truth of the moment: what it had been in the beginning it could never be again. Sienna was glad Hawk could not hear the sound of her heart beating. If he could have, he would have known how deeply his story had affected her. She knew he would never accept pity, and there was no pity in her heart for him, only love. Still, she was apprehensive. In his present state of mind he would not understand.

"And so," Hawk continued, "the transformation took me by complete surprise this time, because it had never occurred during the day. When I finally realized it, it had already begun. I was thankful for the thick fog, and for the mound, where I hoped you and the children would at least be safe."

Sienna thought about how Hawk had appeared different when she first realized who he was, and yet, he was the same. "That means the voice I heard at the top of the volcano was the voice of the sight."

"Yes."

She thought about that, and everything else that had unfolded at the mouth of the volcano, her mind flipping through the scenes like the pages of a book. But what she remembered most prominently was how inspirational Hawk had been just when she needed him.

"The sound was so rich and beautiful, and the message was wonderful," she told him. Aside from the crackling of the flames, the mound turned quiet before she spoke again. "You don't realize it, but without the things you said I don't believe I would have had the frame of mind to carry out my role as The Stonekeeper."

"No." The single word carried a spark of hope. "I didn't realize that."

"Well it's true." Sienna sought to fuel the spark. "And it seems to me that you are a viable part of my mission."

Hawk let go a derisive chuckle. "The purpose of your mission is so magnificent it is beyond words," he said, turning his masked face toward the ceiling. "What has happened to me is the result of my avarice and selfishness. And the growth on my face is a horrible reminder of that. Being forced to use the gift of sight to help others at the expense of my own life, and the lives of those I love, is the penalty."

"It's that way, Hawk, only if you choose to see it like that," she said, trying to reason with him. "The rash that you find so unbearable is proof to you that you're not perfect. But none of us is. We're all doing the best we can, and that's all I believe is expected." She moved closer to his right side and rose up on her knees. "Now, I am tired of speaking to the man behind the mask. I want to see my Hawk, no matter what shape he may be in."

Sienna waited to see if he would make an effort to

remove the object that stood between them. When he showed no inclination to do so, she slowly reached toward it. "May I?"

Hawk held her off with his hand. Finally, he took hold of the end of the facial mask, as if the mask itself were the enemy. With his head down he moved his hands upward. Sienna's heart was in her throat as the black material slowly cleared his face and, eventually, the ends of his shoulder-length dreadlocks.

Not knowing what to expect, her eyes searched his stony profile in the flickering firelight, but she saw nothing. Gently, she turned his entire face toward her, and as she did, she saw his eyes close and his jaw tremble. That was when she saw it, the growth that was the outward manifestation of his gift, and a reflection of Hawk's fears about himself. Sienna looked at it in all its hideous splendor, and her lips curved into a tender smile as she felt her love deepen.

Sienna leaned forward and kissed his eye that had slanted downward, the tip of his nose that inhaled so rapidly, and finally the side of his mouth that was puffed and anxiously silent. "I love you," she said softly. "All of you."

Hawk swallowed hard before he opened his eyes, and they studied each other's gazes anew. Each saw the depth of the love they shared in all its uniqueness.

Finally, Hawk replied, his voice deep with emotion, "I love you, so much. I never want to lose you."

Sienna and Hawk wrapped their arms around each other, holding on for dear life, daring anything to tear them apart.

"We're going to lick this thing together, you and I," she whispered in his ear.

"Do you think so?" His voice was calmer, more relaxed.

"I know so," she quickly replied, "because there's nothing greater than the power of love. You've just got to believe it, deep down in your bones." She closed her eyes and moved longingly against him, until she could feel the love flow between them, a real force to be reckoned with.

Tenderly, Hawk extracted her arms from around his neck and held her out at arm's length. "You better watch that. You know I'm somewhat of a sick man," he said teasingly, but his eyes showed his feelings of self-rejection were real.

Still basking in the waves of emotion, Sienna slowly opened her eyes. For a second she was immobilized when she looked into his unblemished face. Overcome with joy, her mouth trembling, she said, "Not anymore, you're not," and a tear trickled from her eye. "You're free, at least for now."

"What?" Confusion blanketed his handsome features.

Lovingly, she took his hand and guided it to the side of his face. She watched the lines of strain melt away, and his eyes turn into a smoldering yellow-green. Hungrily, his lips kissed the inside of her palm.

"You're right, my Black Queen, there is no greater power than the power of love, and I'm going to love you for as long as I can."

They went into each other's arms, sealing Hawk's promise with a kiss.

About the Author

Eboni Snoe was born Gwyn Ferris Williams in Gary, Indiana. Her love for reading, dance, public speaking, and performing helped her graduate from West Side High School with honors. She attended Fisk University, then began a career as a journalist. Now she spends her time tending to her family, maintaining her writing career, and conducting workshops about public speaking.

COMING IN MARCH 2001 FROM
ARABESQUE ROMANCES

__EVERYTHING TO GAIN
by Marilyn Tyner   1-58314-128-6 $5.99US/$7.99CAN

Caroline Duval was sure that she had put her devastating breakup with Derek Roberts behind her. But it only took one chance encounter to re-ignite a passion she had never forgotten. Now, with time running out, Caroline must walk a dangerous line between desire, trust, and heartbreak if she is to find the truth—and true love.

__TEMPTATION
by Viveca Carlysle   1-58314-170-7 $5.99US/$7.99CAN

When Danita Godfrey's uncle announces he's retiring from the board of the family-owned boutique chain, she's thrilled at the possibility of succeeding him. She's horrified when he tells her that she must work closely with sexy Stuart Lowell, her childhood rival. And she's shocked to discover that beneath the competitiveness lies a powerful—and undeniable—attraction.

__SHADOW OF LOVE
by Marcella Sanders   1-58314-166-9 $5.99US/$7.99CAN

For Tracy Wilson, a weekend trip to the Bahamas seemed a welcome respite from her struggle to overcome her husband's untimely death. But from the minute she encountered mysteriously sensual businessman Evan Maxwell, she found her heart at irresistible risk. With time running out, Tracy and Evan must learn to trust again if they are to claim true love.

__DESPERATE DECEPTIONS
by Linda Hudson-Smith   1-58314-141-3 $5.99US/$7.99CAN

A little romance is the perfect prescription for Erika Edmonds, still reeling from a devastating loss—and mired in the responsibilities that come with being an OB-GYN resident. Her innocent flirtation with Dr. Michael Mathis soon leads to something more . . . She senses he is hiding something, but it definitely isn't his feelings for her . . .

Call toll free **1-888-345-BOOK** to order by phone or use this coupon to order by mail. ALL BOOKS AVAILABLE MARCH 1, 2001.

Name_____

Address_____

City _____ State _____ Zip _____

Please send me the books I have checked above.

I am enclosing $_____

Plus postage and handling* $_____

Sales tax (in NY, TN, and DC) $_____

Total amount enclosed $_____

*Add $2.50 for the first book and $.50 for each additional book.
Send check or money order (no cash or CODs) to: **Kensington Publishing Corp., Dept. C.O., 850 Third Avenue, New York, NY 10022**
Prices and numbers subject to change without notice. Valid only in the U.S. All orders subject to availability. **NO ADVANCE ORDERS.**
Visit our website at **www.arabesquebooks.com.**

ARABESQUE
The Soul of Romance

Arabesque and BET.com
celebrate
ROMANCE WEEK
February 12 — 16, 2001

Join book lovers from across the country in chats with your favorite authors, including:
- Donna Hill
- Rochelle Alers
- Marcia King-Gamble
- and other African-American best-selling authors!

Be sure to log on **www.BET.com**
Pass the word and create a buzz for *Romance Week* on-line.

Do You Have the Entire Collection of
MARCIA KING-GAMBLE?

__A Reason to Love   1-58314-133-2 $5.99US/$7.99CAN
Pediatrician Niki Hamilton is approaching burn-out. Niki is in need of a vacation. But when an emergency leaves her in charge of her pal's dating service, Niki meets the sexiest single dad she's ever laid eyes on.

__Eden's Dream   0-7860-0572-6 $5.99US/$7.99CAN
Eden Sommer had a perfect life until the tragic plane crash that resulted in her husband's death. Suspicions about the crash haunt her. Refusing to believe that it was an accident, she resolves to discover the truth. Only the mysterious man who moves in next door is able to divert her from her worries.

__Illusions of Love   1-58314-104-9 $5.99US/$7.99CAN
Skyla Walker is a respected journalist. Creed Bennett is the prime suspect in the disappearance of several women. But as Skyla searches for the truth, she discovers an attraction that threatens to compromise everything she's worked for.

__Remembrance   0-7860-0504-1 $4.99US/$6.99CAN
As a radio talk show host, Charlie Canfield was used to fan mail. But now someone has crossed the line of devoted fan into the realm of obsession. So when she spots an invitation to attend her college class reunion, she decides that some R&R could be just the thing to calm her frazzled nerves. Little does she know that Devin Spencer will be there . . .

Call toll free **1-888-345-BOOK** to order by phone or use this coupon to order by mail.
Name_____
Address _____
City_____ State _____ Zip _____
Please send me the books I have checked above.
I am enclosing $_____
Plus postage and handling* $_____
Sales tax (in NY, TN, and DC) $_____
Total amount enclosed $_____
*Add $2.50 for the first book and $.50 for each additional book.
Send check or money order (no cash or CODs) to:
Kensington Publishing Corp., Dept. C.O., 850 Third Avenue, New York, NY 10022
Prices and numbers subject to change without notice. Valid only in the U.S.
All orders subject to availability. **NO ADVANCE ORDERS.**
Visit our website at www.arabesquebooks.com.